ALICE THROUGH THE MULTIVERSE

BRIAN TRENCHARD-SMITH

ALICE THROUGH THE MULTIVERSE
Copyright (C) 2017 by Brian Trenchard-Smith

Cover art & interior formatting
by Kevin G. Summers

ISBN: 979-8-9856747-1-2

This book is dedicated to the love of my life for the past forty-two years, Margaret, whose inspiration, patience, and counsel helped me to the finish line.

TABLE OF CONTENTS

AUTHOR'S NOTE

ALICE THROUGH THE MULTIVERSE was originally published as The Headsman's Daughter. This is the revised edition, retitled to better reflect its genre, with the addition of three new chapters, picking up from where the book ended, offering a new perspective on the story.

Time travel as a concept in fiction and movies has always intrigued me. I wrote Alice Through The Multiverse as a wacky, time paradox roller coaster ride, blending thriller genres in a sardonic take on the twists and turns of history, destiny, and timeless love. There's a bit of metaphysics and political subtext thrown in for good measure. I've tried to embed some serious issues in a ripping yarn. If readers respond, our plucky heroine will have more adventures in the Multiverse…

ACKNOWLEDGMENTS

I would like to thank friends and family members who made essential contributions to this enterprise. Thanks also to Kevin G. Summers for his evocative cover design; to Rob McClellan of Third Scribe.com for his helpful marketing advice. Deepest thanks to my wife, Dr. Margaret Trenchard-Smith, for her advice on the novel as it was nearing completion.

CHAPTER 1

The Family Business

MARCH 1554

A young girl ran barefoot through the forest, her face wracked with anguish and dread. This was worse than the worst of the visions that plagued her. This was happening. There was nothing she could do to stop it.

***

Dark clouds streamed in from the east, mottling the walls of Farnham Castle with an eerie light. A storm was chasing the lowering sun. The gate creaked open, and a cart left the castle under cavalry escort, carrying three young men, their hands bound, sentenced to death. One prisoner remained standing, braced against the rear wall of the cart. James De Fries, in his twenty-sixth year, seemed calm, resigned. The two fifteen-year-old sheep stealers lying at his feet were utterly terrified.

Knowing with certainty when the hour of death will come tends to direct our minds to the question of who is accountable. Not ourselves, of course. Fate is malevolent, others are to blame, the words "if only" echo, impotent rage curdles into self-pity. Not so with James De Fries, born to privilege, now to die a common criminal. So had read the charge, trumped up by his uncle to steal his inheritance and serve as a warning to anyone who might dare to champion the poor. But James was not preoccupied with futile fantasies of revenge. What was done was done. He would meet his Maker pure of heart and soul. God would grant him eternal life. Of that he had no doubt. But would God help him find the courage to endure the coming ordeal with dignity? Could his example ease the wretchedness of these two poor lads? But mostly his thoughts were on Alice, who had loved him at first sight, but must not see him now.

Near the town, half-ringed by forest, the executioner's scaffold stood, six feet high, thirty feet square, with a crawlspace underneath shielded by lattice fencing. Three nooses dangled above a headsman's block, posts and pillories, created for various forms of torment. Soldiers, armed with the spiked axes known as halberds, surrounded the structure. Crossbowmen were positioned at each corner as a warning to the sullen townsfolk. Clearly, the sentence was not popular.

The hostility of the crowd was not lost on Rufus Craddock, the executioner, nor on his wife Harriet or their two sons, Will and Ben, gathered in the crawlspace under the scaffold making final preparations to blades, hooks, leather bonds, the awful accoutrements of their trade.

"Watch your backs in the crowd, lads," Rufus muttered to his sons.

To hang a man to a point shy of unconsciousness, then to rip out his innards and fry them on a griddle before his dying eyes takes the kind of mental discipline Rufus Craddock had always managed to summon on these occasions for twenty-five of his forty years. He was old for a headsman, who often went mad young or drank themselves to death. Rufus had learned from his father how to blot out pity and turn the process into carpentry; chopping, pruning, beveling. All swiftly done, the sooner to return to the cottage with his loved ones, where the family business was rarely mentioned. But today's task would try his professional detachment as never before. The sheep stealers he would quickly dispatch, but Rufus was under orders to ensure that the outlaw James De Fries took a prolonged passage across the river Styx, and the lord of half the county was there to see it happen. Of all people, why this young man? God sets such tests.

Then the lattice gate to the crawlspace swung open, and a barefooted young girl ran inside, wearing a woolen shift tied at the waist with a cord. She was Alice, eighteen summers old, the headsman's favorite child. She stood before her father breathless, trembling, fighting back tears. Rufus looked stricken: "I ordered you to stay away, child."

"I cannot."

Rufus patted a small pigskin pouch hanging round his neck. "He will not suffer, I vow."

"Do you swear?"

"By the Rood."

Her older brother Ben put down the axe he was sharpening. "This is no place for you." Will, the eldest, approached to guide her out before the arrival of the condemned. "I beg you, Alice, go now."

Too late. An angry moan from outside drew Alice to a gap in the lattice. The cart carrying the condemned men pushed through the crowd. Her eyes fixed on James De Fries. Harriet dragged her daughter away. "Don't let him see you! Don't do that to him."

"It wasn't meant to be, girl," Rufus added. "I'm sorry." He made the Sign of the Cross. The rest of the family followed suit. Except Alice, who shook her head, scattering tears.

Her mother offered comfort: "God understands...God forgives."

"I do not." Alice let out a sob suffused with anger.

Harriet clasped her daughter's hands within her own. "Pray, child, pray."

For some time now, Alice had been having difficulty reconciling the goodness of God with the world's cruelty. And the strict moral code that emanated from the pulpit did not resemble the behavior of the most fortunate in the land. Prayer would be no comfort today.

The horses hauling the cart halted close to the scaffold. Rufus and his sons pulled the black hoods down over their faces and went out. Alice peered through the gap in the lattice. James was standing, his back to the scaffold, so that her view of him was obscured behind the head of the nearest horse. Her gaze raked the crowd, then fixed on a nobleman, guarded by a cordon of soldiers. Tall, haughty of mien and richly dressed, hair and beard streaked with silver. This was Sir Giles De Fries, one of the most powerful landowners in the southern counties, James' uncle and the man responsible for his death sentence. "Devil take you, Giles De Fries… I curse you to the end of your line," Alice whispered from the deepest, darkest corner of her being.

Alice had loved James from afar at first sight, although for years their social disparity made contact impossible. Still, a girl can dream, particularly at the age of six. As time passed she would glimpse him with other young nobles riding through the village, on their way to the hunt. So it was with astonishment, as she brought water to last year's harvest workers, that she came upon him scything down corn, shoulder to shoulder with the village lads. Their eyes met. Something coursed through her body so strongly she nearly dropped the pail. She knew that he saw it. Did he feel it too? She wondered this because he asked her name, and addressed her not as a wench, but in the respectful tone in which a man of his station would address a lady. This was his way with all, she learned, which was why he was much loved in the village, and hated by his uncle, Sir Giles De Fries.

The quarrel between uncle and nephew, a family matter initially, intensified until it became the talk of the county. Sir Giles claimed that his nephew was in league with Protestant rebels, and sent men to arrest him. He was to be killed for resisting. Yet James escaped, fleeing wounded into Farnham Forest, a haven for outlaws, who, his uncle hoped, would delight in finishing him off or would perhaps hand him back for reward and pardon. So they might have, had Alice not found him first.

Alice had always walked the forest in safety. As the headsman's daughter, outlaws dare not harm her. They counted on her father's mercy should they ever meet him on the scaffold.

Agony prolonged or curtailed; executioners have their ways. Alice was set apart, too, by odd visions of an unnatural world that came to her at times, but since she seemed otherwise sane and clever, people left her to herself. So for many years the forest had been Alice's playground, where she picked flowers and delighted in the antics of birds and foxes. But as she walked its secret paths, she was aware that hidden eyes were upon her.

Then, one day, there he was: James De Fries, bathing his wounds in a stream. It had been a dagger fight. He had left three dead behind him. Her eyes met his again, and Alice knew for sure that he felt as she did. What might he be feeling about her now, Alice wondered, about to receive death at the hands of her father and brothers, a new thought joining others tormenting her mind.

The executioners moved past the angry crowd, held back by soldiers. Ben remembered the applause of the crowd the previous week, when they slowly flayed and dismembered a child murderer. Ben had felt proud to be an instrument of justice then, enjoying the brief approval of townsfolk who generally avoided his family. He had not yet acquired his father's dispassion and acceptance of their social isolation. The fickle nature of people when they form large groups like the one that surrounded the scaffold dismayed him. A further shock awaited Ben as he reached the back of the cart: the age of the younger prisoners, five years his junior.

"So young...it's not right."

His father hustled him on. "They say what's right, not us. Quickly now."

The wind gusted, the storm rumbled closer. Watched by the portly county magistrate, the executioners dragged the condemned up steps onto the scaffold. Avoiding looking him in the eye, Rufus took James. His sons took the two boys. The sight of branding irons on hot coals made the shorter thief lose control of his bladder. Sir Giles noted this. A smile creased his tight mouth.

Three powerfully built armed men, mercenaries, marked by the scars of foreign wars, watched from the fringe of the forest unnoticed by the crowd. Cedric, Andrew, and Gareth, companions since youth, had been away for five years, serving in the army of Philip of Spain. Now the Prince needed eyes and ears in England, to judge when the rebellions had been crushed, and it was politic for him to marry the English Queen, Mary Tudor. This had been a golden opportunity for the three men to return home and become rich. They had been assigned to the service of a Dominican Inquisitor named Córdoba, proud and haughty as Spaniards were, but perhaps the cleverest leader they had known. It was good to be back in the old country. There were worse tasks than to observe an execution at his behest. Cedric, the tallest, regarded the sky, hoping that proceedings would be underway before the storm broke. Faugh! Certainly, English weather had not changed.

Rufus and his sons secured the prisoners to posts in readiness for the ritual of torture and dismemberment. James surveyed the crowd, to see whether his uncle was attending. Yes. There he was. Sir Giles De Fries, surrounded by a squad of his personal guard. Uncle and nephew stared at each other coldly.

Arrogant whelp, thought Sir Giles, how brave will you be, as fingers and toes are snipped from your body? He had sent the headsman a list of the torments he wished to see. He cared nothing about the imminent storm. He would stand in the rain for an hour, if need be, to ensure that each and every punishment was inflicted. Sir Giles was a man who took cruelty seriously.

Unseen by the crowd, and shielded particularly from Sir Giles' view, Rufus took the pouch around his neck, and squeezed the contents, a dark sticky mixture little more than a spoonful, into the palm of his hand. He raised it to James. "Open your mouth. It will numb the pain."

"Nay; give it to the lads," replied James, with a toss of his head, as if to shrug off the temptation.

"It's for you."

"Look at them, man! I will not have it."

"I gave Alice my word," the headsman insisted.

James was shocked. "Alice? Do you know?" James stared into the executioner's eyes. "I did not dishonor her." Rufus nodded. He knew his daughter.

"Tell her I died well."

"You won't die well, 'lest you swallow this," growled Rufus.

Ben stepped up beside his father: "Da?"

"Keep 'em busy."

Ben distracted the crowd by displaying a favorite instrument of torture, a metal ring for tightening round the skull till the eyeballs popped from their sockets. The crowd roared its disapproval.

In the crawlspace, Alice flinched at the sound. Her mother tried to comfort her. "Be strong...be strong..."

" 'Fore God, I demand justice," Alice whispered fiercely.

On the scaffold above, James again refused the opiate. Rufus shook his head. "Alice is here...below." James was aghast. "Why?" Rufus had no answer. The prospect of Alice hearing him give in to pain was more than James could bear. "Why?" James asked again.

"She is willful...I forbad it. For her sake...and for yours."

"Send her away!" pleaded James.

"It is too late." Rufus raised the potion in his hand.

"Please..." James breathed deeply, summoning his last reserves of courage. He gestured the young thieves. "Give it to them, sir!"

The pause in the proceedings escaped Sir Giles, who had lapsed into a triumphant reverie. Not before time, he thought, the final impediment to his brother's estate was about to be removed. He had hated the elder Reynard, their parents' favorite, who after their deaths was frequently away on the late King's business, leaving Giles to steward the estate to which he should rightfully have been heir. Instead, Reynard had married late in life and had bequeathed it to his stepson, James. Sir Giles indulged himself in these ruminations, the more to savor the punishment to come: "...that strutting popinjay, befriender of peasants and pamphleteers...soon his head, full of radical poison courtesy of a Parisian education, would be cleaved from his shoulders, thanks be to God...nay, James was not fit to rule lands that bridge three counties...better yet, his death will deter this town from joining the rebellion to the south." A single drop of rain brought Sir Giles back to the matter in hand.

The officiating magistrate noted the thunderclouds now rumbling overhead and waited no longer. He unfurled a scroll, signaling for quiet from the crowd, which jeered in response. His eyes flashed with anger at the disrespect. Clearing his throat, he bellowed for silence at the top of his lungs. Before the second syllable had ended, an arrow slammed between his teeth. He sank, gurgling blood. The crowd roared its approval.

Lightning flashed from the clouds and the storm broke, disorienting the crossbowmen scanning the crowd for the hidden archer. Arrows thudded into three of them, as more men in the crowd opened their cloaks to reveal longbows and let loose a deadly volley. James' heart leapt. He had not expected rescue. Horsemen and foot soldiers were overwhelmed. Years of suppressed rage against injustice had exploded into bloodlust against all authority. Sir Giles was shocked, angry, but saw that he was outnumbered. His guards closed ranks about him and commenced a fighting retreat.

Two of the mercenaries wanted to intervene, but Cedric stayed them with a look. Their orders were to observe and it was clear that the three of them, strong soldiers though they were, could not affect the outcome against so many.

Rufus signaled his sons to hide below. Ben reached the steps first, just dodging an arrow. He missed his footing, and slammed into a post, falling dazed downstairs into the crawlspace. Rufus and Will rapidly followed, shedding their hoods. They grabbed headsman's axes to defend themselves against the crowd now tearing through the lattice. Harriet cradled Ben in her arms. Rufus turned to yell at Alice: "Run, child! Run!"

Two of Sir Giles' guards, cut off from escape, used their halberds to chop through the lattice into the crawlspace. An arrow felled one at Alice's feet. Picking up the fallen halberd, Alice moved to protect her mother. Too late. A townsman clubbed Harriet unconscious, while others advanced on Alice. She swung the halberd. They backed away. Then the invading crowd's attention was diverted by the sudden overpowering of the executioner and his other son. Alice heard a villager's voice cut through the din: "String 'em up!"

As her family were dragged up the steps to the platform, Alice and her father shared one last agonized glimpse. She knew now that she must run or share their fate. Using the halberd as a battering ram, she smashed through the lattice. Torrential rain pelted down. Thunder and lightning split the air as Alice dashed from the rear of the scaffold. She looked up, trying to learn the fate of her family, but cheering villagers obscured her view. James would save them, she hoped desperately, if he was still alive. She saw the young sheep stealers, released from their bonds, bolt free. Then someone tried to grab her. She ducked, and ran towards a group of townsfolk sheltering at the tree line. Her coif slipped from her head and her bright hair streamed behind her in the freshening wind. The villagers gaped through the downpour as her shape loomed, wild-eyed, howling like a banshee and swinging the halberd. The men scattered.

Alice's escape into the trees had been observed by the mercenaries. Cedric decided that there was a little flexibility in their orders. "Some sport, mayhap?" he offered. Without hesitation, they headed along the tree line in pursuit. Unaware, Alice ran through the forest as nimbly as her bare feet allowed until she was a good distance away. She stopped under a gnarled oak, her panting giving way to miserable sobs. She looked back, but the storm and descending twilight obscured her pursuers till one burst through a bush a few yards away, a thin-faced pock-marked man with curly red hair, holding a short length of rope.

Alice immediately understood his intentions. She grabbed the halberd and turned to run. Another appeared on the path ahead of her, dagger drawn. Then a third closed in from her flank. Jabbing with the spear point of the halberd, she held them off, till they all rushed her at once. She swung the weapon in a wide arc. Her targets ducked. The axe head embedded in the trunk of the oak. They were on her before she could free it.

The mercenaries had often shared peasant prey like this throughout their travels, and fell into a familiar routine. Gareth grabbed her wrists and sought to bind her. Andrew used his dagger to cut the cord at her waist. Cedric ripped off the soaking woolen shift. Alice was now naked, but slippery. As they put their hands on her, she twisted out of their grasp. They lunged at her but she was too quick. She snatched up a fallen tree branch, parried a dagger thrust, and then swung the branch into Gareth's groin, before backhanding it into Andrew's temple. Both fell stunned. Cedric recoiled and slipped in the mud. Alice took off in the opposite direction. Before her attackers could collect themselves, she had vanished into the swirling rain.

As Alice hurtled through the forest, the storm reached a paroxysm of sheet lightning and explosive thunder. Disoriented, she slammed into a tree and fell. Her vision blurred, colours changed. Everything slowed. Echoing sounds assaulted her ears. A thick hedge appeared in front of her. She crawled through it, only to tumble down a steep grassy slope, rolling onto a hard, smooth, rain swept surface. Then a distant noise made her freeze. Moving lights pierced the rain ahead, dancing along the opposite hedge, approaching with extraordinary speed. Dizzy with exhaustion, Alice tried to get up. The lights became two eyes of a hulking roaring Beast approaching fast. Her strength gave out; she sank to her knees. The roaring became a screeching, like the caw of a monstrous crow. The Beast twisted a little in its path as it closed on her, stopping inches from her face.

Alice could feel the pulsing heat of its body, breathing on her from a narrow slit between the intense light of its glowing eyes. There was a clicking sound. What was this hellish creature? The flank of the beast swung away from its body like a wing. Feet descended, not as though a rider were slipping from its back; rather, they emerged from the very bowels of the creature.

The Beast was a car. A 2020 model Toyota Land Cruiser, to be precise.

Certain that Satan himself was standing above her, Alice lapsed into unconsciousness.

CHAPTER 2

Heaven, Hell, or Purgatory?

WITH A RASPING intake of breath, Alice awoke and sat upright. Did the beast eat me up, she wondered, am I dead? A blur surrounded her till she blinked it away. Instinctively, she clutched at her body to find that she was clothed. In a gown of soft fabric such as the gentry wear, thought Alice, now convinced that she was alive. But how? And where? Her eyes darted about, taking in a small room, little bigger than the one her brothers shared at their cottage. This was a place the like she had never seen. Or had she? The padded bedframe on which she lay seemed to extend from the walls without support. There was a light in the ceiling, yet no sign of flickering flame from candle or rush light. Seeing a window at the bedside, she drew back the curtain. A pane of impossibly flawless glass revealed a manicured lawn lit by slanting mid-morning sunbeams. Could this be Heaven? She saw people, clothed like herself, playing a game with hoops, mallets and coloured balls; others were wandering the damp grounds wearing the faces of The Lost. Not Heaven, perhaps.

Fearful, Alice cautiously slid off the bed, and there before her was another wonder. Clean water half-filled a gleaming metal bowl, which, like the bed, jutted out from the wall. Alice swallowed reflexively and realized that her throat was parched.

She knelt down to examine it more closely. She dipped her hand into the water, sniffed, licked her fingers. Satisfied, she bent into the bowl and drank deeply.

Ceiling cameras relayed high angle images of all ten cells in the isolation ward to a bank of monitors at the Nurses' Station. The day shift Duty Nurse, June Daly, noted the unknown patient satisfying her thirst.

"5B thinks she's a dog."

"She's awake?" asked Doctor Anthony Picton, Chief of Farnham Psychiatric Hospital, who had just come in to examine her file.

Although the water had none of the sweet tang of the Farnham River, Alice was relishing every gulp. Then a command issued from above: "Do not drink from the toilet bowl." Alice recoiled. The authoritative voice continued: "Bacteria remain in the bowl. You might make yourself sick." Alice dived under the bed. Was this the voice of God? Perhaps she really was dead after all. "I'm coming in to see you."

Dr. Picton strode down the corridor. Why, he wondered, is she conscious? Tall and a distinguished forty-nine years old, Dr. Picton regarded himself a leader in the psychiatric field, and expected his staff to follow the procedures he laid down without question. He checked the file again to find the name of the doctor on duty at the time of the patient's admission. Ah! The American.

Alice had pressed herself into the corner behind the bed, terrified. There was a whirring sound and the door slid open. All Alice could see was a man's legs stepping inside. Crisp trouser pleats, polished black shoes. Uniformly tied laces. Had she ever seen such garments? Again the voice.

"I am Doctor Picton. I'm the chief psychiatrist here." Alice blinked, her mind in turmoil. "Don't be afraid...we're here to help you...come out now...no one is going to harm you." No response. "Do you know who I am?" The tone of his voice made the question sound important. Again, silence.

Alice wrestled with the question. "Are you ... an Angel?"

Dr. Picton smiled. This would be easier than he had first thought. "I try to be." Alice, becoming more frightened, intoned a prayer: "*Gloria sit ad Patrum, et ad Filium, et ad Spiritum Sanctum...*" Picton interrupted, finishing the prayer. "*... per omnia saecula saeculorum.*" Alice was encouraged, which was his intention. "*Amen,*" she whispered.

Picton made the antiphonal response, then probed some more. "Don't hear much Latin these days. Certainly not from one as young as you...What is your name?"

"Alice." Dr. Picton wrote it down.

"Am...am I in Heaven?" she stammered.

"You're...in the best place you can be, Alice, so please come out, so that we can talk properly."

Alice cautiously emerged, curiosity and fear fighting for dominance. She looked at the tall man, his hair silvering at the temples, his demeanour radiating authority. "Come on," Dr. Picton said in a kindly tone, "sit on the bed."

Alice sat down. The doctor sat beside her. "Gramercy, Sir, is my family here with me?"

Dr. Picton's brow furrowed: "Family?" A jolt of recollection brought tears to Alice's eyes. "I don't know what's become of my family, Sir..."

"What is your father's name?" The intensity of the Angel's gaze was beginning to frighten her. Had she not seen a face like his before?

"Craddock..."

"Full name."

"Rufus Craddock, Headsman for the Farnham Assizes..."

Picton stared at her.

As the conversation in Room 5B continued, the Duty Nurse watched the monitor and listened fascinated on headphones. This was much more interesting than the latest panda bear birth on YouTube. Then a man's hand tapped her lightly on the shoulder. June looked up, smiled, pleased to see Dr. Montgomery, the hot young visiting American who had just joined the hospital as an intern. Late twenties, lean muscular build. Black hair and green, green eyes. Umm, umm, umm. All the nurses liked him. He had brought the day shift boxes of chocolate twice this past week. And he seemed to be paying particular attention to herself. June took off the headphones and handed them to him. "This is amazing. You couldn't make this stuff up."

Dr. Paul Montgomery nodded thanks, applied the headphones and listened in for a few minutes. He had a feeling that he was going to be in trouble with Dr. Picton.

In Room 5B, a tearful Alice was recounting the events of the previous night. She ended with: "…then I fell a-swame, and the demon beast came, blinding me with its glowing eyes…and I can't remember no more…"

Dr. Picton stood and spoke as if to a child: "Understandable. So this is what we are going to do. First you'll be examined by a medical doctor. A woman, of course."

Alice gaped. "A woman…is a doctor?"

"Dr. Unwin. You'll like her. So come with me. She's just down the hall." Picton swiped his key card, and the door slid open.

Alice watched this magical act, agog. As he led her out by the hand, an embarrassing thought occurred to her. "Is she a midwife? 'Cos I'm not with child...that's for sure…I'm a maid, Sir, I swear."

"Of course you are. Now come along." He led her up the corridor toward the Nurses' Station, where he spotted the doctor named in the patient's admission file. He called out. "Ah, Dr. Montgomery. Would you join us, please?" Paul Montgomery, the visiting American intern, left the Nurses' Station, hastily summoning a confident attitude.

As the young man coming down the corridor reached a pool of light, Alice reacted, startled. Her heart raced. Her mouth slowly opened. She took three quick breaths. This went unnoticed by Dr. Picton.

"Why did you curtail this patient's medication?" he demanded as Dr. Montgomery approached. When annoyed, Dr. Picton layered a glacial tone over his precise articulation.

On these occasions, which rarely occurred because his staff were highly motivated not to annoy him, he exuded disdain.

This was Paul's first week, but he had already heard stories of Picton's Pique. Nonetheless, Paul was undeterred. He was going to test the boundaries. "She was a new admission. I don't sedate patients heavily until I've examined them."

Paul noticed that the girl was staring at him intently. What was it about this girl, marked for evaluation and transfer? She was pale, with an arresting ethereal beauty. How had she come to be in a small private mental hospital with no family in attendance, and without identification? Paul had taken special note of the "Transfer Patient" designation on her file. He had taken her pulse. Her heart rate was quite low. The standing directive to place indigent transfer patients in restraints upon admission and to medicate them heavily every four hours seemed unnecessary and potentially dangerous, and Paul had chosen to countermand the orders. Paul knew that there would be consequences, but perhaps that would serve his agenda.

Picton's temperature was rising: "Why did you not follow the protocol? She could become violent." Before Paul could answer with a prepared excuse, the girl, who had been staring at him wide eyed, cried out.

"JAMES?...JAMES! YOU'RE ALIVE!"

Alice could not believe what she saw. His black hair was short rather than long and he talked strange, but his nose, his mouth, his handsome face, were the same, and above all his green eyes were the eyes of James De Fries. Without a doubt.

Dr. Picton watched astonished as Alice flung her arms tightly round Paul, mixing kisses with breathless questions. "What came to pass? Oh, my love, how did you escape? Is my Da safe? Tell me, I pray you."

Dr. Picton interrupted. "Do you know this patient?"

Paul sensed the girl's emotional fragility. He took Alice gently by the cheeks, stopping her from kissing him. "Never seen her before in my..."

Alice interjected. "James! It is I, your Alice! You know me..."

Picton looked concerned. "Are you sure you do not know this person?"

"Yes, I'm sure!" Paul said with alacrity, then softened his tone to Alice: "Look, I'm sorry. You must be mistaking me for someone else..."

What does he mean? Who else could he be? thought Alice, her joy withering, panic growing. "James, please, why do you deny...?"

Dr. Picton called out to the Duty Nurse. "Nurse Daly! Dr. Unwin. Thorazine, please. 100 mgs."

Paul continued to deal with Alice's mounting distress.

"James, please!"

"Sorry, my name is Paul. Dr. Paul Montgomery..."

Alice was bereft. "James, do you care not for me? Why do you treat me so? Why?"

Their interchange continued in this vein till the Duty Nurse arrived, syringe in hand, followed by Dr. Rose Unwin. Alice saw the tiny spiked weapon in the hand of one of the strangely-dressed women. She turned to run but Picton grabbed her. Alice started screaming and kicking.

"AAAGH! Unhand me!"

Paul held her by the shoulders. "Calm down, please" he urged. "No one's going to hurt you."

"This cannot be Heaven. I must be in Hell!" Alice wailed.

Two Male Nurses arrived. Together they held her as Dr. Unwin administered the injection. "Don't be afraid, dear," she soothed. "Everything's going to be fine."

"NO! NO! James...I beseech you to help me!"

The girl's eyes seemed to bore into him, accusing and imploring. It was clear to Paul that she was convinced they knew one another; and that he was one James De Fries, the local Robin Hood character about whom Paul had overheard her speak to Picton through the patient monitor headphones; apparently, that James was the love of her life. This was an unexpected wild card thrown into the game he was playing, one that could endanger his plans. But something made Paul want to soothe her. Quite normal in a doctor, although Paul was, in fact, no doctor.

"It will be alright, I promise," he found himself saying.

Dr. Unwin extracted the needle. The Duty Nurse followed with a swab and a Band-Aid: "Charted at 11:10 a.m., February 6th, 2020."

"Please, James...I love you, James. Please, my love..."

Alice's eyes closed and she gradually lapsed into unconsciousness.

***

Her eyes opened to daylight filtering through leaves. She looked up to see a horse and rider rimmed by the sun. Three other horsemen stood nearby, unrecognizable in the back light. She was naked, splattered with dried mud, in the middle of a rutted track between hedgerows. The nearest rider threw a ragged cloak at her.

"Cover yourself," said a deep Spanish-inflected voice.

Alice sat up, wrapping the cloak about herself, confused and disoriented. Two horsemen leapt down from their mounts. As they dragged her to her feet, she recognized them as two of the men who had attacked her the previous night. The third attacker, the tallest, remained mounted and observed her. The other two lashed her wrists together with a thong. Alice cried out to the rider looming over her, silhouetted against the sun.

"Sir, these ruffians accosted me! Yesterday eve..."

"Silence her!" came the gruff response.

"How have I offended?" Alice asked.

Before she could say more, a filthy rag was thrust into her mouth, and she was gagged. The rider leaned down towards her, no longer a silhouette, revealing a man a little older than her father. He was the Inquisitor Fernando Córdoba, a black-robed priest of the Dominican Order, acting on behalf of Fernando de Valdés y Salas, Archbishop of Seville and Grand Inquisitor of Spain, who was himself answerable to Prince Phillip. Alice had a chilling intuition that the man was evil to the core, like a snake lurking in a field of weeds. She knew this instinctively. Never before had a stranger's malevolence struck her so forcibly. Then he spoke.

"You are a witch, and you will burn in hellfire everlasting!"

CHAPTER 3
Ghastly Yuletide Ornaments

MALE NURSES PLACED the unconscious Alice on a gurney. Dr. Picton, quietly seething and quoting from his folder, reproved the American intern. "This is why she was to be kept sedated and restrained: 'Found naked and unconscious 1:30 a.m. on the Farnham Road. Attacked assisting paramedics.' A danger to herself and others. All of which is in your own admission report."

"The strength of the sedative seemed excessive in view..." Paul tried to explain.

Picton interrupted: "No doubt things are done differently in the U.S., but if you wish to continue to work at my hospital, never act unilaterally again." He turned to Dr. Unwin: "Rose, give her a thorough physical, then call me." Dr. Unwin said she would.

Paul thought that some humility—which didn't come naturally to him— might improve the situation: "I do apologize, sir. I never meant to offend. I was using my best judgement." But Picton was walking away.

Dr. Unwin gave Paul a rueful smile: "Welcome to Farnham Psychiatric Hospital, Dr. Picton's personal fiefdom, and don't you forget it."

Paul responded, "Only my first week. Guess I was out of line."

"We expect that of Americans," she said drily.

The gurney took Alice down the hall. Her eyelids flickered in her sleep

***

The four riders led by Córdoba trotted up a steep wooded hill. On the last horse, Alice sat astride the lap of Gareth, her wrists secured to the pommel of his saddle. He liked tying girls up. It excited him. Neither he nor the other mercenaries were aware of the progress Alice had made toward loosening her bonds.

Gareth had for some time been trying to resist lustful thoughts, as his priest would expect. But the movement of the horse was causing Alice's body to rub against his thighs, and he could no longer resist temptation. His loins had a will of their own. Just a little taste, perhaps, he thought, as he took the reins in one hand and slipped the other inside the cloak that covered Alice. She squirmed as he groped for her breasts, quietly grunting. But she was powerless to stop him. Giving the reins more play so that he could have access to her with his other hand, he whispered into her ear: " 'Tis said a witch's tit is cold. Not so. Be good to me tonight and I'll set you free." A false promise to a witch was hardly a sin.

Alice thought for a moment, then bent slowly forward, lying down on the horse's neck, pressing her rump into Gareth's lap. Gareth took this as a good sign and leaned forward. Without warning, Alice jerked up, smashing the back of her head into his nose. He recoiled, dropping the reins; she twisted in the saddle, got a leg up, and kicked him in the chest with all her might. He tumbled off the horse, hitting the ground hard, snorting blood from his nose. But one of his feet remained caught in the stirrup. Alice snatched the reins, expertly turning the Barbary mare, and cantered into the woods, dragging the wretch Gareth behind her. All done in seconds, before the astonished Córdoba could cut her off. Then Alice ripped the gag from her mouth, and with a yell of defiance turned the horse again, causing the dragged man to arc around, snagging onto a tree stump. The connecting stirrup snapped, allowing the horse to leap away at full gallop, leaving Gareth groaning in its dust. Córdoba and his men rode past, their horses' hooves missing him by inches.

A furious chase twisted and turned through the trees. Alice had been taught to ride a farm horse at the age of five. But her pursuers were skilled cavalrymen. She wheeled this way and that, plunged through bushes, but could not shake them off.

Cedric managed to get ahead of her, turned and charged her head on, while Córdoba and Andrew closed in from behind. Córdoba swung his sword. Alice ducked just in time. Andrew took evasive action, but was unable to avoid a low-hanging branch and was swept from the saddle with a mighty thwack. Alice used the moment to steer her mount into a gully. Córdoba looked round. She was gone.

Alice rode down the gully towards a cluster of trees. Slowing the horse, she reached into the low-hanging branches and pulled herself up. The horse continued to canter without her, disappearing into a hazel thicket. Alice hoped that it would lead her pursuers away. A moment later, Córdoba and his men galloped beneath her and circled round the thicket wall. Alice decided to continue her escape out of sight through the tangled tree canopy, before finding her way back to the village. She nimbly leapt from branch to branch and from tree to tree, till she thought it was safe to drop to the forest floor.

Grabbing a supple young branch of a broad oak that would bend under her weight and let her down closer to the ground, she swung down through the leaves only to collide with the dangling body of a hanged man. The bending branch she held snapped. Instinctively, Alice clutched the hanging man, his eyes bulging, his face purple, swollen and wheezing. He was not yet dead. Her added weight spared him further agony. His neck snapped with an audible crack. She shrieked and dropped to the base of the tree.

Dazed, Alice lifted her head. She found herself at the edge of a clearing full of soldiers making camp. The bodies of three villagers hung from the branches of the trees above like ghastly Yuletide ornaments. Alice gasped with horror. These were people she had known all her life. Then the spike of a halberd was placed against her throat. Alice slowly turned. A tall guard with a craggy face glowered at her. Standing beside him was Sir Giles De Fries.

"Ah! See what has dropped from Heaven…Seize her!" Others from his personal guard rushed forward, still smarting from their humiliation of the day before. They roughly grabbed her and bound her wrists behind her.

At that moment, Córdoba and his mercenaries rode into camp. Gareth, scratched and bruised, shared a saddle with Cedric. Sir Giles called out: "Inquisitor! Over here. See what I have found!" Córdoba and his men rode up and reined their sweating steeds to a halt, snorting and pawing the ground in front of Alice, now on her knees. Córdoba gave her a withering look. Alice understood that protest was useless. She was doomed to the same fate as hung above her in the tree.

"My nephew's harlot," said Sir Giles cheerfully, "the second blessing of the day."

"And the first?" asked Córdoba dismounting.

"News from the Palace. The Princess Elizabeth has been taken to the Tower, by order of the Queen." Alice was shocked.

Córdoba was exultant. "God be praised. That heretic bitch will never see the throne."

"If all goes to plan, she'll see the headsman's block," Sir Giles gloated, "like her whore of a mother."

Alice's heart sank. That would be a black day for England.

CHAPTER 4

The Devil's Teat

ALICE LAY UNCONSCIOUS on Dr. Unwin's examining table, loosely covered by a sheet, under a pool of light in a smallish room with tiled walls. Paul stood at an appropriate distance. Trying not to stare at what Dr. Unwin was doing, he looked at surgical instruments in a metal tray visible through a glass cupboard door. Then Alice made a little whimpering sound, which Dr. Unwin attributed to the exam she was receiving.

Paul saw the sedated girl twitch and give a little moan. A thin red mark appeared on Alice's arm unnoticed as they talked. "Any indication of sexual assault?" asked Paul, wondering why she had been found naked and unconscious in the middle of the road.

"I've examined her to rule that out and actually she's...a virgin." Dr. Unwin rolled off her latex gloves with a snap as punctuation. "Unusual amongst runaways or the homeless. What's her problem?"

"She believes she is Alice Craddock, daughter of a 16th century executioner."

"Interesting," said Dr. Unwin.

Paul studied Alice's face, her delicate features and lightly freckled cheeks, a sadness in the set of her jaw. How does the poor girl fit into this? Feelings of sympathy were somehow seeping through his customary wall of pragmatism. He forced them back. Dr. Unwin continued.

"Other than what we've given her, I haven't been able to detect drugs in her system, legal or illegal. No surgical scars, dental fillings. Remarkable teeth, in fact. Nor does she shave bodily hair, as you can see," she said, lifting the sheet on armpit and pubic hair. "No anachronism you could use to contradict her delusion." Dr. Unwin had also noticed a mole on Alice's left side, the only one on her whole body. Her skin had a milky quality. No sign of pimples or sunbathing.

The girl moaned again in her sleep.

***

Alice lay in a dank room with moist walls, her hands and feet strapped to a bench. Her pain was intense. A man's fingers were intruding roughly inside her most private place. He was a pallid man wearing a shapeless hat, with rotting teeth and donkey's breath. Adding to Alice's humiliation was the presence of the priest Córdoba, and of Catherine, former Abbess of a Cistercian convent once attached to the now-dissolved Waverley Monastery. Catherine had known Alice since childhood. Not even her own mother had seen Alice's bare body after she had reached puberty. When they bathed together in the river before Sunday Mass or during her monthly cycle, Alice always wore a shift. She had done no wrong, yet felt such shame.

"I tell you, she is intact," Catherine insisted, inwardly fuming.

"That my man will confirm," was the curt response.

The erstwhile Abbess noted in disgust that the Inquisitor was making no effort to avert his eyes. The examining apothecary, who also served as the town barber, delivered his verdict: "*Vagina intacta.*"

I told you that, you cream-faced loon, Alice was wise enough not to say aloud. James had never taken advantage of her devotion, despite her invitation. They kissed and hugged, but all

James would say on the matter was that it would have to wait until his estate was restored and the banns of their betrothal were read.

But the apothecary was anxious to please the high-ranking cleric who had scowled at his pronouncement. He knew what was needed. "But note, Father, she has a mole on her left side...a sure sign." Córdoba lifted the cloak covering Alice with a short cane. He bent down and studied the mole, located on her ribs beside her left breast. He extended a finger and slowly brushed its edges. Alice flinched. "The Devil's teat," Córdoba concluded with grim satisfaction.

Catherine glared at the self-serving apothecary. She understood only too well the implications of the mole. "I have known Alice since she was a babe. She is no witch," she asserted.

Córdoba looked at Catherine as if she were a simpleton. "A whole town does not commit the sin of rebellion without Satan's hand. Witches are his emissaries."

"Why do you accuse this girl?" asked the Abbess pointedly. Corrupt clerics had been known to threaten accusations of witchcraft to force sexual favors.

Córdoba resented her insinuation. Simplemindedness he could tolerate, it was the state of most females, but disguised insolence angered him. She would not reclaim her position when this benighted country was reconfirmed in the one true Faith. "She is known to have strange visions. Further, she is the whore of the rebel leader."

Alice cried out: "I am not his whore!"

Córdoba continued. "Found unclothed in the forest after cavorting with the Evil One."

"How" the onetime Abbess interrupted, "can she have lain with the Devil when she is yet a maid?"

"Satan delights in unnatural practice."

While Alice did not understand his implication, she was still outraged: "I've lain with no one!"

"Silence!" Córdoba lashed her left arm with his cane.

CHAPTER 5

Ghost Detainee

IN THE EXAMINATION room the discussion continued. Paul stated: "Her dissociative symptoms might indicate somatization disorder, psychogenic amnesia, schizophrenia. Or we might be looking at an idiopathic form of DID." He permitted himself to feel a little smug saying this. Paul's abbreviation of dissociative identity disorder, the proper term for multiple personality, had an authoritative ring to it. While it might take nine years of training to become a doctor in mental health, it had taken Paul a mere week to learn to sound like one.

A voice from behind interrupted: "*We* are not looking at anything. She is not our concern."

Dr. Picton had walked into the room. Picton tended to reduce life to a series of analytical metaphors. Other people at his hospital, for instance, he regarded as cogs and levers in a machine of which he was both the driver and the central drive shaft. If the cogs meshed with his instructions, he was content. He admired precision. It made him feel the master of his environment. Yet every machine, however powerful, can be undone by a tiny piece of grit.

Twice now the young doctor from America, taken on for a short term internship as a favor to an eminent colleague at

New York University's Department of Psychiatry, had shown a particular interest in this patient, whose paperwork categorized her as being prepared for transfer, for which there was a strict protocol, the subtext of which was—temporary goods, process and forget. Was a professional degree no longer a barrier to stupidity? But a more disturbing question arose as to whether Dr. Montgomery's interest signaled another agenda, one that could endanger Picton's highly lucrative untaxed revenue stream. Was this Dr. Montgomery in fact some media snooper? Could he be one of those wretched Scientology activists trying to gather dirt on the psychiatric profession? Dr. Picton decided to conceal his suspicions, and conduct such conversation as was necessary in a good humored tone.

Paul made a respectful response, hoping to facilitate his own objective, which was to get time with this patient alone. "But sir, with respect, she needs treatment."

"And she'll get it," replied Dr. Picton, "but not by us. Her behavior indicates that she might be a danger to herself or to others. In addition, she presently has no identity and therefore no money. This is a private institution, dependent on profit. Therefore, she falls outside our charter. However, I have colleagues in London who do pro bono work on behalf of such patients. I am going to transfer her to them. You need not concern yourself with her any further." With a nod of dismissal, he turned to Dr. Unwin: "So how do you rate her physical health?

"Excellent." Dr. Unwin gestured Alice's shoulders. "It's strange, considering she's probably a runaway. She obviously goes to the gym. Look at her biceps."

Then they all saw the reddened stripe on her left arm. Dr. Unwin turned to her notes. "Something I missed."

"Probably happened when we sedated her," Dr. Picton pronounced, anxious to conclude the discussion. "When she wakes up, give her a bath, return her to isolation, give her some clothes, and have her eat something. I will decide on her sedation level later." He looked at Paul as he turned to leave. "I'm sure you have other work to do, Dr. Montgomery."

"Yes, sir," said Paul, with an apologetic nod. He immediately left.

In fact, Paul's next task was to hack into the hospital database to obtain more information on patients marked for transfer, and this one in particular. To do this he needed a staff level computer, not the relic the hospital had assigned to his basement cubicle. Paul sidled up to the Duty Nurse's station, and offered to take over the desk while she took her lunch break. June Daly accepted gratefully. When she was out of sight, Paul called up Alice's file. Name unknown. There was no photograph of her, normally required for a no-ID admission. Alice was simply designated as being prepared for immediate transfer, a feature of other cases Paul was investigating. A skim through files confirmed that such patients passed through the facility on an irregular basis, departing always within forty-eight hours. Ghost detainees. Alice was another one. Paul wondered: Why a clearly delusional girl? There was no recognizable pattern as to what these rogues were trafficking in. A search for more information produced: "Level 5 Password Required."

Paul was just beginning to hack his way round this obstacle when he heard footsteps approach. But he was ready. He hit a key and a First Person Shooter game previously on pause filled the screen. "Die! Die! Die! Sucker!" Paul exclaimed, hammering the keypad, as laser blasts blew chunks off an alien monster.

June Daly entered, carrying a stack of files. "Not you, Nurse!" Paul grinned, shutting down the game and the file he had been examining. June wasn't sure whether to be miffed or flattered by the trespass. But it was a clear sign that he wanted a relationship beyond the professional. She chose to be flattered.

"Well, don't mind me. Make yourself at home."

Paul offered his excuse: "Sorry...but I hadn't realized until I sat here that you're a First Person Shooter fan, too! That cubicle in the basement Picton gave me doesn't have a decent computer. Challenge, when your shift ends? Warn you, I'm a bad ass."

Things are going well, thought June. "Bit of a bad ass myself," she said, deliberately dropping a file. Paul bent down to retrieve it. He let June see him cast an eye on her rear end; not bad at all, and he let her know it. He took the stack of files from her so that she could have both hands free for filing, which made her smile with appreciation. "Thanks."

As the filing continued, Paul decided to take a risk: "Help me out here. Why would a patient be marked for immediate transfer? Where are they sent?" This prompted a sardonic look from the Duty Nurse. "Why do you ask?"

Paul offered a reason that he thought sounded plausible. "Listen, I don't want to screw up again...I see 'Transfer Patient,' what do I do?"

"You carry out the orders in the file," she said pointedly, moving closer to reach a shelf.

Their proximity allowed Paul to look directly into her eyes with his most engaging look. "Please, if she's anonymous, found on the street, how come she has pre-set medication?"

June frowned. "Don't go there."

"Why not?" he asked.

"Look, this is a reputable hospital. It'll look good on your resume."

"I know it is, that's why I'm here. Come on. Enlighten me."

"What did they once say about 'Loose lips...'?" she asked, holding his gaze.

"... never make me think of sinking ships," he responded, returning her look.

She knew she had him. Subconsciously her lips parted. He knew he had her. Not for sex, just information. He never mixed business with pleasure. June Daly did frequently. "OK," she said. "Occasionally a patient arrives under sedation, stays in isolation for a few days, then he's gone."

"He?"

"All male so far. Until now. If you repeat any of this, I'll deny it."

"Trust me," said Paul, with apparent sincerity. "Anything you say is in total confidence."

Two men with headphones smiled at that, as they monitored the conversation with sophisticated listening device technology. June's voice continued: "I think sometimes…we do a little government work." They heard Paul's reply. "Government work?" The listeners were operating inside a dark green van with tinted windows, parked in a clearing surrounded by trees, about two-hundred yards from the hospital.

"Maybe for your government, too." Now that it seemed they were going to be special friends, June felt safe repeating rumors as if they were closely-guarded secrets. "I think that apart from its usual work, this facility may be a waystation for persons of interest to the government…"

"Whoa!" said Paul. "You know what? My curiosity just vanished."

"Very sensible," she replied, happy the matter was closed, and she could move the conversation to sharing a drink after work at the end of the week.

From down the hall, Dr. Picton spotted them chatting and decided to break up what appeared to be developing into a chummy relationship. He'd have none of that. Picton strode up to them and ordered: "Dr. Montgomery, you've worked double shifts. Take some time off."

The listeners in the green van exchanged a look. One scribbled notes on a pad while the other shed his earphones and slipped out of the van for a smoke. As he lit up, he looked through a gap between the trees at the object of their surveillance. Across an adjacent car park, was a two-story building ringed by a high brick wall, outside which a laundry service delivery van waited for the automatic gate to open. A sign on the gate read: FARNHAM PSYCHIATRIC HOSPITAL—VISITORS BY APPOINTMENT ONLY.

32

CHAPTER 6
Trial by Water

SOLDIERS GUARDED THE crowd that had gathered beside the Elstead Bridge on the River Wey. Among them was the former Abbess Catherine, anguished but powerless. The townsfolk were outraged, but mindful of the swords and spears that surrounded them. Alice was kneeling at the center of the bridge, tormented by the thought of her forthcoming fate. What sin had she committed? Why had God abandoned her? A length of rope was bound to Alice's waist and secured to a post; her right thumb was tied to her left big toe with a cuir boulli thong. The mercenaries Andrew and Cedric stood guard beside her. Gareth was spending a day in the village stocks as punishment for his carelessness.

Inquisitor Fernando Córdoba and Sir Giles De Fries paced toward the center of the bridge. Now out of earshot of the crowd, they resumed arguing over Alice's fate. "These proceedings are uncanonical. Maleficium is tantamount to heresy; she should burn in the market square as a witch and a heretic," stated Córdoba with finality. He wondered why his king wanted to marry into such a weak-willed nation.

"We are not in Spain, Inquisitor. The stake would require a trial; a trial, time," Sir Giles countered. "We must act now. Half the county's in revolt."

"Hang them!" was Córdoba's automatic response.

"I do," said Sir Giles, "but we can't hang every yokel who spits at us. Who will work the fields?" Córdoba realized that this was not an argument he was going to win, at least not until the souls of these miserable Britons came under the spiritual control of his Order. Sir Giles continued: "No, the trial by water is the answer."

"To the rebellion?"

"It will melt away, when word spreads that wives and daughters face testing for witchcraft."

Córdoba grasped the strategy, satisfied at least that punishment was still involved. He absolved himself of the present irregularity. Despite the Church's condemnation of the trial by ordeal, "swimming" was popularly used for witches and malcontents in his country also. "If you choose to test her, I have no power to stop you."

Alice had overheard this cynical exposition but pleaded anyway.

"Spare me, Sires, I am no witch!"

"It is for your soul's benefit, child," said Sir Giles, relishing his hypocrisy. "This is a judgement of the Church, which it is my duty to enforce. Pray. Pray for God's mercy."

Alice considered what her last words should be. She looked from Sir Giles to the Dominican. "By God's vengeance, I curse you both to the end of time. You shall pay."

Sir Giles noted the fierceness of her gaze: "Indeed, she is a witch." He held up an hourglass containing enough sand for perhaps three minutes and addressed the crowd: "People of Farnham, by my order, the accused will undergo trial by water till the sands run through the glass. If she is righteous, she will be accepted by the water and sink. If she is rejected by the water and rises, she is a proven witch and damned for all eternity."

A groan came from the crowd, and a few shouts of derision. His soldiers slapped their shields with the flat of their swords as a warning. The rabble will curb their tongues after this, thought Sir Giles. He signaled Cedric and Andrew, who tossed Alice into the water headfirst. Then, in no particular hurry, Sir Giles inverted the hour glass, and placed it on the bridge within the view of the townsfolk.

As Alice cleared the hair swirling in front of her face, she saw the sandy bottom of the river. Flailing on her descent to the riverbed, Alice resolved not to drown. She would fight to the end. To escape death, she would have to manage to loosen the thong that prevented her swimming. Yet even if she were to break free and save herself, her "guilt" would be proven. So far strenuous efforts with her free arm and its opposite leg had merely made her spin like a whirligig. Her taxed lungs expelled a cluster of bubbles.

The death agonies of a young maiden, though curtained off from view by sun-dazzled water, were vivid in the minds of the townsfolk standing behind banks of reeds and cattails at the river's edge. Led by Catherine, they sank to their knees, trying to block out the horror with prayer. Some in the crowd wept openly. Alice was beloved in the village. Sir Giles and Córdoba remained standing, each lost in widely different thoughts. Sir Giles imagined that the girl struggling in the water below was writhing naked beneath him. She was a pretty thing for a peasant. He felt a stirring in his codpiece. Córdoba studied the water anticipating the retrieval of the body. For a deterrent to be effective it was important to display the corpse.

Sir Giles looked at the hourglass. Half the sand yet remained. A breeze rustled the banks of reeds that lined the river.

Alice's struggle to untie the hardened leather joining thumb to toe was futile. Pain seared her lungs. She was tempted to give up, to breathe in water and hasten the end. Sensing a movement, she whirled round to see James floating beside her, who began cutting through the girdle of rope and the tormenting thong. James was alive! Joy at the prospect of rescue intensified the pain in her lungs. Clamped between his teeth he held hollow reed stems. Alice's mother had told her that people who love each other deeply could read each other's minds. It was true.

She knew instantly what James wanted her to do, as clearly as if he were whispering in her ear.

Her lungs were ready to burst, but she knew that she must remain underwater; she dared not use the reeds till they reached concealment in the thicket of foliage beside the river bank. If she surfaced now, which all the fibers of her lungs were demanding, they would both die. She launched herself not upwards but clawing her way hand over hand along the river bed. James grasped her under the shoulder to help her along. They both clawed and kicked and swam like frogs till they reached sheltering cattails. James saw her chest heaving. He quickly placed hollow reeds in her mouth with one hand, while raising her head with the other. Their reeds broke the surface, spouting accumulated water. Then came the sound of sucking air, but the attention of the crowd was on the rippling water by the bridge.

Alice and James knelt facing one another on the sand, their heads arched toward the surface, one hand holding up reeds, the fingers of the other intertwined. As soon as James felt her breathing slow, he squeezed her fingers and pointed in the direction they must swim. No one noticed the reeds moving away. James, swimming skillfully underwater, guided Alice along the dappled riverbank. They surfaced behind the thick foliage of an overhanging willow, now some distance from the bridge. Catching their breath for an instant, they hugged tightly.

"Your family's safe and well," James whispered. Alice kissed him deeply, lovingly. She had known that he would save them if he could. Then she broke from her kiss. There was something he must know. "The Princess Elizabeth..."

James put his fingers over her mouth. He already knew. "Taken to the Tower. We must go to London Town."

"They've blocked the river," warned Alice.

"We'll get by. Quietly now."

They crawled stealthily onto dry land and hid behind a bush. James cupped his hand and made the call of a skylark. Alice was surprised afresh that one so highborn knew country ways. A few seconds later, the light crunching of leaves signaled someone approaching through the nearby thicket. Alice's brother Ben appeared carrying two cloaks. Brother and sister embraced wordlessly. Then Ben wrapped a cloak about her, before turning back into the thicket. Alice and James followed him. Alice, now in a state of giddy happiness, half wished she could stay to see Sir Giles' face when her escape was discovered.

On the bridge the glass had been empty for several seconds. Sir Giles held it up, inspecting it for any last recalcitrant grains. He enjoyed tormenting the crowd. Then he waved to Cedric and Andrew to pull up the rope. It held nothing. There was a gasp from the townsfolk, then a cheer. Córdoba stared astonished. Sir Giles hurled the hourglass into the river, cursing in French: "*A foutre cette con de vache!*"

Córdoba scanned the river, thick forest on both sides. He turned to Sir Giles: "Alive or dead, she must be found, tried and burned."

***

Two nurses charged with getting Alice bathed were puzzled by her distress. Giving the drowsy girl a shampoo, they had dunked her head for no more than three seconds, yet she had come up as if on the verge of drowning. The older nurse had offered maternal comfort. "There, you see, isn't that better? Did you get soap in your eyes?"

Her eyes were indeed stinging, but Alice's distress was not merely physical. Her visit to this frightening world, unlike the odd visions of it she had glimpsed throughout her lifetime, was prolonged. It seemed that she was now living in that strange place, interrupted by fragments of the life she had known. And with each waking, a new contradiction. The kindly older man who had first greeted her, the man she had thought might be an angel, she now recognized. Changed though he was in his hair and attire, he was Sir Giles De Fries. And worse, James De Fries, the love of her life, no longer knew her. As the daughter of an executioner, Alice had witnessed desperation, and she did not wish to wear that face. She must force herself to be calm. She would make sense of all this soon, through prayers for guidance. "One more rinse, dear. Shut your eyes, now," said the large woman standing over her, as she grabbed Alice's neck and pushed her head under once more.

CHAPTER 7
Nelson and Brandt

A CAR DROPPED Derek Nelson off outside a government building in Whitehall, then drove on. Nelson, Lead Security Agent for the British Division of the European Security Taskforce (EST), fastened the lower buttons of an expensive double-breasted suit coat. The morning's work had gone as planned, though he expected mild carping from his superiors in the U.K. and on the Continent that the suspect had not survived for interrogation. But that could easily be written off as operational necessity. Politically bulletproof results were all Whitehall and Brussels wanted, which Nelson consistently delivered.

Nelson was the son of a war hero, an officer from a distinguished military family. Disabled while fighting in Northern Ireland, his father had received the undying gratitude of his nation but its inadequate support. The boy had looked up to his father as to a deeply resented idol. Lieutenant Colonel Nelson had ruled the household as a petty tyrant who aimed to toughen up his only son through unrelenting criticism and punishment. Derek's cowed mother surreptitiously spoiled and cosseted the boy. Together they made out of their promising son a narcissist and sociopath.

Derek Nelson had always known that he was destined for success. When his time came, he would die old, rich, and universally admired. He was certain of that. A scholarship student at one of England's top public schools, his peers were the scions of the wealthy. Their class instinct was to look down on him, but Nelson demanded their respect, distinguishing himself in every field: he was a top scholar, rugby team captain, head prefect. His training at the Sandhurst Royal Military Academy was no exception. Nelson had never found his lack of conscience an impediment to advancement—quite the contrary, and since he was shrewd enough to conceal his prodigious self-regard, he was well-liked.

Like his father before him, Nelson had graduated 2nd Lieutenant at the top of his class. Just in time for Iraq. As the war came to a close, he was almost involved in a firefight in Basra, but his unit was ultimately held in reserve. While his men were looking forward to returning home, Nelson feared that hostilities would end before he would see combat and have the legal opportunity to indulge his lifelong fascination with the taking of life. In the confusion and darkness, he isolated a group of six prisoners, commandeered a vehicle, and told them that due to prisoner overload and the imminent end to the war, he had been ordered to drive them down the road a way and release them. The weary Iraqi soldiers were relieved and grateful, until a while later, in a deserted place, they saw the M9 Beretta in Nelson's hand. Just to make the challenge more interesting, he told them to run before opening fire. By the light of a half-moon, he put them all down inside twelve seconds. Checking the bodies, he found that one was still alive, so Nelson put him in a chokehold and strangled the man. Nelson found the experience empowering. He drove back to his unit feeling God-like, leaving the fate of the dead men to be obscured by the fog of war.

On his return to England, Nelson saw an opportunity to transfer into intelligence and grabbed it. His keen mind and total fearlessness ensured swift promotion. Now he was Britain's top scoring domestic anti-terrorist commander for the newly-formed European Security Taskforce, set up in the wake of Brexit to co-ordinate British operations with those of their continental counterparts. Within the U.K., harsh measures were beginning to gain a level of tacit acceptance from a British public wearied by a string of terrorist atrocities across regional cities. The Nottingham truck attack. The York computer school bombing. The Bristol supermarket outrage. Anger over continuing attacks by sleeper cells made Nelson's penchant for wet work forgivable. So Nelson was given a sweeping brief and a generous measure of autonomy, which had opened up the possibility of hiring out his expertise to private clients.

Nelson's Number Two, Angus Brandt, understood that some of his work for Nelson was entrepreneurial; the other operatives thought that they were carrying out government-sanctioned missions, even though they understood that some of their operations were off the books. A tall powerfully-built Scotsman, Angus Brandt had begun his career at Scotland Yard, where professional jealousy had stymied his advancement, and he had made a lateral move to the EST. There, he and Nelson had formed a fast friendship. Nelson had picked up on Brandt's bitterness and thwarted ambition, and when Nelson decided to freelance on the side, he had had no trouble enlisting Brandt's aid. Brandt was further motivated by the need to provide a fine house for his family and put his three kids through public school. No way would he let them experience the social humiliation he'd gone through as a lad. His wife had no idea how they managed so well financially. Brandt wanted to score big this time, pull out ahead of the game. Retire to Edinburgh's Old Town. Not bad for someone who'd started out life in Possilpark.

Another of Nelson's close associates, a wiry, acne-scarred, red-headed Yorkshireman named Ian Selwyn, was not in the know. It wasn't necessary to fill him in on Nelson's commercial sideline; Selwyn wasn't a man inclined to question orders. The third member of the inner circle was young and relatively untried—Willem Jones. He suspected that some of their work wasn't legit but was prepared to do whatever it took to get ahead.

Nelson's entry into the conference room was greeted by spontaneous applause. Word traveled fast in anti-terrorism circles. At the dawn raid in Walthamstow, although, regrettably, a high-value target had been killed, material evidence had been recovered that promised to yield a trove of useful intelligence. Nelson smiled with feigned modesty, nodding thanks as he strode to the podium. He adjusted his cufflinks and signaled for the applause to stop. It did immediately.

Selwyn measured a quarter teaspoon of sugar into a cup. Nelson was as particular about the precise degree of sweetness to be accorded to Darjeeling as he was about the cut of his suits. Selwyn stirred the cup, then handed it to Nelson, who sipped, then nodded approval.

"Alright then. Let's get started. Preliminary examination of the computers and cellphones we've recovered indicates there's a new crew in town, one of them experienced in explosives. In view of the heightened threat level, all leave is canceled for the time being. I'll be issuing new surveillance assignments later today. Here's what we know at this point..."

After the briefing, Brandt brought cheese and chutney sandwiches in to Nelson's office for a belated lunch. They chewed together silently while scrolling through images on Nelson's computer. The subject was Pamela van Doren, a young woman with a direct gaze and striking red-gold hair. She would be arriving in London the next day for a brief visit to the U.K. before attending a conference in New Delhi.

Pamela van Doren was the young inheritor of old money, from a respected family in upstate New York. Her father had assiduously augmented the already considerable family fortune, and had left his daughter in control of *serious* wealth. Egalitarian by instinct, Pamela was regarded by others in the top tier as a class traitor. Mid-twenties, hip and attractive, with her signature flame-colored mane, Pamela devoted her time, energy and fortune to various progressive causes, but what mattered most to her was promoting the availability of adequate, sustainable and wholesome food and water to the world's population, opposing the privatization of human necessities. Her indictment of corporations that absorbed public water supplies, opposed labeling GMOs, drove farmers to suicide, poisoned bees and other wildlife, etc., was unoriginal. What made her different was having the charisma, the profile and the means to energize activism against them globally. She had made powerful enemies.

44

CHAPTER 8

Strike Three

THE DOOR TO Room 5B whirred shut. Alice, hair wrapped in a towel, sat on the bed in her hospital gown, a tray of food and a mound of clothing beside her. The glimpses of the life she knew had ended when the strange women had stopped bathing and dunking her underwater. Did they not believe her when she told them that she had been baptized? These women had kept hissing at her like village geese. Nattering about the 21st century, whatever that meant…Alice's mind was reeling from contradictions. She had not died, or at least she had no memory of death. James' saving her from death was her last recollection. Yet here she was in another world. Certainly not Heaven, nor did this seem the molten pits of Hell. Was it Purgatory, mayhap? Lost and frightened, Alice put her hands together, bowed her head and began to pray. She begged God to forgive her lapses of faith. She should have trusted Him to rescue James, as He did. She prayed for strength to beat back doubt and fear that she might face the trials to come.

Alice surveyed her cell. She glanced dubiously at the clothing by her side. She was unsure how to put on the narrow breeches they had given her, and why she should be asked to dress as a man. She regarded the tray of food balanced on an unsteady stand. She had pecked at the meal, but the potato was a watery pulp and the meat had no blood in its fibers. It was bland, neither sweet nor rich to the taste, unlike the victuals her mother put on the family table. The memory filled Alice's eyes with tears. Was her family safe? Where were they? Alice took another bite. There was some taste to the food. That told Alice she was not dreaming. Was this to be her real life now, and the life she had known before just a dream that started and stopped? Nay; the smell of the horse she had galloped through the forest was real, the pain of her bursting lungs, the joyous reunion with James and Ben, all real.

She watched the toilet bowl refill once again. Its function had been explained to her, in a tone that conveyed she was meant to know such things, though Alice felt that mullein was far better for cleaning oneself than the flimsy white fluff they gave her, that tore and crumbled at her touch. But, to be sure, this was the grandest privy she had ever seen. Like a child with a new toy, she had pressed the metal button on top of the cistern over and over. But the novelty of the swirling, gurgling water was wearing off. Her spirits sank under the weight of unanswerable questions. She curled up to avoid them in sleep.

Hours later, Paul was back at the hospital after a nap and a snack at The Bishop's Table Hotel, his official residence during his internship at Farnham. He paused beside 5B and watched Alice through the one-way glass portal in the door. Further contact with her was a risk. But Alice was the key to his investigation. He considered quickly slipping inside the room and asking her questions before she could be transferred—to the pro bono clinic in London or wherever else. But there was too much traffic up and down the corridor. The swing shift Duty Nurse was probably aware of Dr. Picton's prohibition. Paul considered leaving it for later. No, he finally decided, he couldn't risk Alice being spirited away. Now was the time.

Paul casually glanced behind himself. The nurse at the other end of the corridor was busy with paperwork. But someone else was watching Paul as he observed the patient in 5B.

June Daly looked up from her video game, wondering why the American's interest in the transfer patient persisted.

Alice's prayers had foundered; she was again experiencing a momentary crisis of theodicy. What was her great offense that God should punish her so? As if to scold her for a blasphemous thought, the door to her room slid into the wall with an unsettling hiss. She startled. There, standing in the doorway, was James. Not the James she knew, who had, but an hour ago, saved her from drowning, before she was thrust back into this strange world of bright light, smooth polished surfaces, and doors that opened and shut themselves. This was the James who denied her.

Paul looked at the sad frightened girl. How did she fit into the puzzle? "May I come in?" He stepped inside without waiting for reply. Alice watched the door miraculously slide itself shut.

"I see they've brought you some clothes," Paul said, seeing the sneakers, leggings, and tunic top still neatly piled on the bed beside her. She was silent. "Let me know if they are not your size." It was the first of a series of questions he would pose to probe the sincerity of her delusion. If she was playing a part, he needed to know.

"I thank you, Sir."

"It's 'Sir', now, not James?"

Alice shrugged, disconsolate. Paul pressed for an answer. "You don't think I'm James anymore?"

Alice stared at him for a moment. "You share his countenance and form...but you talk funny."

"In America we'd think *you* talk funny." His attempt to lighten the mood fell on stony ground. He sat down at the end of the bed. "America, that's where I'm from." Alice stared at him blankly.

After a moment, she responded. "Am I dreamin' or has someone put a spell on me?"

"That's a good way to think of it," Paul offered. "You are under a spell, but with your help we are going to break that spell and give you back the life you should be having."

Alice shot him a quizzical glance. "Life..?"

Paul watched her carefully as he continued to set his traps. "Friends...your job…"

Alice looked confused by the word. "Job?"

"Work. For money."

"My Da gives me three pence every week." Thoughts of her family turned her silent again. Paul tried another approach.

"What king sits on the throne of England?" Paul asked, matter of fact.

"No king. A queen."

"Really?" Paul wondered if she referred to Queen Elizabeth II. Was this the first crack in her story? Paul realized that in fact he preferred her to be deluded, not a dissembler.

"Mary reigns now."

Mary? Then he tracked her logic.

"Mary? You mean Bloody Mary?"

"I would not call her that, not if you know what's good for you." Alice's mood sank further. Tears welled in her eyes. "I am not in Heaven, am I?" Her voice quavered for the first time. "I am in the other place 'cos of what my Da does..."

"What's that?"

"He's a headsman."

"An executioner?"

"Like his father before him, and his granddad. You're born to it...there's no shame...till someone you know is to be put to death. Till it was you..."

"Me?" Paul was stunned. Obviously she meant this James, the love of her life. Executed by her father? Interesting. Was there a Freudian factor at work in her condition? Paul wondered. Alice fought back the tears.

"Am I cracked? Am I a mad girl?"

Dr. Picton's face hardened as he listened to Paul's reply. Although it was nighttime, he had not yet left the hospital, due to a visit from June Daly. She stood beside him, observing 5B's security camera output enlarged on a separate screen while he listened in on headphones.

"We don't use words like that," Paul was saying. "It's Alice, that's your name, isn't it? Alice, you are sick, but we're going to get you well again."

Paul knew how to impersonate a doctor. He gave her a comforting pat on the shoulder, as a doctor might. Something about this girl was reaching through his defenses. Underneath the delusion she had genuine warmth, purity of heart, considerations it was wise to ignore in his line of work. She looked at him piteously, clutched his hand and kissed it. He allowed her to hold it for a moment, then disengaged it slowly.

Picton's voice issued from the ceiling speaker: "Dr. Montgomery, come to the Nurses' Station straightaway."

Alice shrank into a corner. Paul froze. He had weighed the options, chosen the bold move because time was pressing, but his play had not worked out as intended. Fancy footwork was ahead of him.

"He plots an evil deed," whispered Alice.

Paul looked at her. What does she know? Was there some reality buried in her delusion? Once again his instincts kicked in. Yes, there was. It was a hunch, but a powerful one. Picton spoke again, the tone more acidic.

"Dr. Montgomery, now...please."

Paul gave Alice an encouraging nod, then left the room. He walked up the corridor to the Nurses' Station, where he saw a grim faced Picton, watched by a sheepish-looking June Daly, who had decided, with considerable regret, to put job security before recreational sex. Two security guards stood nearby.

"It is becoming clear that this arrangement is not working out."

"Sir, may we discuss this privately?" offered Paul in the most conciliatory voice he could muster. He had a cover story prepared about a specific need this patient could fulfill for his research.

"There's nothing to discuss. You disobeyed my direct orders. Again. Three strikes and you're out, isn't that the way you Americans like to put it? Well, this is the third time you have displeased me today. Strike three. I shall inform NYU that you had inappropriate contact with a patient and had to be dismissed."

"I did no such…"

But Picton swiftly interrupted: "Witnessed by staff and myself, recorded on this monitor." June Daly had rewound the image to freeze at the moment when Paul and the patient appeared to be holding hands. "Not an argument you will win if you choose to pursue it."

Dr. Picton did not need any more complications in his life right now. He had not, at any rate, wanted to have an American therapist, however purportedly brilliant, walking around his facility, but had been pressured into it by an influential emeritus at NYU. Picton had taken an instant dislike to this cocky young man. Today's behavior was definitely suspect. Could he be picking up some spending money from a tabloid for snooping? A disgruntled patient had set the dogs on his hospital once before, but happily his colleagues in the British Medical Association had stood by him and it had all blown over. He recognized that he was probably ruining a young doctor's prospects for a top career, but the man was clearly a loose cannon, whom he did not want interfering with his work for an important client. Besides, an example every now and again was good for staff discipline.

"Hand over your security pass and leave the building immediately."

CHAPTER 9

Compromised

ALICE WAS CONFUSED and dispirited. She would try to sleep again now. Turning her head to the pillow, she shrank back into the fetal position. Perhaps when she awoke the nightmare would be over.

Dr. Picton watched her on the monitor. He would not sedate her again. He would leave that up to the men who would come to collect her, a day ahead of schedule in light of his concerns. And they would be arriving soon.

The security guard gave Paul a look of deep contempt as he passed through the small steel gate in the hospital wall out into the car park. The gate clanged shut behind him. Paul walked on, then began talking in a wry tone, apparently to himself. "That went well, as no doubt you heard... A lot more going on here than we thought. I'm headed for my car, so call me on my cell."

Paul sat in his late-model BMW, stripping off his white coat and removing the listening device he had been wearing. He extracted the transmitter from the small of his back, while speaking into the microphone taped to his collarbone. In this way, his colleagues had been able to record all his conversations, and any observations he passed on privately. Previously, they had spoken briefly about the risks of the step he was contemplating, which had now become reality. He had been told to go for it. Now a new plan was needed.

"Come on guys, check in."

He opened the glove compartment. It was where he kept his Tanfoglio Force 9mm, an eccentric choice of weapon, but he liked its 850 gram weight, and its magazine carried twelve rounds. The pistol sat on top of an envelope. Paul extracted its contents, duplicate hospital key cards to the ones he had handed in. He put them in his pocket. Staring at his phone did not make it ring. A beat later he speed-dialed on his cell. Voice mail. What were the guys doing? He got out of the car, clipped the pistol to his belt, and headed into the nearby woods.

Paul moved swiftly but cautiously through the moonlit trees. Various options for what was happening, and strategies for dealing with it, competed for priority in his mind. The current game was speed chess, at which he normally excelled. He had made a bold gambit, and been checked. Now his choice lay between retreat and an even bolder move. He needed input from his boss and mentor, Section Chief Rick Almaraz, who had recruited him at Georgetown to join the CIA and pushed him through years of training, before bringing him into his own department at Central Intelligence, the Internal Affairs Investigation Unit under the Office of the Inspector General. Rick Almaraz' brief was to hunt down rogue agents. In national security circles his unit was known as The Ratcatchers. Not a great way to make friends. But Special Agent Paul Montgomery had recognized its importance and embraced it with zeal.

The unending war on terror had expanded the ranks of intelligence services all over the world. This inevitably attracted agents with an entrepreneurial bent, which with the rise of corporatist ideology in government encouraged the abuse of power at all levels. Lucrative opportunities for pliable senior agents were available from transnational corporations and corrupt regimes with problems that required solutions outside legal channels. Globalization had conveniently muddied jurisdictional waters. A whistleblowing employee or a business rival could be removed for interrogation, then disappeared to some secret foreign prison until the dispute was resolved, or fed alive to pigs. Although the cowboy days were over, pockets of rogue agents remained, and Paul's department had the job of hunting them down.

Now it seemed that there was rogue activity in the U.K. A protected source in London had alleged that a group of unknown agents from the European Security Taskforce had been making sporadic visits to Farnham Psychiatric, a private hospital, for a number of years. The informant, who had briefly hooked up with an indiscrete nurse at the facility named June Daly, suspected a kind of human trafficking, involving the clandestine use of patients designated for immediate transfer. Given the inflammatory nature of the allegation, before Washington could alert Whitehall, the Ratcatchers were to provide hard evidence that agents of a loyal ally were corrupt.

The informant also suspected that something new was about to go down. There was no time for orderly preparation. Section Chief Almaraz had selected Paul to infiltrate the hospital and had given him a week to absorb enough information to play plausibly the role of a new psychiatric M.D. who needed to serve an internship at a foreign mental health facility in order to fulfill requirements for a major grant. An obliging senior academic, whose requests were never refused in psychiatric circles, made the call to Farnham Psychiatric. Paul joined the staff ten days later. He waited to see whether a patient would be marked for quick transfer. Last night the girl, Alice, had mysteriously turned up.

Two fellow agents had accompanied him to England at the outset of the investigation and recorded Paul's daily interaction with staff from a van parked in nearby woods. Now Paul could dimly see their vehicle through the trees ahead, parked in a small clearing. He walked swiftly towards it, still turning over in his mind how he was going to explain to Rick what had just happened. Paul needed to use the secure satellite phone in the van rather than his cell. It was going to be embarrassing to have to explain his expulsion from the target of surveillance in front of his subordinates, both of whom had more field experience than he did. But it had to be done. Rick Almaraz, whom Paul deeply respected, was not going to be happy that an impulsive maneuver had hindered the investigation, so selling him on an even bolder move wasn't going to be easy.

Paul pushed through the bushes surrounding the clearing at the end of a rutted track, and approached the van where his colleagues were waiting. He knocked on the driver's window. No response. He put his hand on the door handle and slowly pressed the button. Click. It wasn't locked. Then it started to push open. Paul stepped back, drawing his weapon. A dead man with his throat cut lurched halfway out of the door, restrained from falling to the ground by his lap belt. This was Jim Hart, the senior agent.

A jolt of shock, then his training kicked in. Paul whirled round in a firing position, scanning the trees. In a second he had whirled back, covering the dark interior of the van. Blood still trickled from Jim's severed windpipe. Dead only minutes, Paul determined. For some reason his killers had left, but they could return at any second. Carefully, gun leveled, his forefinger lightly brushing the trigger, Paul moved to peer over Jim's body into the van. A half-eaten cheese sandwich lay on the floor. Then another man came into view, Hank Wolnitz, father of three, sitting in front of the hi-tech equipment, his head rolled back, a screwdriver protruding from his left eye socket.

Ice spread through Paul's body. The faces of Hank's wife and daughters flashed into his mind. What could he say to them when he got back from this mission? If he got back. He had never been on a mission with casualties before. Rather his experience was of gentlemanly games of surveillance, deception, infiltration, putting the opponent in a corner where surrender, compliance or flight were the only rational options. Not this time. Paul was a virgin to wet work. He realized he was now the sole survivor of ambush by unknown assailants.

A realization came to him with instant clarity, as it sometimes does to people who stand resolute at a moment of crisis. This was what his education, his skills, his whole life had been building towards. Since childhood, Paul had believed in the concept of personal destiny. Now, it seemed, he had just run headlong into his own. He had stumbled onto a very serious secret. So serious that the rogue agents he was tracking would kill agents of a friendly power to protect it. Something bad was in the works that he was in a unique position to prevent. Inside him were two voices, one that gnawed at his self-esteem and asked *Are you as good as you think you are?* and one that said *Yes, I am.* Paul could fall apart, or he could pull himself together.

Through the rear window of the van, Paul saw distant headlights winding their way up the track to the clearing. He pushed Jim's body back into the driver's seat and shut the door. He scurried to the tree line unobserved. Paul watched as an SUV pulled up. A figure got out of the passenger seat, moved to the van, opened the driver's door, and shoved Jim's body into the back, revealing a blood-soaked seat. With the skill of a dry cleaner bagging a suit, the man covered the seat in plastic sheeting, then got in behind the wheel. Both vehicles drove away down the track. Paul was left hiding behind a tree, his mind in turmoil. These were professionals. The implications were ominous. A rogue was active within The Company.

CHAPTER 10

The Coracle, the Longboat and the Sloop

BACK IN THE isolation ward, the swing shift Duty Nurse sat beside the screens that monitored the patients' rooms, reading her Kindle. A news program played silently on her computer. A Harlequin Romance was unable to stop her ruminating on the scandal of the day, to which she had responded with a heady mixture of moral high dudgeon and prurient fascination. Her day shift counterpart, June Daly, had told her that that nice American doing an internship had been seen groping a patient and had been escorted off the premises. Hard to believe. Just goes to show you can't tell anything about anybody these days. She glanced at the screen showing 5B, the room where the victim lay. Poor girl. That's right, you sleep. Rest is what you need.

But Alice's sleep was far from restful. She was panting as if engaged in strenuous exercise.

***

Breathing hard, Alice and James were paddling a coracle downriver, by the light of a three quarter moon. Resembling a round, black, upturned seashell, the coracle moved with the current swiftly, but would not outrun the longboat, full of sol-diers, closing on them from behind.

James glanced back. He estimated that they would shortly come within range of crossbow or musket fire. He peered for-ward into the gloom. He saw the prow of a large sloop anchored at a bend mid-river, with swivel cannon mounted fore and aft. Excise men looking for smugglers. No sign of crew or watch-men. Perhaps they had not heard of his escape. Perhaps they were all asleep. With luck, there wouldn't be a practiced gun-ner amongst them. It was a chance they would have to take. Alice knew that the means to escape could only come from one quarter, the Virgin Mother. Alice silently beseeched Her to intervene.

In the moonlight, a narrow tributary was coming into view feeding into the main river, with forest on either side. Could they reach it ahead of the longboat, Alice wondered, and dis-appear into the trees? Then torch bearing horsemen appeared along the riverbank. A quick exchange of looks. Now their best chance was to disappear from the pursuing longboat's view round the starboard side of the anchored sloop, and hope that its crew did not see them till they had turned into the tributary and had reached a patch of total darkness under hanging fronds of trees.

Reward was on the mind of the Sergeant in charge of the longboat pursuing Alice and James. The gold coins promised for the capture of the felon and the witch would feed his family for years to come. A lifetime spent in the service of Sir Giles was about to pay off.

The Sergeant saw the coracle change course. He could guess what the fugitives were up to. This posed a dilemma. If he sounded the alarm, the excise sloop might capture them and claim the reward. But the risk of losing his quarry was too great. He pulled a sounding horn from his belt, and blew it with as much wind as his lungs could muster. James groaned as he heard it. The horn roused one watchmen, then another, and quickly the coracle was spotted as Alice and James paddled past the bow of the sloop. Its captain appeared on deck and bellowed to the coracle to stop. In a pig's ear, thought Alice. She looked back toward the longboat. It was gaining.

A grizzled gunner had arrived at the starboard bow swivel cannon of the sloop. A naval veteran, he had fired every cannon in the arsenal, though he had not used a swivel cannon since a tangle with a Dutch privateer eight years before had robbed him of his left hand. He normally wore a wooden hand, gloved, with stiff outstretched fingers. He would take it off each night before sleeping, as he had tonight. But his pride would not let him leave his post to fetch it. He thrust his stump into the ring mounted on the left side of the barrel, placed his right hand on the other ring, and swung the barrel towards the coracle. It swiveled stiffly. Evidently the ball joints and shaft had not been greased for a while. This cannon was ideal for a moving target, such as the one paddling furiously towards the tributary at the bend. He reckoned that several moments must pass from when the fuse was lit until it ignited the powder in the barrel below. Throughout that process, the gunner must adjust the cannon to maintain his aim. He cursed the captain. A farthing's worth of pig grease would have made for an easier shot. A crewman brought up a burning brand. The gunner called for the fuse to be lit.

Alice and James heard the call. They dug into the river with their paddles in a renewed effort to accelerate and throw off the gunner's aim. The fuse, enhanced by grains of gunpowder, sizzled into life. As the flame came close to the ignition point, the coracle drifted from between the cannon's sights. With a sudden jerk, the gunner swiveled too far ahead of his target. As he wrenched the handles back to correct, the cannon fired.

James and Alice turned, still paddling furiously. They could hear the whistling sound of the approaching cannonball. Doom was on the wing, thought Alice. Were they heading into the shot or away from it? James looked at Alice. No words were necessary. She knew what he needed her to do. Instantly they reversed their paddling to stay the coracle's progress. James felt a glow of appreciation for how Alice's instincts so closely mirrored his own. It boded well for the kind of life they were going to be leading together. If they lived through this night. A spout of moonlit water erupted beside the coracle, just ahead of the bow, splashing them both. Perhaps the Blessed Virgin had chosen to intervene. Slashing at the water, they renewed their forward paddling. They shared a glance, then James started breathlessly chanting "*Ave Maria gratia plena dominus...*" Alice quickly joined in.

The gunner ran to the aft cannon. Just as stiff. Hang this ass of a captain! As he swung the barrel towards the disappearing coracle, he called again for the fuse to be lit. There was no time to waste; he would have to find his aim inside three seconds. A flaming arrow then slammed into the gunner's back, puncturing his right lung. Other crew members turned to see a volley of more burning arrows rising up like a flock of glowing birds out of the wooded darkness, where a group of outlaws had been concealed awaiting James' arrival. A practiced archer could loft a shaft every four seconds, and these men were experts. The gunner lurched against his cannon, as other arrows fell upon the sloop, splintering wood like the beaks of a dozen angry crows. A cry of agony indicated another victim, but the gunner could not see where, as crewman scurried about, shouting for pails of water, the escaping coracle forgotten.

The gunner knew from the blood in his mouth that his wound was mortal. Even if he survived the night, the apothecaries and doctors would finish him off for sure. This was an unexpected end, he thought. The excise business was meant to be a quiet life, ideal for an old salt who had survived the Battle of the Solent. He struggled to reach the arrow that extended from his shoulder. His hand gripped the burning oil rag knotted beneath the arrowhead, searing his fingers, but the pain was too great to pull out the shaft. Perhaps this was God's final test for him. Perhaps it was his destiny, if he chose to ignore his pain, to sink this fugitive boat, about whose occupants he knew nothing. Surely their significance, if he stopped their flight, would be revealed to him at the Gates of St. Peter. He would perish doing his duty. The gunner set the barrel leveled at the dead center of the coracle, before sinking to his knees. The cannon fired. He died proudly, unaware that the ball had hit a choppy patch of water at an angle that had caused it to pass just above James' head like a stone skipping over a pond.

In the pursuing longboat, the Sergeant's final moments were a sorry contrast. A rain of arrows from the opposite bank pelted the boat from stem to stern. Panic ensued. The dead slumped, the wounded clutched at the biting shafts, others who could swim stood up, shedding breastplates and helmets before diving overboard ahead of the next volley. Too many lurched starboard, causing the longboat to capsize. The Sergeant clutched at the bow rope as he pitched into the cold dark water. His hand had managed to grip the thick hemp when the weight of the chainmail, which he wore to display his rank, disregarding its risk when navigating water at night, tore the bow rope from his grasp. He sank to the bottom, struggling to tear off the symbol of status that was killing him, all the while knowing that it was futile. It had seemed such a simple task to drive the fugitives towards the armed sloop at the bend in the river. The sloop would do the hard work. He would recover the outlaw and the witch, alive or dead, and take the credit. Now, within moments, the prospect of prosperity had been replaced by the agony of drowning. Worse, he would die unshriven.

Still paddling fast, Alice and James looked back and saw the longboat sinking, the sloop dotted with spots of flame. They were exultant.

"*Gratia tibi Domine!*" yelled James.

Alice truly believed her response: "The Lord of Hosts is with us!"

"And a few of my men!" added James. They laughed.

Alice scanned the looming shadows, then heard him call her name. She turned. Again she heard her name whispered quietly: "Alice..." Yet James was not speaking. He was breathing hard, concentrating on his paddling. Yet clearly she heard his voice call to her again. More insistently this time. "Alice!"

Alice opened her eyes to find a hand covering her mouth. A man was lying on top of her, holding down the sheet between them to imprison her arms. His face was beside her ear, his breath tickling the hairs on the nape of her neck. Then she heard his voice again: "Alice, you are in danger. Great danger."

CHAPTER 11

Boys' Clothes

THIS WAS NOT the James with whom she had been paddling with all her might down the River Wey, evading capture a few moments before. This was the new James. She was back in that unnatural world that she had seen in fragments since childhood. If not Heaven or Hell, was it indeed Purgatory?

Paul had thought hard about what he would say to her, and settled on simplicity. Securing her speedy cooperation was essential. He concealed a small spray canister in his palm. "You must leave this place now. I will help you, but you must trust me, because I truly care for you." Paul knew which buttons to press, and her struggling ceased. Yet the words he had selected to cater to her pathology did not feel manipulative to him. He did truly care for her. His training suppressed but did not eliminate empathy. She was an innocent, and mentally ill at that, caught up in something beyond her comprehension. By taking control of Alice, he would flush out the person or persons who were behind the illegal activity at this hospital and the murder of his fellow agents. Removing her from the hospital was not only good strategy, but had the uplifting quality of rescue. Paul realized that there was an uncharacteristic emotional component to his decision; he would have to watch this in himself. If he had to abandon her for the sake of the mission, he would have to do it without compunction.

"I will explain later," Paul continued, "but for now you must do everything, absolutely everything I say." This was the critical first step if his plan were to succeed. To extract her willingly would be a major advantage in making it to the safe house in London.

With his canister he had gassed, then hidden, the unconscious bodies of every person he encountered on his swift re-entry to the building using his cloned access card. First the security guard patrolling the grounds, then two nurses in the corridor to the isolation ward. He had hidden them in a storeroom. Next the startled June Daly as she emerged late from her office, reviewing the events of the day and thinking that she had been right to report the new doctor's interest in the hospital's inner workings. Suddenly there he was, extending what looked like a cigarette lighter towards her face. Paul had sprayed her like a bug. June had gasped, then staggered, her vision narrowed to a point. Paul had caught her as she fell, then stashed her out of sight in her office. The gas was relatively harmless but brought about unconsciousness within seconds. The target would wake some time later with a headache, and the embarrassment of chemically induced incontinence, which had the added benefit of slowing down pursuit or retaliation. Paul hoped he would not have to spray Alice.

He lifted his head and looked down at her. "I want to take my hand away from your mouth. Do you promise not to scream?" Her eyes grew less wild. Alice responded with a nod. Paul slowly took his hand from her mouth and released his grip on her arms.

"You are indeed James, are you not?"

Paul decided to answer with a question. "Do you trust me?"

Alice nodded. "I have prayed and now grasp God's will; you are here to set everything aright."

Paul wondered what she meant, but did not want to pursue the matter and delay a rapid exit. He stood up and gestured at the leggings, tunic top and sneakers the hospital had given her, now scattered on the floor. He had brought a smart windbreaker and a cap that he had taken from a cupboard in the nurses' recreation room. He gathered up all the clothing and handed it to her. "Put these on. They should be your size. Shoes may be a bit big, but they'll do for now."

Alice stared at the clothes.

"We must hurry," Paul urged.

She fingered the leggings. "Breeches?" Then a realization hit her. It was to be a disguise. "Is this what your manservant wears? Aren't you the clever one?" She pulled the hospital gown up over her shoulders. She felt no shame in exposing her body to James. Paul averted his gaze.

"You'll have to clothe me," said Alice, "I know nothing of a boy's clothes."

"Alice, put them on," Paul said, facing resolutely away. He looked at his watch. Close to ten. The longer this took, the greater the potential for staff from another part of the hospital stumbling across his handiwork.

"Not without your aid, I can't," came Alice's insistent reply.

It was quicker to comply than to argue. Paul turned and started dressing her as he would a child.

"What a handsome doublet!" Alice exclaimed as the tunic slipped over her hips. For a microsecond, Paul was struck by how beautiful she was in the night lighting of the cell. It was impossible not to notice the curves of her body. Paul pushed such thoughts aside as he struggled to help put on the leggings. As he slid socks over her toes, Alice marveled at their softness. Paul slipped a sneaker onto each foot and tied the laces. She liked the way the shoes gripped her toes and the arches of her feet.

Paul exited the cell with his spray cylinder in one hand and leading Alice out with the other. She looked with curiosity at the swing shift Nurse lying across her desk.

"Has the Lady taken ill?"

"Just sleeping."

Alice did not notice the security guard lying face down under a bush, as Paul hustled her through the garden at the run. They reached the steel gate in the wall outside the car park, monitored by a security camera. If Dr. Picton, still at work in his office, had happened to glance at the bank of security monitors, he would have seen the American intern abducting his mysterious patient. Instead, Picton was intent on texting his most important client, confirming their earlier phone conversation. He reported in oblique terms the suspicions he had about this American's interest in the patient in 5B, and that he had immediately terminated said doctor, whom he theorized was in the pay of a muckraking journal. He wanted the man checked out and attached his information. So Paul's abduction of Alice, currently Picton's prime commodity, went unnoticed by him, something so inauspicious that the doctor could not even have conceived of it happening.

Alice gawked at the lights above the hospital's main gate. She had never before seen lamps that burned so brightly that it hurt your eyes to look at them. Under the glare of the overhead Zenon, Paul swiped his cloned key card, and scrutinized the darkened building behind them for movement. The LED went green and Paul pushed the gate open. There were no cars left in the car park other than his BMW, which was in the shadow of the trees that ringed the facility. As they raced across the asphalt, Alice enjoyed the spring in her feet that this strange footwear gave her. Then a shape came into view and she slid to a halt. Paul whirled round to see her face frozen in fear. He followed her gaze. His BMW stood a short distance away. To Alice, it was like the creature with glowing eyes that had loomed over her in the storm.

"Armoured beast! Nay!" She tried to back away, then Paul put his arm round her, and whispered soothingly: "Don't be frightened. It's...my carriage." Alice shot him a dubious look. "Where are the horses then?"

Paul pressed the button on his key. The headlights flashed, the interior light went on, accompanied by an electronic squeak.

Alice recoiled with a gasp. "This is sorcery..." Paul knew that they had to get moving as fast as possible. He took his spray cylinder out of his pocket, keeping it concealed in the palm of his hand. If she became difficult, he would do whatever was necessary.

"Again, I ask...do you trust me?"

Alice had no defense against such a question. She nodded.

"Then do exactly what I say." He hustled her over to the passenger door, and opened it. A voice from behind him barked. "Stop right there. Don't move."

68

CHAPTER 12
Two Hand Cannons

A WIRY MAN was standing in the shadows. It was Nelson's subordinate, Ian Selwyn. Other than Brandt, neither Selwyn nor the other agents in Nelson's section knew the ultimate purpose of any of the tasks they were carrying out on this mission. Selwyn only understood that they were striking another blow in the global war against terrorism. It wasn't his place to sort out the complexities of intelligence work.

Nelson had handpicked Selwyn in part because he was a third-generation Pentecostal Christian, who believed that the End Times were at hand. His loyalty could be counted on. Selwyn was a man fully prepared to die for a cause. He had joined the SAS, deploying to Afghanistan, and had distinguished himself in battle, earning the Military Cross. Charging a heavy machine gun got you a medal or a body bag. Often both. Selwyn's commanding officer knew that he had a death wish lunatic on his hands from the first day Selwyn saw action in Khunduz. But every platoon needed a death-or-glory boy, as inspiration to others. Selwyn got the medal, not the body bag. In his work for the EST, Selwyn saw himself as a warrior for God in the final battle against the forces of Satan, his experiences in Afghanistan confirming that the End Times were following their prophesied path.

However, this was not going to stop him enjoying the pleasures of life: beer, Irish whiskey and soccer. But there was no steady girl in Selwyn's life. Sex for him was furtive and guilt-ridden. Bang and bolt was his motto. There was no point in committing to a permanent relationship, when he knew he would be taken up in The Rapture before he reached forty. And if he was killed in action ahead of time, it was his privilege to be at the cutting edge of God's sword. Life Everlasting was the one that mattered. But he was troubled by the events of the evening. These were not Islamic radicals they had killed. These were Americans. Of course there had to be a good reason for it. It would be explained to him later, he was sure. But he had followed his training. Doubt was the enemy's friend.

Selwyn set his mind to the task ahead. He had been expecting to accompany the ambulance to collect the suspect in the usual manner the following morning. But Nelson had received disturbing information that evening from their contact at CIA headquarters in Langley, Virginia. Nelson communicated to Selwyn that the hospital was under surveillance by a rogue team. The observers had to be neutralized at once. How much they had found out would be evident when the recordings and computers in their van were examined. Now it appeared there was a third enemy agent involved and he was making off with the package they were scheduled to collect the next day. Selwyn had seen Paul and the girl crossing the car park and whispered into his lapel mike for instructions. Capture and hold was the response from his colleagues, who were transferring the bodies of the men they had killed to a meat wagon and making the van ready for disposal. They would join him as soon as possible. Selwyn drew his Glock 26 and stepped confidently forward into a patch of moonlight, which revealed his pock-marked face.

Paul focused on the man's posture, his earpiece, the way he held his weapon. A professional. Paul knew that he could not outdraw the man at this stage and would soon have his weapon taken from him. He would have to pick his moment carefully.

What Alice saw, as light fell on Selwyn's face, was Gareth, the pox-faced man to whose saddle she had been tied, who had molested her so foully, and had paid for his sin with a painful fall. He was the same man, yet now dressed in strange garments, like James'. Had their enemies pursued her into this new life? Frightening though that thought was, it made some sense out of the swirling nightmare around her. They would all have to be destroyed.

"Don't worry Alice, I'll straighten this out," whispered Paul. He launched into his bluff, as the gunman approached. Paul deflated the natural strength in his voice to a pitch that seemed as nonthreatening as possible. "There must be some mistake. I am a doctor at this hospital."

"Stow it," snapped Selwyn. "Hands in the air!"

"Look, I'll show you my ID," said Paul, slowly moving his hand towards his jacket, not so fast as to provoke a shot.

"Stop!" came the immediate response. A bullet in the head was a hair trigger away. "I will shoot unless you do what I say. Now turn around."

"Don't shoot! Please. I'll cooperate." Paul turned his back, muttering indignantly. "This is ridiculous. You're making a big mistake. You'll be sorry about this, I warn you..."

"We'll see who's sorry," said Selwyn, patting Paul down. He extracted the Tanfoglio 9mm from Paul's belt. "Nice piece... Doctor," Selwyn said pointedly, dropping the gun into his jacket pocket. He would add it to his collection. Alice took a step forward. Selwyn snapped at her: "You! Step back! Any trouble and you'll be sorry too."

Alice obeyed. She recognized the metal object jutting from the man's hand as a weapon. A hand cannon, as they were called. She knew of them, but had rarely seen one. Then her eye fixed on a small metal object in her lover's hand which his fingers were turning upside down. Her James was up to something, as she knew he would be.

Selwyn stepped closer to Paul's back, pulling a looped plastic handcuff from his pocket. Paul half-turned his head in his adversary's direction, gauging the distance.

"Eyes front!" said Selwyn tersely. Ex-soldier, noted Paul.

"Cross your wrists."

"OK. But I have a question for you..."

"Really? What's that?" said Selwyn contemptuously, about to slip the plastic loop over Paul's wrists. In a nanosecond, Paul had swung his right hand up to his shoulder blades and sprayed Selwyn full in the face. Selwyn recoiled, gasping and choking. Paul took a pace away to avoid any contact with the dissipating droplets. Selwyn tried to raise his gun but it fell from his fingers.

"Who's sorry now?" taunted Paul.

What weapon was this that could fell a man with a puff of fine mist, wondered Alice, as Selwyn sank to the ground. Alice ran up and kicked him hard in the stomach. Totally unconscious, the man barely reacted.

"Burn in Hell, you cur! You shall not touch me again!"

So she thinks she knows him, thought Paul, as he retrieved his Tanfoglio and pocketed the fallen Glock. Alice was pleased to see that they now had *two* hand cannons.

Paul pulled Alice towards the car, and opened the passenger door. He had to push her inside and slam it shut, nearly catching her fingers, when she did not immediately get all the way in. Her wail of protest stopped as he took the driver's seat, put the Glock in the glove compartment, turned the key in the ignition. Alice tried to climb out of her seat as the engine roared. He pulled her back with one hand and secured his own seatbelt with the other, then floored the accelerator. Alice was wide-eyed, as they sped out of the car park down the narrow lane away from the hospital.

The speedometer climbed to sixty. "Buckle up," snapped Paul. Perhaps in the heat of the moment she would comply automatically and expose her archaic persona as a conscious charade. But there was no response. "Seat belt, Alice!" he said more insistently, but Alice remained mesmerized, squatting cross-legged on the leather seat. Paul reached across and strapped her in, before propelling the BMW into a sliding turn through a junction onto a deserted country road. Paul's adrenaline was in overdrive and it made him impatient. He needed answers.

"That man, Alice, you knew him...how did you know him?"

"Name's Gareth. Chased me through the forest, him and the others, but I got away. He's one of thy nuncle's men."

"My uncle?" Paul exclaimed. His only uncle had been dead for years.

"I didn't recognize his face at first, but here you call him Dr. Picton."

"Dr. Picton?"

"Sir Giles, you doddypol, stole your land and half the county, made you an outlaw."

"Oh, Sir Giles, of course," said Paul unable to suppress sarcasm. "Hundreds of years later, still alive and kicking. Come on Alice, time to come clean."

"Clean?" cried Alice, unable to understand the shift in his tone. "I am clean. Those women bathed me nigh to drownin'."

Paul reacted to something a few hundred yards ahead. An SUV slid out of a junction and stopped short blocking the road. Paul braked hard and slowed to a halt. He looked in the rearview mirror. Behind him the road was deserted.

"Enemies, fore and aft," said Alice without looking round.

Paul looked round again. Nothing. But an instant later the lights of another vehicle crested a rise in the road behind, then stopped. He looked at Alice. Spooky.

Paul weighed his options. To his left was a break in the fence, giving entry to a track between plowed fields. He could disappear down that track, and while out of sight find another way to slip through the net that was evidently closing on him. But then he might just end up cornered in a dead end.

But Alice knew what to do. Although there was much that she did not understand about her new life, she was recognizing parallels with the life she had known. Their escape down the river flashed into her mind. God was testing them with the same challenges. They must trust in Him.

"Not there," said Alice pointing to the track.

"Why not?" Paul wondered how she could have known what he was considering.

"No way out. Charge through. God favors us, and your men will come to our aid."

So she knew he had back up? But did not know they were dead? Or did she mean that Robin Hood's Merrie Men would leap from the hedgerows and shower his pursuers with arrows? She was crazy. But maybe she was crazy right. With screeching tires, he roared away. Chicken it is. Let's see who blinks.

The driver of the SUV ahead was a junior agent recently added to Nelson's department. He was surprised to see the BMW heading towards him. He had thought that surrender was imminent. He looked at the ditches on either side of the narrow country road. No vehicle could squeeze past his without tipping over. But as the BMW sped closer, it stayed resolutely in the center of the road, with no sign of choosing one side or the other to slip past. The junior agent started to panic. He had been given no information as to who their adversary was. Just that he was to be taken alive. What if this was a suicide run? Reflexively his hand moved to the gear shift. There was a girl he wanted to marry. Was this worth dying for? Although he had just transferred to counterterrorism, he had always thought that dying was what the enemy did. The oncoming lights started to blot out all other detail. Impact was a second or three away. Then his hand and foot took on lives of their own, independent of the debate in his head, slamming the shift into drive, and stamping down on the accelerator. The SUV plunged into the ditch ahead, cracking the radiator, and giving its driver whiplash. As he bent over stunned against the wheel, pain radiating from his neck to his shoulder blade, he realized that his career with Nelson's counter-terrorism section was over. Then a wave of relief hit him, momentarily overwhelming the pain. He had never really wanted the job. He had only taken it to please his father. He would please himself from now on. He would resign tomorrow.

Paul had been ready to clip the tail of the SUV and take his chances on the ditch behind it, but with a deft flick of the wrist he found the gap and shot through, skirting the rim of the ditch with an inch to spare.

Alice had seen none of it. She had simply shut her eyes, put her hands together and prayed. As the car fishtailed back into the center, she looked up and saw that the road ahead was empty.

"*Gratia tibi Domine!*" she yelled exultantly, looking at Paul.

But his eyes were on the rearview mirror. One down, one to go. Sure enough, the second SUV was in pursuit, roaring past the car in the ditch, the driver not bothering to check on the fate of his colleague. Paul would have to lose him and get onto the motorway to London unobserved. As he wracked his brain for a plan, his car phone hummed in its cradle. Paul ignored it.

Alice looked in wonder at the glowing object. She startled as it spoke with Paul's voice.

"This is Dr. Montgomery. Leave a message."

Alice went rigid, clutching the sides of the seats. After the beep, another voice; Nelson in acid tongue. "Doctor Montgomery, or whoever you are, you have taken something that does not belong to you. I strongly recommend that you return it."

Paul smiled. The bigger fish were coming out of the reeds.

A shiver ran through Alice. She'd heard that deep, evil voice before. The accent was different but it was unmistakably that of the grim Dominican, Córdoba.

76

CHAPTER 13

To London Town

PAUL HIT THE talk button. "Who should I say is calling?"

Oh, a smartarse, thought Nelson. He was making the call from the basement of an abandoned building scheduled for demolition. It was his forward HQ for the operation in hand. Nelson's anger was straining at the leash but he contained it as he cautioned the thief. "Just know that there will be serious consequences if our property is not returned or is damaged in any way."

"Then call off your dogs," replied Paul, hanging up. Click.

When Nelson was frustrated, he clenched his teeth and growled through his nose, a sound familiar to his second-in-command, Angus Brandt, taking notes from a call on his headset across the room. It was a spartan office: bare concrete walls, a small fridge, folding chairs, picnic tables full of laptops, and a pair of suicide vests. Brandt had been sewing each vest into the lining of upscale coats. Nelson was privately amused that a man as tough as Brandt was deft with a needle and thread, a skill Brandt said that he'd learned from his granny. The woman's coat was finished, the man's just begun, when news had come in of the unexpected drama at the hospital.

Nelson signaled to Brandt, who put the caller on hold. Keeping the chief continuously updated was a 24/7 priority, which made him the best backup man Nelson had ever had. Brandt was six-foot-six inches of muscle; barrel chest, craggy face. They had been a successful team for seven years now, with Brandt happy to defer to Nelson's leadership, for which he was amply rewarded.

"They know who ordered the snoop. Farrell says he's been neutralized. No leak, no damage, they say."

"They say," growled Nelson. "They're not doing the heavy lifting...Bloody Yanks! Why didn't they tell us about this sooner? Typical!"

"I'll have more details in a moment."

"Find out who this Dr. Montgomery really is," said Nelson replacing his headset. He returned his attention to the chase that was continuing down the A331 highway. The other elements of the team sent to West Surrey to destroy the surveillance post were disposing of bodies or bringing the vehicle back for analysis, leaving Selwyn to supervise the pickup at the hospital, with Jones and another new recruit cruising separately nearby. They had been totally blindsided by the kidnapping. Now only Jones had the suspect in sight.

Nelson was pleased with Jones' performance so far. Willem Jones had proved to be a gifted agent provocateur at political rallies, with an affable manner that masked inner detachment. Jones had intuited the for-profit nature of some of Nelson's work. It did not bother him in the slightest. The junior agent had let Nelson know that he was up for anything. Anything. Now Nelson was giving him his shot at field work. He had to test the boy's stomach. Jones for his part knew that he was being evaluated. He had taken no part in tonight's killings due to his lack of experience, but had viewed the bodies, and his stomach was just fine. Tonight's sudden turn of events was an opportunity to distinguish himself. Neutralize this wild card that had suddenly jeopardized their operation. Do it without backup. The other car had chickened, now it was down to him. Jones hit the accelerator and drove as fast as he dared.

Once Jones had closed within fifty yards of the BMW, he took the gun, a standard-issue Glock, out of his shoulder holster, opened the driver's side window, and maneuvered to a position where he could get a shot at the BMW's rear tires. In training his shooting scores had been high, but this was the first time he would use a weapon on active duty. His orders were clear. Follow them. Capture alive. Hold them till backup arrives.

Paul could see what his pursuer's game was. So Paul turned it into zig versus zag, never allowing his rear tires to align with the gun extending from the pursuing driver's window for more than a second. This frustrated Jones' aim.

Alice gasped as the car's motions jostled her in her seat, but she did not look afraid. Even while his whole focus was in pushing the car to the max, Paul nonetheless caught the expression on her face. A nine-year-old girl on her first roller coaster ride. Petrified with delight.

As Alice's experience of this sorcerer's world expanded, its wonders became more apparent. Such wonders could only come through The Hand of God. Wonders, like moving at great speed, faster than any horse ever could run, while looking outside from inside the belly of a metal beast. Awe eclipsed fear. Satan had no such marvels. She was re-united with James. A new James, now blessed with the powers of a wizard. God had not abandoned her.

As the BMW rounded a bend, Paul saw an opportunity to throw a curveball. He swung the wheel sharply, smashing through a wooden gate into a small field full of sleeping livestock. Jones, in the pursuing SUV, could not turn in time and overshot. But the fact that his adversary had chosen to drive into a dead end was encouraging. Then he heard the blare of a car horn. Tires squealing into fast reverse, he gunned it over the splintered gate into the field, not expecting what came into view.

In the intervening moments, Paul had switched off his lights, and hit the horn repeatedly, as he circled behind the herd of suddenly awakened and grumbling cows. They cantered away from the intruding presence, mooing their disapproval.

Alice giggled. She knew cows well. Obstinate beasts sometimes, so it always amused her when they lost their dignity. Then the entry of the SUV startled them further. The rumps of wheeling cows collided, as Paul circled the perimeter of the herd driving the cattle inward. Jones found himself in the midst of a confused stampede. Dark shapes rushing round him in all directions in bellowing cacophony. Alice could see the trap her James had led him into. She suddenly screamed with laughter, as she had when a pompous tax collector had got himself tangled with a herd of cows on their way to market in Farnham High Street.

Paul looked at her as she became convulsed with laughter. Perhaps the adrenaline built up in her was seeking release. But laughter was a sign of trust. Paul was going to need her cooperation in the hours to come. He folded another group of cows back into the bovine whirlpool he was creating around the SUV, then headed for the smashed gate.

Jones was looking in every direction for his quarry. Then he saw the escaping vehicle going out the way it had entered. Instinctively, Jones swung the wheel. Wrong way. The SUV broadsided with a sickening crunch into an indignant cow, which smashed its horn through the windshield. The glass gave way. The point of the horn stopped inches from Jones' nose. The BMW fishtailed back onto the road, and with it went Jones' chance of early promotion.

Paul checked the GPS. In half a mile he would reach the M3 motorway and blend into the constant stream to London. Alice's laughter had given way to short giggles and loving smiles. She squeezed his arm, and laid her head against his shoulder. Paul decided that it was time to have a serious conversation now that she had seen the reality of their situation. He tried a different tack: "Alice, try to remember who you really are."

"James? You know me..." She could not fathom what he meant.

"These men intend to kill us," Paul said as flatly as he could, but perhaps his exasperation showed.

Why was this James saying what they both knew right well? Alice wondered. Did he not understand what they were fighting for? "They mean to kill HER too! By cunning and lies so no one will know it is them."

A note of unease rang in Paul's mind. "Her?"

"If she succeeds, she will change everything, and they will be swept away." Alice meant that the Princess Elizabeth must become Queen. She must succeed her sister Mary, as monarch, upon Mary's death, which some rumored might be none too far off. But the Princess would not succeed if she were attainted as a traitor, or if she were dead.

Paul pondered Alice's cryptic statement. So far, her intuition had been uncanny. Could she mean that their adversaries were going to kill a woman, before she could "...change everything and sweep them away," whatever that meant?

"They're going to kill ... who?"

"The Princess!" It was Alice's turn for exasperation to show. "The Princess Elizabeth…You know that."

"Jesus Christ!"

"James! Don't blaspheme." Alice crossed herself.

Paul was at a loss. Back to square one. But with a flicker of unease.

"I heard them," Alice added. "They were crowing about it."

"When did you hear them?" asked Paul, sucked back in.

"When they caught me yet again, the knaves, may the Devil seize them!"

Paul was silent for a while, his mind spinning. The BMW entered a long ramp, passing a vandalized sign covered in spray painted slogans which would otherwise have indicated the M3 Motorway North.

"This way to London Town?" asked Alice, hoping the silence had calmed his mood.

"How do you know we're going to London?" Paul asked. The sign had been unreadable.

"You told me at the river, silly," she said with such a sweet smile.

This simple girl was running rings round him. "We're going to a safe house, where they won't find us."

"A safe house. Like a castle?"

"A small personal castle. I'll explain everything when we get there. I don't want to talk any more right now. I need to think. Do you like music?"

"Church music," said Alice piously.

Paul hit the button to the CD player. Music by The Rolling Stones burst from the speakers. Alice nearly jumped out of her skin. He adjusted the volume. But as the band segued into driving rhythms, she calmed and her smile returned.

"Where are the minstrels?" she asked, looking towards the rear speakers.

"Same place as the horses," Paul matched her tone. He pressed a button and the back of her seat reclined. She reacted, then shook her head ruefully.

"More sorcery." She gave him a knowing look.

"Progress," said Paul. "Rest now."

She settled back, wondering whether she would be allowed to learn sorcery, the good kind. She closed her eyes.

Paul glanced at her. She could be the death of him, yet he was drawn to her. As he reflected on this, he saw her foot twitching to the beat of the song.

CHAPTER 14

Safe House

SELWYN AWOKE IN a fog with a foul taste in his mouth. As he slowly sat up, he felt a painful bruise where the girl had kicked him. Then he felt the moisture round his loins. While unconscious he had wet himself. Waves of shame and anger swept over him. He had been about to relieve himself, while waiting in the trees, when he had seen the targets approaching across the car park. No time after he had called it in. He was ex-SAS. Incontinence was not in the field manual, but his trousers were totally soaked. Luckily he kept some old track suit pants in the trunk of his car. The muddied jacket and paint-stained gym pants combo would look ridiculous in front of his colleagues. He would be the butt of their jokes till he could get new clothes. He often was the butt of their jokes due to his religious beliefs. But he shrugged it off, secure in the knowledge they would not be laughing when they were Left Behind. However, he would make that American pay for this affront to his dignity, made worse by the theft of his weapon. He would redeem himself in the eyes of his superiors for losing this contest. Selwyn's lapel was wired with a live feed to HQ, so they already knew about the escape. He volunteered to join the pursuit but was told curtly by Brandt to collect Dr. Picton and deliver him to an address that they would nominate in due course.

Still at their headquarters, Nelson and Brandt disconnected the battery pack that ran the temporary lighting. Jaws clenched, they were thinking furiously. Brandt pulled out a pill bottle, and offered it to Nelson. "Thanks." He took two, and passed it back. Brandt did the same. They chugged half-empty water bottles to wash them down. They knew that they needed to be alert and high-functioning for an indefinite period, and these pills taken daily were designed for that, courtesy of the EST pharmacy. There was a danger of heart attack if used for longer than a week.

"Thirty-eight hours," mused Nelson. He had never had an operation go pear-shaped so close to the deadline.

"Aye, thirty-eight hours," echoed Brandt with a reassuring tone. "We'll get there."

Before ascending to the ground floor, they walked past another room sealed from the corridor by a chain link and razor wire fence which could be slid back and forth across the open doorway. Inside was a cot and blankets. A cell had been prepared.

They exited the graffiti-sprayed building and made their way to a padlocked gate in a high fence that sealed the building off from squatters. Prominent signs warned trespassers of armed response. Next door was a large construction site on which an office block was being built. Work was still going on under floodlights. Brandt had picked the HQ well, a place where their irregular visits would blend with the constant activity next door.

Paul sped into the outskirts of London just before midnight. To insure that they weren't being followed, he drove randomly through its darkened suburbs for about an hour. Then his BMW cruised along a recently gentrified Brixton back street to a row of identical three-story town houses. Paul turned into the driveway of the last one and buzzed the carport. As the sliding door slowly rose, he looked at Alice, now deeply asleep. He was going to have to carry her in. This was not his official address as Dr. Montgomery, visiting American psychiatrist. The hotel on West Street, Farnham was his accommodation for the purported three-month residency. Brixton was his safe house, rented under another alias; his bolt hole, the location of which was known only to him. This was his second visit to it.

Paul carried Alice up the stairs from the garage into a standard town house living room: couch, desk, faux antique rocking chair, TV, bookshelf, wet bar, with adjacent kitchenette, leading to a small garden. A staircase to bedrooms and a landing overlooked the living area. As Paul laid Alice down on the couch, her eyes fluttered awake.

"Go back to sleep Alice. I'll get you a blanket."

"Water...?" she requested in a sleepy voice

"Right away."

Paul got up and headed for the kitchenette. He placed Selwyn's Glock in the kitchen drawer where he kept his safe house weapons. He wanted to get her settled down for the night quickly, so that he could contact Washington and upload the files he had extracted from June Daly's computer. Paul took a blanket from the laundry cupboard, filled a glass with water, and returned to the living room.

The couch was now empty. Paul paused by the wet bar. His head swiveled towards the stairs and landing. Did she go upstairs? Suddenly Alice rose up from behind the counter with a face like fury. She swung a large coffee table book hard at the back of his head. There was a blinding flash in his brain. Paul staggered, then blacked out.

CHAPTER 15

"It's Jane."

AS THE LIGHTS of his mind flickered back on, Paul saw that he had miscalculated. The worst fuck up of his life, in fact. Then the pain kicked in, surging through his head like a fireworks display. He uttered a series of gasps as he forced the pain back into a manageable corner. Then he realized that his arms and feet were secured tightly to the faux antique rocking chair with duct tape. The situation was FUBAR. Paul didn't realize that things would get far worse.

"Alice...?" he croaked.

Alice walked in from the kitchen, holding a cup of steaming coffee in one hand, and a large set of scissors in the other.

"Alice doesn't live here anymore," she said with a wry smile. "It's Jane."

Alice looked just the same as before, but her archaic rural accent, it seemed to Paul's ear, had changed to contemporary British. Paul struggled against the tape. Useless. Jane sat on the sofa in front of him. Her demeanor was confident; super-smart assurance masking anger and fear.

"So..." Paul uttered, trying to sound as calm as possible, "we're not in the 16th century any more, it seems."

"Who are you?" asked the girl who before had been sweetly anxious Alice, but was now coldly contemptuous Jane, as she placed the gleaming scissors across her lap.

"I am Dr. Paul Montgomery," he replied with as much authority as he could muster, "and you are my patient, so please release me."

Jane interrupted. "What's my disorder, Doctor?"

"Multiple personality disorder. It's treatable." Before he had uttered the last syllable, she interrupted him again.

"No, it isn't. Outmoded term." And the conversation continued much in that vein, as they both tried to talk over each other.

"…you've had a transient psychotic episode …"

"…helps to call it by its proper name …"

"It's over now so …"

"… think I've been around more shrinks than you have, 'Doc'," said Jane with a hint of a sneer. Psychiatrists, and she had gone through at least five, were pompous, arrogant know-it-alls.

Paul made a fast recovery. "Dissociative identity disorder. DID. Scores of different personalities have been recorded inhabiting a single patient," he said, finally without interruption. "One is usually dominant. Is that you? I can help if you cut me loose."

For a moment Jane was silent. She lifted a cushion, revealing the Glock and Paul's Walther PPS, an 8 round slim line model ideal for concealed carry. It was his safe house backup weapon. How long had he been out, he wondered. What else has she found? She spoke again.

"Here's a question for you. Hippocratic Oath…How does it go? First do no harm?" She twirled the trigger guard round her finger. Paul hoped he had left the safety on.

"That's for my personal protection."

Jane arched an eyebrow. "From your patients? Doesn't seem like your brand of therapy is working, Doc."

She placed the cushion back over the guns. Paul tried a conciliatory tone.

"Look, I can understand your..." he started to say before being interrupted again.

"Have you had sex with me?" Jane snapped.

"What!?" exclaimed Paul, "NO! Of course not."

Jane left the couch and squatted between his immobilized legs. "Because if you have," she brushed the scissors across his crotch, "snip, snip...off with his head."

"I have not had sex with you, Alice!" Paul yelled, straining against the implacable tape. "Stop this! Alice! Cut it out!"

"Mean it?"

"No, please, Alice!"

"Not Alice, it's Jane," she said, unzipping his pants. "Lucky you caught me in a good mood. I can be mean as a cut snake sometimes. Oops! Freudian slip."

"Jane, you've got to stop this!"

Paul carried on in that vein, but she ignored him. She opened the fly wide. After she knocked him unconscious, it seemed as though something inside her must have snapped. The idea first took shape when she had hidden behind the wet bar. On a shelf in front of her nose was a roll of duct tape. Then after he fell from her blow, it came on her like a fever, she had to do it. Apparently the ground rules to her life had changed dramatically. Were there any rules anymore? Why not? Pretext became necessity, or was it the other way round? Had she been kidnapped by a sex trade gang? She needed information quickly; this was the quickest way. Violating the sanctity of a man's underpants with a sharp instrument. Enhanced interrogation. Choose your euphemism. But still, Jane knew she had really gone off the deep end this time.

Paul bucked in the chair, which Jane immediately stabilized by leaning her weight onto it.

"I wouldn't make a sudden movement if I were you," was her only response to Paul's demand that she stop.

Paul flinched as the blunt edge of the scissors lightly brushed the tip of his penis. Every muscle in his lower abdomen clenched inward. He knew that he had to regain control of this relationship as soon as possible. Somehow he had to maintain the mantle of an authority figure.

"Alice...Jane, I meant Jane, don't do something you'll regret."

"The regret will be yours, if you've used me," said Alice with a dark smile.

"I have not! I swear to you ..."

"You see, I do feel...interfered with."

"I assure you no one has interfered with you sexually in any way..."

She widened the blades.

"You're a virgin!" shouted Paul, "You were examined at the hospital! Internally. A full medical examination, that's all! Doctor Unwin said you are a virgin. Stop!"

This registered. That fact was known only to her and her gynecologist. She withdrew the scissors. Ten minutes ago she had woken up in a strange place, with a vivid memory of what had occurred before she blacked out.

"You're not one of the men who broke into my flat..." Indeed, Jane would never forget their faces.

Paul was relieved; the girl volunteering potentially exculpatory information was a good sign. He was quick to grab the lifeline.

"What men? I can help you. When was that?"

She shook her head slowly. "Who are you...really?" She sipped her coffee.

"I am the best friend you've got right now, Alice," said Paul with quiet emphasis, then an instant later realized that he had misspoken. "Jane! Sorry. Jane."

Jane immediately slid the scissors back into his pants. Paul writhed. "A...hah!" exclaimed Jane. The scissors had found their mark.

"Bingo! Are you circumcised?"

"Jane!"

"I haven't had much practice, but I could take a stab at it."

Paul fought to remain calm. Begging was his only option now.

"Jane, don't do this!...Please!" As he uttered the word, Paul saw his facade crumbling. He realized that he felt just like a torture subject would, about to be violated, trying one last desperate appeal to reach the human side of the aggressor. Like most members of the Agency, Paul was strongly against torture, never more so than at this moment in time. "Don't do this, please, you're in danger, don't do this..."

"Danger?" Her implacable look returned. "What's your game?"

Paul's last option was the truth: "I work for the CIA."

"Of course you do!" snorted Jane with a derisive laugh. "You're a secret agent and *I'm* the loony toon. Glad we got that straightened out...Jesus wept!"

But the fear on Paul's face was so genuine, it gave her pause. And then it hit her. She'd seen his face before. But when?

Dear God. He was James. Alice's James.

At that moment the front door burst open as far as the thick security chain would allow. A big man, 280 pounds of steak-fed muscle, looked inside. Jane jumped up, scissors in hand. The Giant Man. Paul could see instantly that she recognized him.

"Get away from me!" she screamed, raising the scissors. The big man grinned as he put his shoulder to the door with increasing force.

"Run!" Paul yelled. But she had hesitated too long. This time the intruder's collision with the door wrenched the chain apart. He lunged in, closely followed by a shorter slightly older man. Jane bolted for the kitchen. Paul watched as she barely made it through the doorway before one of them grabbed her hair. She swung the scissors. The big man blocked the thrust and slammed the side of her head into the fridge door. Jane slumped to the floor semi-conscious looking up at the two faces bent over her, their outlines flickering, their voices slowing into unintelligible guttural growls. They, whoever they were, had caught her again. For what purpose she still could not imagine.

CHAPTER 16

Crazy Jane

IT SEEMED TO Jane Benedict, before she blacked out yet again, that only a short while before she had been sitting at her computer in her bathrobe, freshly showered, energized, ready to write up her research for a paper to be entitled: "Erasmus' and Machiavelli's Distorting 'Mirrors for Princes'." It was late on a rainy Wednesday night.

As long as she could remember, Jane had been fascinated by the 16th century. So it was natural for her to gravitate toward Early Modern European History after her admission to the University of London. There she had attracted the attention of tutors and professors because of her preternatural insight into Early Modern quotidian village life in England. She had enjoyed lively office-hour debates with one tutor in particular, an unmarried man in his early thirties. Then Jane sensed that his interest in her was becoming personal. Nothing he did, nothing he said, but a change in his body language. He rarely looked away from her as he had done when she had first visited during his office hours. So Jane stopped attending them. Nothing was ever said. She could see him tense up beneath his smile when she asked a question during a tutorial.

It was better, Jane had decided, not to get too close to people. Relationships of anything but the most superficial kind led only to pain. She recognized that she was a borderline reclusive, but who cared? She was quite content with her own company. Jane managed to put her tutor off without incurring unpleasantness, believing that she was doing the man a favor, in fact, because if he truly got to know her, he would run a mile. He would discover The Secret. It was a pretty open secret within Jane's immediate circle. Namely, that she was nuts. Bats in the belfry. Barking. Choose your pejorative.

From earliest childhood, Jane would herself acknowledge, she had always seemed a little strange. Intense. Remote. She would on random occasions either wake from a nap or zone out for a few seconds, then snap back and breathlessly recount what she had experienced in an English country village of the mid-sixteenth century. Initially, such a playful and imaginative child delighted her parents and her two older brothers. But when these episodes started to occur in front of extended family and friends, when nine-year old Jane insisted that she really had traveled back in time for a few moments, and that the whole olden day village of Farnham knew her as a girl named Alice, her parents became concerned. Perhaps, as the youngest child, she was making these stories up to get attention? The vivid images of antiquarian rural life, they reasoned, she probably derived from books, movies and television. They decided to play along and ride it out. Their daughter had an IQ in the 160s. Perhaps it was an extreme form of pre-pubescent hormonal rumblings.

Then, the summer she was fourteen years old, Jane's parents and brothers were killed in a holiday motoring accident, when their rented station wagon took a bad turn on a Cisalpine pass. Images of her family members hideously injured and dying in the hours before rescue came were burned into her mind. Jane herself escaped with minor injuries, but suffering intense survivor guilt and PTSD, and the loss of the people on whom she could rely to accept her idiosyncrasies without judgement.

Her paternal uncle and his wife became her legal guardians and she went to live in their home. Although she was fond of her uncle and aunt, their relationship with her was rather formal and forced. Their hugs lacked warmth. Jane swiftly learned that she could not confide in them. For their part, they did not know what to make of this singular child. Her visions disturbed them. So there had been a mutual sense of relief when she turned eighteen and was emancipated from their care. Thanks to them, however, her inheritance had been prudently managed and was adequate to provide for her university education and a middle-class living standard. Unfortunately, after leaving their home, Jane had embarrassed her conservative uncle and aunt by getting arrested. She and they hadn't had much to do with each another since.

To compensate for the emotional deficit of her teen years, and hoping to solve her personal conundrum, Jane had applied herself indiscriminately to the getting of wisdom. As a voracious reader of history, science fiction, philosophy, psychology and the paranormal, she had considered mystical explanations, like reincarnation, but none seemed to fit. She thought about psychological causes, but her mental quirk failed to conform to the features of DID or of any other pathology she researched. Ultimately, Jane had embraced the quantum physics notion of the multiverse. Life was not confined to one universe, rather, it existed in a series of parallel universes, each either slightly or vastly different from the one she inhabited, all stacked one upon the other in a sort of cosmic hard drive, containing all the options of Being.

Or as one of her classmates had said: "Oh, like a stack of vinyl 45s on my granddad's stereo?"

"More like a CD that skips," Jane had replied, ignoring his snarky undertone.

Hanging out with fellow students at a campus coffee shop, Jane had turned the usual talk of politics to the mysteries of the cosmos. Unwisely, given the looks of sly derision she observed, she offered theories based upon her own experience. She revealed how images of another life in an apparent past inter-mittently invaded her. She defined them as a glitch in the cosmic computer, an unintentional momentary download from one of her other selves. A file swap, as it were. But metaphysics was beyond the ken of her group of acquaintances. It was as though Jane had said that she had been abducted by aliens whom she had discovered making crop circles. Jane read their faces. To hell with them. She rarely spoke about the things that interested her. They would have to listen to one of her raves for a change.

If there was a multiverse, she continued, it prompted larger questions. How was it created? Did God create it? And for what reasons? Did God have to have reasons? What is God? How can we, mere bipedal sentient life forms, hope to fit our limited intellectual apparatus around a concept as vast as that of a Supreme Being? How can we hope to understand the cosmos, when we impose upon that understanding a patriarchal hierarchy that mirrors society's control structures? An elderly but all powerful man with a long white beard sitting on a throne, dispensing judgment, to be obeyed without question. Theologically unsound, but an enduring image. Wasn't Xenophanes right—people create gods in their own images? And a throne? Constant obeisance? God, creator of the universe, needed the trappings of earthly monarchy to reflect his status as Supreme Being? Give me a break! Were people really supposed to accept on faith a system of rewards and punishments for the way they led their lives—the promise of Heaven and the threat of Hell—the two options in the rulebook of life, as defined and administered by society's elite for their own benefit? Please...

Jane often spoke much as she wrote, in complex paragraph-sized streams of consciousness. No, God, as defined by religious leaders, was a hoax. Religions were just competing corporations. But, that said, was there a guiding intelligence behind existence? Jane was not 100% ready to rule that out. In truth, Jane felt that mankind was at the earliest stage of groping towards the answers to these questions. She remembered asking Teresa, the last person left at the table by this stage, was existence linear? Was it just what you could see and touch? Or was there more that we were not yet equipped to understand? But Jane could see that Teresa's eyes had glazed. She was not buying it.

"The multiverse. It's science fiction, Jane. No offense," she had said, hurrying to finish her meal.

"What if it's science? " Jane had countered, "We've invented computers and the Internet. How come? Because they reflect our multilevel cosmos in miniature. Isn't that plausible?"

Not to her friend, who fled the cafeteria, having suddenly remembered a book she needed to check out of the library. Existence is a computer, Jane decided, and computers get glitches. Pop-ups from a past life that somehow bypass the firewall. Or maybe there were nihilistic cosmic hackers scattering viruses and messing with lives. Who really knows shit? Whatever. That was Jane's best explanation for what intermittently happened to her. It was preferable to the stigma of having a mental illness.

When in her mid-teens Jane had first brought up these theories, her guardians had taken her to a series of psychiatrists. One suggested that their niece's fugue states, obsessive behavior and irrational ideation resulted from a treatable imbalance in brain chemistry. Initially Jane had refused to take medication, but finally succumbed to pressure. The prescribed cocktail had reduced her "delusions" and smoothed out her mood swings, to everyone's relief. But Jane stopped taking it when she gained independence. She felt that it was getting in the way of her studies, stopped her mind flowing free. Bollocks! People shouldn't be forced to take psychoactive drugs if they didn't want them, she had told herself.

And that's when impulsivity and obsessive thought caused her to throw a cream pie in the face of the corporate CEO of a bottling company in a demonstration outside his office. When her uncle paid her bail and testified about her mental condition before the Court, he made it clear that she was completely on her own from then on. The Court mandated psychiatric treatment, cognitive-behavioral therapy, and community service.

Jane reclaimed her solitary life, reentered university, and settled into her studies.

Then the evening had come when her doorbell had rung, interrupting her creative engagement with Erasmus and Machiavelli. Of course. Just when you're ready to concentrate, somebody bothers you. Jane tied the sash of her bathrobe. If it was that man in the flat down the hall again, pretending to be helpful while angling for a date, he was going to get the rough end of her tongue. Not the way he was dreaming of, either. But when she looked through the security peephole, Jones was standing there, or Jonesy as people seemed to call him because he wouldn't tell you his first name. A recent acquaintance she'd made at school.

She opened the door with a mildly peeved expression on her face.

"Yes, Jonesy?"

"I was in the area," he said deadpan, then burst out laughing.

Jane wondered—was he drunk or on drugs? Jonesy stepped aside and a Giant Man appeared, wearing a paramedic's uniform. He pushed her back into the apartment. It all happened in seconds. Another man, Red Curly Hair with Bad Skin, in the same uniform as Giant followed, pushing a wheeled stretcher. The Giant pulled her to him and pressed a cloth over her nose and mouth. As she drew breath to scream, she inhaled a sharp acrid smell that spun her head. Vision blurred as she lapsed in and out of consciousness.

Even with her mind blowing fuses, Jane realized that she was being kidnapped, and that the stretcher was a means to spirit her out of the apartment block in plain sight. Not that any of her fellow residents knew her beyond a figure hurrying in or out of the building with her eyes down. Was this some kind of crazy practical joke arranged by her fellow students? Pretty sick, if it was. Then Jane found herself lying flat, with Jonesy tying a restraining belt across her waist.

He leaned into her face: "Hello, Crazy Jane."

Jonesy wore his usual grin, now with a sardonic edge. This cut her to the quick, because Jonesy had ingratiated his way into her friendship, overcoming her customary reclusiveness, and she had confided in him about her past and its problems. He himself had urged her to drop her medication again, release her creativity.

"Bet you're not such a smarty pants now, are ya?" he sneered.

There was more going on here than a man's resentment of a smarter woman. She was in genuine danger, she realized in a snap. But quickness of mind did not activate resistant limbs. The drug had taken hold.

Blackness alternated with flashes of a man peering down at her. He was in his forties, wearing top of the line Armani. It's funny how a suit will stick in your memory. She could tell from his demeanor that Suit was the man in charge. Again consciousness faded.

A crashing sound brought her back. Jane awoke to see herself being propelled on her stretcher out of the open doors of an ambulance, feet first, into a ditch in drenching rain. Sheet lightning revealed forest on both sides of the road. Dark night, pools of light. A raging storm. She looked back to see that the rear of the ambulance had broadsided into a tree, buckling the doors open. Instinct dispelled the fog of anesthesia. Run and hide. Her hands felt the belt and unclipped it. She tumbled from the stretcher into the ditch.

Jane looked back. A tree lay across the road blocking the path of the ambulance. Beyond the tree, a Toyota Land Cruiser had stopped in the road. Men were emerging from the vehicles: The Giant Man, Curly Red Hair, and that rat bastard Jones.

Another lightning flash, and suddenly she was racing through the trees. Then Curly Red Hair jumped out from behind a tree right in front of her. Jones and The Giant grabbed her bathrobe. She twisted out of their grasp naked and ran on. She remembered thinking if these men wanted to rape her, why hadn't they done it in her apartment? Why had they brought her out here? Bastards! They meant to murder her.

A paroxysm of lightning assaulted her, then all went black.

Those were the last memories Jane had had before she had awoken in this strange townhouse, God alone knew where. She realized that she must have been in Alice's life, but could recall very little. Normally, these spells had only lasted a few minutes, an hour at the most, yet this time it seemed from the date on the digital clock behind the wet bar that a day had gone by. And here she was on the couch of an unknown apartment in some-one else's clothes in the middle of the night, with a torrent of anger pouring within her. The man she had knocked out cold while he was coming out of the kitchen was going to give her some answers. Perhaps strapping him to a chair and threaten-ing him with castration was going a bit too far. But all her life, Jane acknowledged, she had had a tendency to go too far. She would not have gone through with it. Well...unless she found out that he had raped her. Maybe. Then she had recognized him. His black hair was shorter, but he had the same bone structure and those remarkable green eyes. Alice's James.

All these thoughts were ricocheting round her mind in the few seconds of consciousness she possessed after The Giant Man bashed her head against the fridge door. Then Jane's world went dark once again.

CHAPTER 17

A Bucket of Murphy's Law

AS NELSON DRAGGED Jane's limp body back into the living room by the arms, Paul called out "Don't hurt her!"

Brandt looked down at Paul, taped to the chair, his zipper undone, a piece of his shirt protruding from his fly. What has been going on here? Brandt wondered, as he pocketed Paul's Walther PPS. This just gets wilder and wilder.

"Hope the blow job was worth it."

"Fuck you!" snarled Paul, bound into the rocking chair, trying to project strength rather than the helplessness he was feeling.

"Au contraire. Fuck you..." Brandt slapped Paul, pitching him back in the chair, before he rocked forward into a backhand. "Ole!" said Brandt, "I can do this all night. Keeps me fit."

Nelson flashed a cautionary look. Not too hard. Make it look like an accident. Brandt nodded his understanding. Not that some mild contusions on the face would matter. The autopsy would say anything they wanted it to.

Nelson processed what had certainly been a strange turn of events. The pickup needed to be as close as possible to the blast date lest the target be declared a missing person. She would be stored at Picton's clinic, medicated in the usual manner, and retrieved shortly before the operational deadline. Then it seemed that a bucket of Murphy's Law had been tipped over their heads. They knew that a storm was coming; they had not expected the worst storm in years. Bloody global warming. A tree had fallen, just missing his Land Cruiser, but right in the path of the ambulance Selwyn was driving, with Jones riding shotgun. Selwyn had swerved, lost control, and slammed into a tree. Somehow the cat got out of the bag. But she wasn't loose for long. Twenty minutes later, courtesy of another dose of desflurane, everything was back on track. Or so they thought. The next evening, the second half of the drop and pickup from Picton's clinic, something that had gone through without a hitch numerous times before, had completely unraveled, largely due to their U.S. clients being caught on the hop and failing to flag a problem till the last minute.

They had done their part. There was no doubt in Nelson's mind about that. On short notice, too. The junior member of the team, and resident chameleon, in the guise of Jonesy, had befriended Jane, providing that moment of trust necessary for the team to gain access to her. Jane possessed a combination of desirable attributes. A history of mental illness had been the starting point.

Dr. Picton had his ways of obtaining the files of psychiatric patients throughout the U.K., and had selected Jane Benedict/Alice Craddock for Nelson's use. Her personal history and pathology made her a choice candidate. As an introvert unconnected to family, few people would ask questions when she disappeared. The pie incident was, as they say, cream. Other useful elements were Jane's radical leanings in her academic work, her political activism, and general instability. A body with the right profile. Should the Alice personality take over, so much the better. Malleable clay. When Nelson and the others had subdued Jane, they added an email to her computer, drafted but not sent, to be discovered later. It stated that she had to do something to make Britain feel the pain it inflicted on the rest of the world.

As Nelson dragged the girl across the kitchen floor, her head swung, banging into the bottom stair rail. Paul saw her eyes pop open and react to seeing him bound to a chair.

"Villains!" she screamed. "Release him!"

Alice then saw Nelson—to her, the Inquisitor—above her. She sprang up, attacking him with her fists.

Paul saw that she was Alice again, her outmoded accent restored along with her fierce loyalty to himself. Nelson was taken aback by the girl's sudden resurgence. He too noted the reversion to the Alice personality. A flash of anger overcame Nelson as she kicked him hard, and he only just stopped himself from breaking her nose. But he needed her unmarked to the end. He regained control of himself, quickly put her in an arm lock, and dragged her kicking and screaming up the staircase.

Paul craned his neck till she disappeared from view. Again he shouted "Don't hurt her!" A look from Brandt told Paul they needed her unharmed for some purpose.

Paul heard Nelson shut her inside the tiny bathroom on the landing. Alice continued to scream and bang on the door. Nelson quickly reentered. Grabbing her by the hair, he hissed: "Make another sound and I will cut off his ears." Alice had seen her father do that to a man judged guilty of lewd acts with children before he was driven from the village. She immediately fell silent.

Nelson studied her for a moment, as he had the previous night. She was a pretty girl, even in the harsh bathroom light. Impulsively he turned the dimmer down till her skin tones turned to honey. He saw innocence and sensuality in her frightened elfin face. It was a pity that circumstances would prevent them getting better acquainted. Nelson left her in the soft light, thinking it would keep her calmer, shut the door, then quickly secured the handle to an adjacent clothes closet with a length of bungee cord.

Alice calmed her breathing and looked around her new cell. Yet another privy. Was there one in every dwelling? she wondered.

A search quickly provided Brandt and Nelson with information supporting what they had already been told by their client. Brandt scrolled through Paul's laptop, taking note of data about Dr. Picton's hospital, hacked from its computers. But no outgoing email dispatching files. No email at all. By the time Brandt had finished skimming the data it was after three a.m. He wondered what the mysterious Dr. Montgomery knew and didn't know.

Nelson, seated on the sofa across from Paul, had gone through the passports of four different nationalities all bearing Paul's photo. He held Paul's spray cylinder in his hand.

"Bet you're wondering how we knew about your safe house, aren't you?" he asked in mock sympathy. "There's a tracking chip in this. They didn't tell you that, did they?" Paul said nothing, inwardly furious. He would have dropped it in the parking lot if he had known. "Intelligence sharing is a wonderful thing," Nelson observed dryly. He signaled Brandt to join him in the kitchen, where they conferred in tones too hushed for Paul to hear.

"How much does he know?" Nelson asked.

"More than we want him to." They both thought for a moment, then Brandt looked up towards the landing at the top of the staircase. Nelson nodded. Hang him from there.

Nelson came out of the kitchen, and sat beside the rocking chair. "Who else have you told?" he asked with acidic joviality.

Paul played it deadpan. "That information is on a need to know basis."

Nelson's temperature was rising. "We could work something out."

"You mean...if I become a greedy animal, wallowing in my own moral filth, like you?"

"Don't be a comedian," snapped Nelson, "or pleasantries are over."

Brandt now left the kitchen, wearing latex gloves and carrying a length of coiled electrical cord under his jacket. Out of Paul's sight, he reached up, and with his fingertips looped the end of the cord through the landing stair rail. He sat down on the floor behind the rocking chair, working on an efficient noose.

Paul continued his provocative attitude, probing for clues in the response. "You're a national security officer. You swore an oath…"

Nelson shook his head. "Spare me the Pollyanna bullshit. 'Nationality' is for soccer hooligans to brawl over."

"Doesn't the land of your birth mean anything to you?"

"You can wrap yourself in the flag if you wish, but, bottom line, we all sell our skills to the highest bidder."

Yes, Paul thought, the classic "It's human nature" excuse. In the couple of years of ferreting out rogue agents, he had found that they all fell back on that. "You sleep well at night?" Paul asked flatly, which Nelson returned in kind.

"Sure, by dreaming of incalculable wealth almost within my grasp." Indeed, if Nelson scored what he thought of as The Jackpot, his wealth would admit him to basement squatter level of the Global Players Club.

Upstairs, Alice noticed water dripping from a piece of metal that protruded from the strangely gleaming piece of pottery built into the wall. The hand basin faucet in the bathroom on the landing had a slow leak. She realized how thirsty she was, and bent down, licking at the drips. She steadied herself against the tap, which turned, releasing more water. Alice twisted the tap back and forth and grasped its purpose. Water you don't have to fetch.

Her thirst satisfied, she looked out the window. The back garden was all of thirty feet below. Alice knew that she would be hurt if she jumped. Then she heard the front door open. She pressed her ear to the keyhole.

Dr. Picton was less than happy as he walked up the steps to a Brixton townhouse where he had been told he was to meet Nelson. He had made his feelings known volubly to the two underlings in Nelson's employ who were accompanying him during the journey from Farnham. One of them, who looked young enough still to be at school, they had stopped to pick up from beside a wrecked car in a field, for God's sake. The other, most inappropriately dressed, had the slight odor of urine about him. What kind of a circus was Nelson running? Picton had made it a condition of their arrangement that he not be involved in their activities. He did not want to know what they did with the subjects he selected or warehoused for them. It was always to be a simple arm's-length transaction. Tonight, despite this clear understanding, he had found his staff in seeming mass hysteria. A patient had been kidnapped—by the American intern whom he'd already suspected. Then Nelson's men had roused him from inadequate sleep on his office couch in the wee hours of the night. He hadn't a clue where they were taking him, or why. All Nelson's underlings would say, whenever he paused in his complaints, was that Nelson was the only person who could answer his questions. Dr. Picton was not accustomed to be refused by staff, anybody's staff, and demanded that they get Nelson on the phone. Then their mood changed from routine politeness.

"Hey, Doc" said Selwyn, in a sharper tone, turning from the driver's seat. Picton hated it when anyone abbreviated his title. "Do us a favor?"

"What?" asked Picton, sullenly.

"Shut the fuck up. No more chitchat till we get there. Got it?"

Picton then realized that these men was not his chauffeurs, but his captors. He was silent for the remainder of the journey, but a small furnace of anger had been building inside as he mounted the steps to the townhouse, carrying his medical bag. He wanted answers.

Selwyn led the doctor in. Jones closed the door behind them. Picton stood there in shock at the sight of the man he had dismissed from his hospital the evening before as a possible media snooper, and the subsequent kidnapper of a patient, now taped to a rocking chair. Anger was doused in an instant, replaced by icy fear. What on earth had he got himself mixed up in?

"Good morning, Dr. Picton," said Paul with a steely look. "Long night for you, I see."

Nelson told Selwyn and Jones to help themselves to anything in the fridge. He noted Selwyn's track pants with a mocking look.

"This yours?" asked Nelson deadpan, handing Selwyn back his Glock.

"Sorry, sir. Won't happen again."

"Indeed it will not," Nelson said.

The two junior agents snorted their "Who's sorry now?" derision at Paul as they passed, then headed into the kitchen.

Picton was aghast. Things were going from worse to terrible. Now there was a hostile witness able to tie him to Nelson. Picton did not want to contemplate the implications. The electrical cord dangling from the landing, and Brandt tying a noose, had not yet registered.

"What...are you doing?" Picton stammered to Nelson, after a moment. He was rarely at a loss for words, but he had just caught sight of Paul's open fly.

"Cleaning up your mess," replied Nelson.

"Look, none of this is my fault," Picton insisted, knowing that the opposite was true. "An old friend at NYU asked if I would take on this..."

Nelson interrupted. "He's not NYU. He's CIA."

"Dear God..."

"Bit of a brawl going on there right now, Doc. All under the radar of course. But you'll be pleased to know that our side is winning."

"Don't count on it," Paul interjected. Bravado was his only weapon at the moment. Nelson glared at him.

Picton avoided Paul's gaze. He turned to Nelson, talking in hushed tones as if it mattered what the man tied to the chair overheard. "Where's the girl?"

"Locked in the upstairs bathroom," replied Nelson. "Quite a little firebrand."

Typical selective memory, thought Picton. "You read her file. Of all the patients I offered, she is the one who best fit your specifications. You approved her."

"Oh no complaints about...*her*," said Nelson pointedly.

"What are you going to do with...?" Picton's words dried in his mouth.

"Ask him some questions. Watch. You might learn something." Nelson walked over to Paul.

"Question time. I recommend you respond truthfully."

Paul switched to conciliation. "Of course, then what?"

"Not much," said Nelson breezily. "You'll just hang around here for a bit, till our client decides what to do with you."

Brandt suppressed a smirk. Nelson was in fine form tonight.

It was then that Picton noticed what it was that Brandt was doing; wrapping a hand towel around a noose made from electrical cord and taping the towel in place. Less of a mark was left that way by practitioners of autoerotic stimulus by temporary asphyxiation. Padded nooses were often found at the sites of such accidental deaths by hanging. Brandt would make sure that Paul's fingerprints were all over the cord later when it was over. From Picton's aghast expression, Paul realized that something was going on behind him.

Nelson moved to the kitchen door, snapped his fingers, signaling Selwyn and Jones back into the room, then he leaned towards Paul.

"I want the truth."

Paul tried to play for time. "Can't be truthful if I'm dead."

"Oh, we will drain you of every drop of truth. Before we're done, you'll beg for death."

Brandt quickly got up and slipped the noose round Paul's throat, applying a metal clamp behind the knot. Selwyn and Jones hauled the rocking chair to a spot below the landing rail.

Dr. Picton snapped out of his paralysis. "Now, steady on! This has gone far enough...!"

They ignored him. Selwyn and Jones cut the tape securing Paul to the chair. Brandt pulled down on the cord, lifting

Paul off the ground. His arms sprang free. He managed to get three fingers of his left hand and two of his right under the towel-wrapped noose, relieving some of the pressure on his windpipe. Just enough to suck in a lungful of air as Brandt tied off the other end of the cord. Paul now hung, wheezing, his feet swinging two feet above the floor.

Nelson nodded his approval to Brandt. Nicely done. Nelson turned to Paul with a smile. "Once, this sort of thing would attract crowds. People would bet money on how long the condemned would dangle, fighting for a few more moments of wretched life."

"I'm not having any part of this!" blustered Picton. "This is not our arrangement." Picton turned to leave. Selwyn and Jones blocked his path. Nelson barked at him: "You take my money, you do what I say. Go upstairs. Sedate that girl. Now!" Picton was cowed. He headed upstairs to the landing. A rasping intake of breath came from Paul. Nelson stepped closer.

"Used to be the breathing difficulty you're now experiencing was sometimes just a warm-up, before castration, disembowelment and quartering, all of which is ahead, unless you tell me who else knows." He was bluffing of course, if only in relationship to marking the man's body, but such extreme statements at the outset often gave him the measure of his victim. Certainly as a message to those who sent him, this interloper had to die the most disgraceful and embarrassing accidental death possible.

Paul could find irony even in extreme situations. To convince them that he was now the only person who had put the pieces together would insure a quicker end to his pain, but he would die knowing he had probably helped them succeed. His mind raced to construct a story sufficiently convincing to keep himself alive long enough to find an opportunity to turn the tables. The balance of probabilities was not in his favor.

On the landing above, Picton unwound the bungee cord securing the bathroom door. He opened cautiously in case there was a raging harpy within. He found the cubicle empty and the window open. He lunged forward, puts his head out of the window, and saw Alice's means of escape—a drain pipe within arm's reach.

Picton ran onto the landing and shouted: "She's gone!" He rushed downstairs.

Brandt moved to the living room window. The garden back gate was open. Nelson saw it, too. He snapped orders to Selwyn and Jones, as Brandt charged through the kitchen to the garden. "You! Circle the block." They ran through the front door to Selwyn's car across the street.

Nelson turned to Picton. "Doctor! Keep him breathing till we get back." Picton's head shook involuntarily. Nelson approached with a dangerous look in his eye. "Leave him hanging, but he must not die, got it? Not! Die! Yet! Have you got that?"

"This is insane!" gasped Picton.

Nelson stepped right into his face. "Do it or you'll be next!" he hissed, leaving Picton in no doubt that he meant it.

Paul saw Nelson grab the laptop, containing all his accumulated evidence, and run out the front door, slamming it behind him.

Picton stared at Paul's twisting body, unsure what to do next. He had to play along. Just survive the night. Once they caught the girl, he could disengage himself, and never have anything to do with these people again.

CHAPTER 18
Wicked Knots

ALICE CROUCHED ON the townhouse roof beside the brick chimney, looking down. Nelson entered the Land Cruiser. Selwyn and Jones boarded the SUV. The cars took off to circle the house from different directions. Although she understood that in this world they had different names, she recognized the men getting inside the mechanical beasts as the Inquisitor Córdoba, Gareth, and Andrew, who for some reason had reappeared as her enemies here to torment her. And to threaten her James.

Alice turned toward the garden. Brandt—Cedric, to Alice—was outside the open gate, looking up and down the back lane. She had opened it to lay a false trail, before climbing back up the drainpipe to the roof, bringing with her a piece of broken tile. She lobbed it into a garden two houses away where it skittered along some paving stones.

The big man's head whirled round. He immediately seized the top of the fence, and with surprising dexterity for a man of his size, swung himself over. Gymnastics as a teenager had brought him in contact with police volunteer sports coaches, which in turn eased his way into the Force. Brandt enjoyed its rough and tumble and maintained his fitness rigorously. Right now he was hungry; he had not eaten for ten hours due to the complications of the night. He needed to get his blood sugar up, so, Brandt told himself, the sooner he caught this little bitch, the sooner he would get himself a good gyro with humus.

Meanwhile in the living room, Paul continued to strain against the noose, taking its pressure off his windpipe, as he formulated his next move. Appealing to Picton's greed seemed the best option. He managed to gasp out a few words. "Whatever they're paying...I'll treble...cut me down..."

But fear trumped greed, and brought a haughty response from the psychiatrist, a pure defense mechanism: "You've brought this on yourself. Nothing I can do..." Dr. Picton was starting the process of absolving himself of culpability. Something he was accustomed to doing, but never before had torture/murder been the subject of absolution. His shoulders gave an involuntary shrug as he exited the room, as if shedding the moral burden.

Paul strained to loosen the noose but the metal clamp rendered his efforts useless.

Washing his hands at the sink, Picton looked through the kitchen window in time to see Brandt give up searching the adjacent back gardens, then swing himself over the fence into the lane as Nelson's Land Cruiser pulled up.

Brandt got in. "Check the local police?" he asked, pulling out his cell.

Nelson nodded. "Start planting the seeds. Escaped mental patient. A history of violence...Fucking hell!" Things were not going well. Better start working on Plan B. Nelson's credo: You never run out of options, they just get harder to find.

A similar thought was running through Paul's mind. A new move was needed. Something that would get Picton within reach.

Alice sensed that it was time to make her move, too. Sure that her enemies were now out of sight, she grasped the drainpipe with her hands and feet and started climbing down. If this was a kind of ladder people built to get to the rooves of their houses, she did not think much of it. It was smooth and slippery. So she had to go carefully, knowing all the while that James was in dreadful danger. Then she froze. She saw a figure stepping out onto the back doorstep thirty feet below. It was too late to climb back onto the roof.

Picton was scanning the fence line. Where was Brandt? He did not want the appalling responsibility he had been given for any longer than was absolutely necessary. Alice's foot slipped, dislodging a leaf wedged behind the pipe. It fluttered down towards the man below, who took another step into the light of a garden lamp.

A cold chill washed over Alice. It was the man with the face of Sir Giles de Fries.

Alice watched the leaf continue its gently spiraling descent. It seemed as though it would pass right in front of his face. If the villain looked up, she would have to drop straight down on him with uncertain outcome. He would pay. They would all pay in time. But for now she must secure herself here, quiet as a wee mouse, and pray that the man did not see her. She squeezed her eyes shut. Then her prayers were answered. Picton turned to step back into the kitchen, not noticing the spinning leaf passing behind him. After a pause, Alice continued down the drainpipe. Once at the bottom, stealth would be necessary till she could find a weapon. Surely there were farm tools lying about? Then there would be blood.

Paul had assessed the odds. Sooner or later his arm muscles were going to give out. But right now the weakest member of the conspiracy was left alone to guard him. Paul committed himself to a do-or-die gambit. As he saw Picton returning from the kitchen, Paul deliberately slid his fingers out from under the noose, knowing that he wouldn't be able to get them back in again. The noose clamped across his windpipe, closing it. He hung writhing, clawing at the noose, as he strangled. Picton gasped.

"Pull yourself up! Pull!"

But still the doctor did not move forward to assist him. He just stood there in frozen panic. Paul's mind raced. A searing pain was expanding from his lungs. White spots flickered before his eyes. How to get the good doctor within range. The supreme gamble was required. After which there were no other options. When you bet the farm, you might buy the farm, as his mentor had once told him. Paul let his arms drop to his sides. His struggles stopped as if he were dead. Irreversible brain damage followed by death was less than two minutes away.

Alice, oblivious to what was happening inside, jumped down. She realized it would be wise to shut and bolt the garden gate again, before running inside to rescue James. She did not want the Inquisitor and Cedric getting back in too easily.

Picton was trembling with stress. He knew he must act. He grabbed Paul round the waist, lifting him up, pulling the noose away from Paul's windpipe as far as the clamp would allow. "Breathe damn you, breathe!"

Picton struggled to support Paul's limp body, when suddenly it sprang to violent life. Paul's risky ploy had worked. In a flash, he grabbed Picton, and hooked a leg around his throat, in a triangle hold, secured by his other leg behind Picton's back. Paul's calf and thigh squeezed Picton's windpipe, cutting off his air.

Paul sucked quick gasps into his tortured lungs, reached for the noose, and discovered the clamp locking the slipknot in place. His fingers tried to pry it loose. At the same time, Picton lunged forward, pulling Paul's body with him. The noose tightened again round Paul's throat. While Picton remained locked in the triangle hold, he had eased the pressure of Paul's leg against his own windpipe enough to be able to take in a breath.

Picton knew that it was just a matter of seconds before Paul would lose consciousness. He just had to keep tugging, not so hard as to snap the man's neck, but enough to regain control of the situation. He would worry about revival at that point.

As she looked in the garden for anything to use as a weapon, Alice heard the sound of a struggle. She dashed for the open back door. She saw just what she needed hanging from hooks in the kitchen. Sword and shield.

White spots were taking over Paul's field of vision when he saw Alice burst in with a frying pan in one hand and a carving knife in the other. She slammed Picton in the stomach with the frying pan, knocking him back and releasing the pressure on Paul's throat. Paul sucked in air, standing on Picton's hunched shoulders as the doctor fell winded to his knees. Alice ran to where the electrical cord was secured to the stair rail and slashed it with the knife. But the blade only made a nick in the smooth white cord. How could it be stronger than hemp? She sawed at it with the serrated edge of the blade. At last it parted and Paul sank to the floor gasping.

"Oh, James, my love! My poor love!" Alice joined him as he struggled with the noose, at last freeing the clamp. Picton got up on his hands and knees. Alice quickly swung the frying pan and clipped him across the side of the head. Picton fell back, out cold.

Rage flooded through Alice. She dropped the pan, took the knife and raised it in both hands, ready to plunge it into Picton's chest. The blade hovered at the apex of the downswing. She had never killed more than a chicken till now. Could she take the life of an evil man, as her father had so many times? But the decision was made for her. Paul lunged across and grabbed her wrists.

"No! Alice! No! Need him alive," he rasped.

"I should carve him like a roast!" said a manic Alice, eyes wild.

Oh, God! She means it too, thought Paul. "Evidence! Need evidence for trial."

"Like there be honest courts in this world, right?" said Alice, calming down. She reluctantly tossed the knife aside.

Paul picked up the electrical cord to tie Picton's hands. The gleam returned to Alice's eye. "Let me, James. My Da taught me wicked knots."

16

CHAPTER 19

Something Dreadful

NELSON'S CAR TURNED into the back lane and cruised slowly along. Brandt scanned the fence line on each side. No sign of the girl. They circled the neighborhood and turned back. Still no sign. Nelson did not want to admit to himself that he was getting worried. Just a glitch, he kept repeating to himself. He could feel Brandt looking at him, trying to gauge the threat level. Nothing in this girl's profile indicated that she could have scaled down the drainpipe. They had been incorrectly briefed by that fuckwit Picton. He would deal with Picton later.

The doctor, in fact, lay gagged and trussed like a turkey on the kitchen floor, painfully regaining consciousness. His first clear image was Paul sipping water from the tap. The horror of his predicament went through Picton like an electric shock. Deep down, he had always known that he was treading on dangerous ground. Yet he had thought that he could justify his work for Nelson as being in the interest of international security. The worst that could happen to him would be some ethics violations, he had thought. Till now. Nelson had deceived him. He would make Nelson pay.

Paul doused his head at the sink as he shook off the fog of his ordeal. Alice looked at him, her eyes welling with pride. God is with us. She was sure now. She watched her James move to a large upright white slab, and somehow pry a section of it open. She felt a puff of frosty air escape from it. You could store winter? Another marvel.

Paul turned to her and croaked through his swollen throat. "They'll be back. We need to get out of here."

Paul had wanted to sound commanding. He needed to take control of this girl, whatever her mental condition, till they could find a safe haven and he could reassess their situation. But Alice nodded quickly. Paul reached inside the freezer, broke open a sealed frozen food packet. Inside, wrapped in plastic, were two additional passports and matching credit cards. He slipped them into his pocket.

Picton's next indignity was to be dragged down the stairs into the garage like a rolled carpet. Alice on his legs, Paul gripping his shoulders, indifferent each time Picton's head bumped a step. The psychiatrist groaned through his gag.

"Should've taken the deal," growled Paul.

Nelson's Land Cruiser had circled back to the laneway behind the townhouse. The gate was not as he had left it. Brandt spotted it at once: "Gate's closed." In seconds both men snapped into high gear. Nelson braked hard. Brandt jumped out. Nelson drove off. Brandt swung himself over the gate, and ran to the kitchen door, drawing his Glock. He entered cautiously, scanned the empty kitchen and listened for sounds. Then he called out: "Doctor?" No reply.

In the garage below, Paul and Alice slid Picton onto the back seat. "Turnabout is fair play, eh Sir Giles?" hissed Alice, with a vehemence that was noted by Paul.

"Don't do this!" Picton bellowed beneath the gag. Paul slammed the door shut.

Brandt reacted to a distant sound, uncertain whether it came from another room or the street outside. Gun at the ready, he raced to the doorway of the living room. The noose was nowhere to be seen. The rocking chair was lying well away from where he remembered it. No sign of their prisoner or that idiot Picton. Brandt swung his gun towards the landing and listened. The next sound told him what he needed to know, the whirr of the garage door retracting. Brandt rushed downstairs to find the door leading into the garage jammed by a crowbar that Paul had strategically wedged. He hurled himself against the door, but it scarcely moved.

At the same time, the rising garage door came into view through Nelson's windscreen, as he swung the Land Cruiser into the entrance of the cul de sac. How had a half-hanged man outwitted a top psychiatrist? Then, as he accelerated towards the townhouse, he guessed how. There was a figure in the passenger seat of Paul's reversing BMW. It was that bloody girl...

Brandt smashed his massive shoulder into the door again and again until it gave way, just in time to see the BMW roar backwards out of the garage, scraping its roof on the still rising garage door, and clipping the rear of Nelson's Land Cruiser as it tried to block the driveway. The BMW spun away, accelerating towards the mouth of the cul de sac. Brandt bolted out of the garage a second later and boarded the Land Cruiser.

"Explain!" demanded Nelson with mounting frustration. Brandt reckoned that the gutless Picton had fled, allowing the girl to come back unopposed.

Paul's BMW flew out of the cul de sac. He clicked Alice's seat belt into place, then he swung the wheel to corner sharply into an older industrial district. "Alice, I will need you to help me." Then Selwyn's SUV hurtled out of a side street intent on ramming the BMW. Paul avoided impact in the nick of time, flooring the accelerator. The SUV just managed to shear off the BMW's rear bumper, before sliding into the opposite curb.

From the passenger seat, Jones shot Selwyn a disparaging look. If *he* had been driving, it would have been a bullseye.

Alice stared wild-eyed at the pursuing metal beast.

The impact had pitched Picton to the floor. He ceased to struggle against Alice's implacable knots. Picton would have kicked himself, if he could. Idiot that he was. He had assumed that he had been taken as a hostage in some turf war about which he knew nothing, and that Nelson's people would ransom or rescue him. Everything would return to normal soon. Then had come the sound of rending metal, and Picton realized that battle had been joined and he was trapped in a No man's land, experiencing that particular level of anguish felt when someone accustomed to power is rendered powerless. But Dr. Picton's situation would get even worse.

From the side window of the Land Cruiser, Brandt opened fire at the BMW's tires, hitting short by a foot. Paul swung the wheel, swerving from side to side, as he opened the glove compartment. They had not searched his car. His Italian 9mm was still there. Brandt's second shot pierced the rear window.

Dr. Picton gasped as glass fragments fell on an ear.

Then Selwyn's SUV swung into view again. Selwyn drew abreast of Nelson's Land Cruiser, steering with one hand and firing wildly at the weaving BMW with the other. None of his shots hit home.

Paul grabbed Alice's left hand, placing it on the steering column. "Hold this...the wheel... the round thing...with both hands! Quickly, now!"

Alice immediately placed her other hand on the wheel. She was glad to see that James' warrior spirit had returned.

"Hold it tight. Keep us straight. Stay in the middle of the road."

Like the reins of a horse, she thought, as she moved the wheel sharply.

Paul snatched it. "Easy!" he warned, and corrected their path. He swiveled round, keeping his foot on the accelerator. "Loud noise coming up! Don't be frightened."

Paul took aim, then fired at the Land Cruiser, shattering his back window completely, raining shards of glass on Picton, who pressed his face into the carpet. Alice screamed, letting go of the wheel. They veered towards a parked truck. Paul reached for the wheel, but Alice grabbed it again, missing the truck by an inch. "Straighten up!" Paul yelled. Alice swung the wheel back, and the metal beast responded. It was easier to control than she had thought. Now she had grasped how to steer.

Brandt fired again. Picton bellowed through his gag, as if this might somehow cause his captors to stop and surrender. Paul took aim at Selwyn, who slid his SUV behind the Land Cruiser for use as a shield just as Paul fired. Alice gasped at the sharp metallic crack of each shot but kept her hands on the wheel. Paul swung his aim to the Land Cruiser. WHAM! The bullet blew a chunk out of the center of the windshield, frosting the glass.

Nelson swerved, Brandt lurched back inside as they skidded to a stop. Selwyn's SUV could not brake in time and slammed into the back of the Land Cruiser. "Fuck!" screamed Nelson. Brandt raised both feet to kick the windshield away.

As Paul redirected his attention from his stalled pursuers to the road ahead, he saw that the BMW was speeding towards a dead end. Alice was reacting too, her arms locked rigidly to the wheel. "James!" she cried. Paul thrust his foot back onto the brake pedal just in time. The BMW fishtailed wildly across the road as Paul took over the wheel, before broadsiding into the curb beside an alley between two warehouses.

The impact smacked Alice against the passenger window. Lights exploded in her head. For an instant her world changed. The wide street they had traveled down became a narrow cobbled road, crowded on either side by dark uneven buildings. Was her old life back? In a moment it was over and she saw the new James, who was searching the floor for his pistol. No luck. Paul couldn't know that with the crash the gun had gone flying into the back, falling at Picton's feet. The psychiatrist strained to reach the gun, but his bonds prevented him from grasping it.

Paul looked up to see the Land Cruiser and the SUV starting towards them again. He grabbed his cellphone and spoke sharply to Alice: "Come on, come on, gotta go!"

But Alice seemed to be in a trance. Paul dragged her none too gently out of the passenger side, then leaned into the back of the car in a last desperate search for the pistol. He had two seconds to find it. But Picton had concealed it beneath his legs.

Alice stared at the metallic beasts bearing down on them. Then lights flared again in her mind. Suddenly they became mounted men at arms, thundering towards her, flanks gleaming, hooves crashing. Like the Apocalypse. Then the horsemen were gone, and the metal beasts were almost upon them.

Paul gave up on the gun. No choice. Leave at once. Yet Alice still seemed in a trance. "Alice, we have to go!" He dragged her into the adjacent alley a microsecond before a bullet smashed into the wall behind him.

Shit! I never miss! Brandt cursed to himself as he rushed forward, stopping abruptly at the sight of a pair of legs bound with white electrical cord extending from an open rear door of the BMW, flailing like a frenzied snake. He recognized the doctor's expensive shoes. "Are you a dickhead or what?" Brandt sneered. Nelson, Selwyn and Jones converged on the car to find Brandt cutting through the electrical cord that secured Picton's wrists, and pocketing the Tanfoglio. "Be ready when we need you, doctor; you're still on call," barked Nelson running past as he led Selwyn and Jones in pursuit down the alley. Brandt severed the last restraint and ran to catch up. As Picton freed himself, he realized that disentangling himself from Nelson would not be as easy.

Paul dragged Alice down the narrow alley between two warehouses, then disappeared round a corner, just as their pursuers came into view.

Alice caught a glimpse of them. In a flash her world changed again. Horsemen in chainmail were cantering down a cobbled street in pursuit, swords outstretched, getting ever closer. Then just as quickly Alice found herself back, running between buildings, the brick walls flashing past. Perhaps she truly was in Hell where sorcery rules and all you encounter mean you harm. All except James, whose hand she gripped hard. But a feeling grew within her, as she ran with all her strength, that something dreadful was around the next corner.

CHAPTER 20

Thieves' Market

ALICE AND PAUL burst out of the alley into an open area abutted on all sides by abandoned factory buildings, in the middle of which was a homeless encampment filled with improvised dwellings made from plastic sheeting, gutted cars, ragged tents. Twenty or more destitute men, women and children took refuge there, the walking wounded of poverty who had formed a community for mutual benefit. Two men, warming themselves by an open fire, shared a cigarette and a bottle. Near them, a woman held two slumbering children close against the pre-dawn chill. Some people were sleeping; others milled about, unable to sleep.

But what Alice saw instead were the outcasts of her own society, thieves with the letter T burned into their foreheads, whores shorn of their noses, beggars and cripples, and a tall man with jagged broken teeth who stared at her intently. Alice realized that she was standing in one world while experiencing glimmers of another. Her old life was still going on. An event had taken place that she was only now catching up with. As memory flooded back, she tugged on Paul's hand. "Thieves' Market! No! This is where they catch us!"

"They will if we stop," gasped Paul.

He dragged her on, scanning for some good cover near an exit. He pulled her down behind a tent, as Nelson, Brandt, Selwyn and Jones ran in. The ruckus roused the camp. The young mother screamed at the sight of their guns and shielded her children. Heads turned. Nelson raked a pocket flashlight across the encampment. He knew how to deal with refuse. "Police business! We are looking for a man and a woman, armed and dangerous; they just ran in moments ago. We need you to point them out. Just point. That's all you need to do."

Nobody stirred. Silence.

The two younger agents moved to impress their boss. Jones ripped open the nearest shelter made of cardboard boxes before Selwyn could get to it, so Selwyn switched to a leadership role and addressed the crowd. "Come on. They're here somewhere. Don't make us take the place apart. Tell us where so we can do our job."

"Give her up, lad," Nelson added as conclusion.

Paul glanced at Alice. She seemed in a trance, though a tear was rolling down her cheek. But she was calm, and that was how he needed her.

Alice's calm was resignation. This is where they were caught before. This is where they would be caught again. Here before her was Thieves' Market, a tiny enclave in the heart of London Town, rarely bothered by the authorities, because this was where the underworld and the overworld met to trade. Again they were surrounded by Córdoba and his men. This is where they would be taken, after much slaughter. As she blinked, a barrage of images assaulted her mind. Blades flashing, blood gushing, children screaming, horses trampling the fallen, James fighting valiantly till overwhelmed, both of them dragged away in chains. Which world was she in? Was she possessed by a demon that could take hold and leave her at will? So Alice wept silently and submitted to the will of God, Whom she believed she would meet soon. Because she had no intention of being taken alive by Córdoba again.

"Fascists!" came a cry from behind Nelson, who whirled round.

Alice snapped back to what was taking place thirty feet away. A tall gaunt man in rags, with long matted hair and jagged broken teeth, walked towards the intruders and yelled at them again. "Rottweilers of the ruling class! That's what you are!"

Nelson pointed his flashlight. The advancing figure had a crazed look.

Brandt leveled his pistol. "Back off!"

"Keep the masses in line, that's your job, so the rich can go on fucking us up the arse!" continued Mr. Broken Teeth, now changing direction towards Brandt.

"I mean it!" growled Brandt louder.

"Easy..." said Nelson, not wanting to have to explain at this critical time the public shooting of a civilian to his superiors at the European Security Taskforce, let alone the British police. There was enough damage control in their wake as it was.

Mr. Broken Teeth stopped inches from the tip of Brandt's gun. "What' ya gonna do? Shoot me? Go ahead. I don't give a shit."

Brandt looked at his weathered face. Could be anywhere between forty and sixty. Maybe a homeless lifer. The man pointed to the center of his forehead. "Put it there. Make my day." Brandt and Mr. Broken Teeth glowered, assessing each other. This dickhead has a screw loose, better be ready, was Brandt's thought. Mr. Broken Teeth sensed his opponent's hesitation and tapped his forehead again.

Nelson noticed many more homeless people standing up, emerging from their shelters, edging forward, muttering. "Calm down. Everybody just calm down."

Paul felt the rising tension. It would work for him. He picked up a smooth shale stone from a nearby pile. If his pitching arm was still as good as it was in college, he could lob it through an empty window frame in the building to their left, and divert attention perhaps long enough to slip away.

Alice saw the stone in his hand. You'll need a bigger weapon than that, James, she thought at first. Then she saw his mind working. Oh, you are the clever one, but how can you change what has already happened?

Paul drew a mental bead on the window frame, its glass long shattered, now a three-foot-square hole. The distance was achievable, but having to throw from a crouch made it harder. If he missed and the rock hit the wall, he would give away their position. The gag would only work if the noise came from the inside. He limbered up his shoulder, then let fly. Loud clangs echoed as the rock flew through the window frame and bounced off heavy machinery. Years of Saturday softball had paid off. Nelson and his team immediately reacted to the noise, and ran to the building, glad to abandon the standoff.

Mr. Broken Teeth smiled triumphantly. He had frightened them off. Nice one Cyril, he said to himself. Not that his name was Cyril. "Nice one, Cyril" was the punch line from a TV commercial that had aired before he was born. Where it came from, he had no idea, but somehow it surfaced whenever he was feeling pleased with himself. In fact, he had no clear idea what his real name was. Nor could he remember his childhood, parents, relatives, anything. All he could remember was The Street. It was as though he had been born onto dirty asphalt already into his teens. Fighting for scraps. Learning how to forage. Teaching his skills to others. Becoming Obi Wan to the homeless in each new camp until he had had his fill of its women and moved on. Once again fate had given him the opportunity to act as protector to his flock. It would reward him.

The moment their pursuers disappeared into the building, Paul grabbed Alice's hand, pulling her towards the nearest alley from the courtyard, just as James had pulled her away from the fighting, but to no avail. "They'll catch us!" wailed Alice as they ran into the dark narrow alley with her other life exploding in her head anew. In front she saw their escape blocked by pike-wielding soldiers. To their right was a wall of advancing swords. She looked round. Cavalry were closing in from behind.

A horseman put a horn to his lips as if to summon hounds. Then an intense sound wiped the image from her mind. A big rig roared past, horn blaring, as Alice and Paul burst out of the alley into a suburban street now busy with early rush hour commuters and pedestrians. "See," said Paul, "they haven't caught us. Now trust me and run."

Nelson stared at the rock lying by a rusty turbine, and knew he had been fooled by one of the older tricks in the game. Demented laughter echoed from outside. They ran out, weapons at the ready, to find Mr. Broken Teeth, convulsed, pointing to the alley at the back of the camp, the only escape route.

Brandt gestured Broken Teeth. Plan B? Nelson nodded.

Paul and Alice meanwhile had run down the street. Paul waved at taxis but they were all taken. Then Brixton Underground Railway station came into view. Seeing a gap in the traffic he grabbed Alice's arm and they rushed across. Alice jumped as one of the metal beasts made a bellowing sound as it passed. Paul steered her to the entrance of the station, his eyes scanning for pursuit. He realized that the next mode of transport would be frightening to her present persona. "This place will get us where we can be safe. I warn you, it's going to feel strange. Come on." Then he saw Nelson and his team across the street. They saw him too. Just another few seconds and he would have lost them. He could still do it if they moved fast.

CHAPTER 21

The Metal Serpent

PAUL HUSTLED ALICE inside the tube station. It was the hour before dawn, when opposites converge. Night shift workers trudging homewards, day shift workers fresh and alert, insomniacs and early risers, the indolent and the ambitious, all on the commute.

What dreadful place is this? Alice wondered. A cavern full of strange colored lights, the sound of giant millstones grinding below, people scurrying in all directions jabbering to themselves. Was this some kind of Bedlam where the mad walked free? Ahead was a barrier through which people passed one at a time. James extended his hand holding something Alice could not make out. The barrier opened. No end of sorcery. James picked her up and carried her through as if they were one person. She delighted in his pressing her against him. This was the closest they had come to intimacy, and her heart swelled. Alice heard a woman shout out her disapproval as the barrier closed behind them. James hurried her towards what looked like a steep staircase, yet it was moving. Gusts of noisome wind wafted up from below.

Alice baulked, but Paul dragged her onto the escalator. Its unexpected movement caused her to lurch and cry out.

Paul steadied her: "Hold onto me." She gripped him tightly. Suddenly she was traveling downwards without walking or falling. The noise of grinding millstones got even louder. Alice felt faint. She let James guide her down the moving staircase, past sullen-looking men and women, most gazing at objects like prayer books or holding them to their ears and mumbling to the air.

Then Alice caught sight of the tiny people cavorting in box windows on the wall as they passed. She had seen little folk many times when the mummers came to Farnham on High Holy Days. They were such wondrous tumblers. Paul realized from her face she was reacting to the animated billboards for consumer goods and holiday resorts. Further down came lingerie models, sinuously displaying their wares. Alice was shocked. Harlots can put their likeness up on walls in public places, what kind of Godless world would allow that? Before she could think further on the subject, they reached the bottom and she tripped getting off. Paul caught her. Alice likened herself to a newborn foal, unsteady on its legs in an unknown world. She would master this place, or any place where she could be with James. Paul steered her towards platforms signposted for the West End of London. Nelson arrived at the top of the escalator in time to see where they were headed.

Paul and Alice arrived at the designated platform. Commuters were hurrying away from a departing train. Paul groaned. Ten seconds earlier, and they would have caught it. The hounds would have lost the scent. At least for a while.

Alice watched wide eyed as the giant metal snake full of people slithered away into a big hole and disappeared with a loud roar.

"They ride within a metal serpent?"

"A train...a subway train. Don't you Brits call it a tube?" Paul asked with baited guile. If she would just let slip one anachronism, then he would at least know what he was dealing with. But no. Bewilderment in her expression.

He led her towards the farthest end of the bustling platform, which was rapidly filling with passengers for the next train. Alice had no idea what his words had meant, but could see that his attention had moved to the entrance from which they had come. Paul was scanning for their pursuers. The digital timetable showed the next train arriving in one minute. He hoped that they would not guess which platform he had chosen. They just needed a bit of luck.

Paul and Alice had reached the far end. The carriages were going to be packed. Soon enough, Paul saw the distant figures of their four pursuers weaving through the crowd, maintaining their separate identities as random commuters. The floating box and converge maneuver.

The train burst out of the tunnel, an intense high-pitched squeal from its brakes. The sound seemed to go through Alice like a knife. She shrank fearfully, blocking her ears with her hands. She bent over. Then, as Paul grabbed her, she suddenly snapped upright, gasping. "Alice? Are you alright?" "I am not fucking Alice! Are you deaf?" she shouted over the noise of the arriving train, wondering where the hell she was this time.

Paul instantly recognized Jane from the choice of words and the fierce stare.

Jane's eyes darted in all directions. What was she doing in an underground railway station with the American who called himself Paul but had James' face? How had they gotten here? And he was still calling her Alice! She had to trust that he was trying to save rather than harm her. It was surreal. "How did I get here?" she moaned, then before he could answer, she recoiled. "Oh, my God, it's them." She saw Suit, The Giant, Jonesy, and Red Curly Hair. Had the American betrayed her? But clearly Paul was not pleased to see them, either.

"Call the cops," said Jane, "Call the police!"

Paul shook his head. "They control the police."

"What?"

The train had stopped. Paul pushed Jane forward against the tide of exiting commuters.

"They're rogue European Security Taskforce agents..." he began to explain.

"EST?!"

"And they're after you."

"Because I'm an activist? Because..."

Paul cut her off: "To be a patsy, take the rap, no argument because you'll be conveniently dead. Or so I think."

"Me?!! Dead?"

"I'll explain later. Move!" He pushed her into the carriage still crowded with commuters.

Nelson, Brandt, Selwyn, and Jones closed in on the open carriage door. Nelson saw that he had his quarry trapped. It would be better that he not participate in the next stage. He spoke to Brandt and redefined their orders. Offer safe passage, then isolate and kill the American. Bring the girl to him. He signaled his men forward and stepped back onto the platform, and pulled out his phone. There was other business pressing.

Paul pushed Jane ahead of him along the standing room only carriage. Brandt, Jones and Selwyn, hard on their heels, had now cut them off from an exit, when two transport police stepped in front of them through the central double doors. Jones and Selwyn stopped, looking to Brandt for instruction.

Fifteen feet away, Paul and Jane found straps to hang onto near four sturdy skinhead girls. Steel-capped boots, tattoos, lots of piercings, and high as kites. Still partying at six in the morning. They giggled and exchanged deep kisses. The doors closed. The train moved off. Jane glowered at Jonesy, who looked back with a contemptuous smile. No point in pretending any longer; besides, very soon she would be back in the bag for good.

Jane's mind was racing. This was a pretty extreme response to minor civil disobedience. Waving a sign, throwing a pie in a face that deserved it? Give me a break. Since that incident, she had complied with the requirements of her probation. Well, except for neglecting to take her medication. Even the most radical anti-authoritarian might look to the police for protection in a pinch. Jane gestured the transport cops to Paul.

"Talk to the police."

"No. I'll talk to 'them'." Paul inclined his head back to where their pursuers were standing. He leaned forward and whispered. "I need you to trust me. Otherwise we are both dead. Do you trust me?"

They locked eyes. Jane nodded.

"You're the best friend I've got, right?" she said echoing his words from their earlier encounter, not entirely convinced. She realized that she had been away from herself, as she privately called it, for much longer periods than usual. Couldn't recall a thing about Alice's world. And she could feel a large bruise on the side of her head.

"Right?" said Paul. Again she nodded. He moved away through the crowded carriage to stop near the transport police. He gestured to Brandt, who slid past the cops, and stood in front of him. Selwyn watched them, as he reached into his coat pocket for the syringe container and unfastened it, ready for the moment when he could discreetly inject Alice with a fast-acting sedative. They would then play the role of Good Samaritans and take a girl under the influence of alcohol and drugs off the train at the next station. But first they had to neutralize this mysterious American. Brandt and Paul conversed in mock-friendly tones.

"You've no idea what you're messing with," said Brandt.

"Yes, I do."

"Then you know you can't win. So my advice is hand her over at the next stop, run to the nearest airport. You can still survive."

"Think you'll survive?"

Brandt glared at him. The American could not be played. They would have to sedate them both. He and Jones would get Alice off the train, leaving the American apparently asleep in his seat. Selwyn would remain behind, to finish him off when a discreet opportunity arose. The short blade of a Swiss army knife into the kidneys needed only three inches of penetration from a precise angle to be fatal, with little external bleeding. The murder would not be discovered for many stations.

"You got about two minutes to make up your mind." Brandt rejoined his team.

Paul moved back to Jane, who was expecting answers, but instead he addressed the skinhead girls, while making it look from Brandt's point of view that he was talking to Jane.

"Ladies…"

"Piss off," said Ms. Tattooed Skull.

"One hundred pounds…" said Paul discreetly pulling out a roll of notes. He had their attention. "I'll give each of you one hundred pounds if you go over to those three men I was just talking to." Paul gestured over his shoulder without turning round. "See them, with the big guy?"

Jane saw what Paul was up to.

"Why should we do that?" asked Ms. Steel Toecaps.

"Well, the first hundred reasons are obvious. Go on, take them."

Paul offered them each a note. They grabbed the money without hesitation, giggling at their good fortune.

"More when you're done. They'll pay whatever it takes for some fun and games with the four of you."

The Skinheads' smiles took on icy venom. Paul turned and smiled to Brandt. The girls saw Brandt's glacial smile in return. Paul quickly continued before they could focus their anger at him.

"See? Now don't be offended, I'm just the messenger, so I'm quoting here. They said they're horny as hell for fat dykes. And they'll pay big. Go on, go see them."

That did it. They exchanged looks. Why not? They set off. Paul flashed a look at Jane. Get ready.

The train left its narrow tunnel to enter the brief junction area where the Piccadilly and the Northern lines intersect. Another train roared past in the opposite direction. Then just as quickly they were back in a narrow tunnel. The loud noise had synchronized with a blur in Jane's vision. Not now! her inner voice pleaded. Then as the sound diminished, her focus was restored. Jane watched as the skinheads, ignoring the transport police, pushed through the crowd towards Brandt. Brandt always avoided eye contact with street scum so he had no inkling of what they were about to do.

Ms. Tattooed Skull landed a straight right to Brandt's nose, while Ms. Steel Toecaps kicked him in the groin; not a knock out, but hard enough to sink the big man to his knees. The other girls sucker punched Selwyn and Jones. Pandemonium ensued as passengers fell over each other trying to get out of the way of flailing fists and feet. The transport cops immediately stepped in to restrain the skinheads none too gently. At the same time Paul pulled the emergency lever. The brakes squealed, the scrum of commuters lurched into further disarray, as the train came to an emergency halt in mid-tunnel. Selwyn yelled that they were antiterrorist agents but the sense of it was lost in the general hubbub. The transport police just heard was the word "terrorist". All skinheads were terrorists to them.

Immobilized by pain, Brandt knew at once what his adversaries had done. The American was smarter than he had thought. Through the crowd he saw the two of them prying open a sliding door the moment the train stopped. He forced himself to his feet to follow, but the transport police, with their batons out, thought he wanted to get some payback on the now subdued skinheads and blocked his path. Although the waves of pain were receding, Brandt could scarcely move or speak. He nodded at Selwyn, who understood that this was his chance for redemption. Selwyn slowly eased himself back into the crowd to disappear from notice.

Jane jumped down from the carriage declining Paul's outstretched hand, which grabbed her anyway and dragged her towards the rear of the train. But she went with it. She had to trust somebody and he was the sole option at this point.

"You're going to call your people in Washington, right?"

"Langley. If they're still alive."

"What?"

"I think there's a coup going down."

"You've got to be..!"

A chill ran through her. Further questions died in her throat, then a glimmer of hope appeared ahead; the tunnel filtered into a junction. It proved to be a cavernous maze of intersecting rails, across from which there was a flight of fire stairs leading to the surface. Paul flashed a look back. No one. Yet. If they could make it across four sets of rails, before any of their pursuers entered the junction, they would have a chance to shake them off. But if they were caught half way across...they would have a choice between gunfire and electrocution. Paul pointed to the fire stairs. Jane's first response was: You're joking, right. Walk over live rails. In a hurry. She shuddered at the prospect.

Paul saw her flinch. The girl now endangered his survival. But he could not cast her aside. He had become emotionally involved, a potentially fatal condition in counterespionage. Yet he found himself saying: "Come on. Watch my feet. Tread where I tread. Don't touch the middle rail. Any rail! We'll do it together."

He stepped warily over the first live rail, then stretched out his hands to her to guide her across. Jane was taken aback by the offer. "You'll die if I..!"

"We both will so make sure you don't!" said Paul, summoning his most confident smile.

That was the moment Paul gained some ground with Jane. Young men, particularly good looking young men, were so shallow, self-serving. She could not imagine a stranger doing this for her. She now saw how much like Alice's James Paul was, essentially. Though it happened quickly, the passage across the rails seemed to take an eternity in her mind. She took Paul's hand, clenching his fingers hard. Her breathing quickened. He watched as she stretched out her left leg, pointing the toe vertically down like ballet dancer in toe shoes. She cleared the 20,000 volt middle rail easily, then did the same with the other foot, this time faster. They exchanged a flash of a smile. One down, three to go.

Brandt was now on his feet, arguing with the transport police, interrupted by the skinhead girls screaming sexual harassment. His brusque manner and sense of superiority to the transport cops when he showed his EST identity card was not working for him. They were going to do everything by the book. Unnoticed, Selwyn pried open the doors and jumped down from the carriage. He could see no one in either direction. They would not have gone forward, he decided. He drew his weapon and swiftly followed the tunnel back towards the last carriage. He would get the American this time.

In the carriage, things went suddenly quiet. Everyone stared at the matte black Glock 9mm in Brandt's hand that had replaced the official ID he had been waving at the transport cops. He was tired of arguing.

"Enough! You've let a terrorist get away. We are leaving!" he shouted.

Brandt and Jones pushed past the transport cops and jumped out of the carriage into the tunnel, following Selwyn's path.

Selwyn had reached the entrance to the junction. He could see his quarry most of the way across to the fire escape. He leveled his pistol, but the girl kept blocking his line of sight to the man he needed to put down, if he was to be the hero who recovered her.

Paul had his foot over the last live rail, when he felt a hot wind play on his face. A roar in the gloom of the tunnel which fed this rail into the junction quickly followed. He could get himself across in time but maybe not her. He overcame the impulse to leave her. He nimbly guided her back outside the rails, as a West Bound train roared out of the tunnel, blocking the final set of rails they needed to cross. Paul made Jane crouch down. He anxiously scanned the gloom from which they had come, knowing that they were open targets. It was too dark to see Selwyn peering round the buttress from which they had set out across the junction.

Selwyn saw them hunched over, the American's head mostly obscured behind the girl's. Best to wait. There would be time enough when the train passed and they stood up. Then Paul heard the sound of another train coming from the opposite direction. Jane heard it too. The distance between the two sets of tracks was narrow. Paul stood up, pulling her to him, to take up less space. Selwyn raised his pistol. A clean shot at last. His trigger finger tightened. Then the other train, from the opposite direction on the adjacent track, thundered through, blocking his aim.

Paul and Jane were now sandwiched between two trains hurtling in opposite directions. Paul caught a blur of astonished passengers' faces. Jane reacted to the screeching wheels, the thunderous noise on each side of her, pressing her hands over her ears, buckling at the knees. Paul pulled her out of harm's way and held her against his chest. As the noise intensified, Jane's vision blurred and pixilated into swirling fragments.

The portal had opened once more.

CHAPTER 22

The Rapture

IN THE TUBE station, the girl in Paul's arms convulsed, then threw her arms up around his neck. "James…"

Oh, shit. She was Alice again. Their eyes locked. She was inviting his kiss. Despite every good reason to the contrary, Paul could not deny he wanted to kiss her. Under other circumstances. He must not kiss her. Yet he must not reject her. He pressed her head against his chest, gently stroking her hair. Alice smiled at his courtly response. They held each other tight, enclosed within a haven of peace amidst the roaring trains, swirling dust, and flashing lights.

Selwyn decided that he had the opportunity to get closer and guarantee his kill shot. The live rail did not faze him. In the SAS he had done extensive minefield training. He methodically navigated two sets of rails, gun at the ready. The moment the nearside train cleared he would terminate the American. He would secure the girl then toss the American's body onto the electric griddle to become a statistic, the result of unwise trespass on railway property. Nelson would make sure that no bullet was mentioned in the autopsy report. His return to Nelson's favor was seconds away. So Selwyn kept his eyes on the approximate position of his target as he stepped onto the next set of tracks. He did not have to worry about the outer rail. Then his foot came down on the edge of a brick that years of vibrations had shaken from the tunnel's vaulted ceiling. Selwyn lurched, and instinctively put his other foot out to steady himself. But there were patches of grease near the rail mountings. His foot slid forward. His shin connected with the middle rail.

For the few instants in which Selwyn's brain still produced conscious thought, even as intense heat and shock wracked his entire being, he did not attribute it to electrocution. Instead he knew that this was the very moment the Lord had chosen to return. The Rapture was sucking the souls of the Chosen toward Heaven. And he was proudly amongst them. It was just that he had not expected The Rapture to be so painful.

The last carriages of both trains passed. Paul turned to check for pursuit. There was Selwyn standing twenty feet away, mouth open, body shuddering, arms flailing, the gun flung from his grasp. Alice stared at the man who had tried to coerce her from chastity, and had chased her into this life. Gareth. Quivering and jerking like a hanged man, yet there was no rope. God must be smiting him that he commit evil no more. Paul saw no distress at the sight in Alice's face. Rather, her jaw set tightly as she crossed herself. He quickly picked her up and stepped carefully over the last live rail. The fire escape leading to the street was seconds away.

Brandt and Jones arrived at the entrance to the junction in time to see Selwyn, a rigid dancing upright corpse, clothes smoldering, eyeballs melting. Beyond him Alice and Paul were almost at the fire exit. Brandt quickly took aim at Paul. Before he could fire, another train thundered through, grinding Selwyn's body under its wheels. "Whoa!" thought Jones. It was like watching a splatter moment in a video game. But it was live. Amazing. Jones had never liked Selwyn, who constantly patronized him because he had not done military service. Didn't help when it came to train spotting, did it, mate? The ladder to promotion suddenly had one fewer obstacle.

The train's brakes squealed, the carriages slowing to a halt across the junction that obscured the fire escape. Brandt, for his part, was shocked by Selwyn's death. He had respected the man. But shit happens; he could not think of that now. His targets were gone, and he had better be gone, too. He needed to reach Nelson so that a press embargo on the accident could be imposed on the grounds of national security till the appropriate story could be manufactured. The pile of rendered flesh that was once their colleague, would, for a media minute, become a homeless, nameless vagrant illegally squatting in the tunnels of the London Underground. Tragic, the media would cluck, but a lesson to all vagrants. His body would be held at the central morgue awaiting claim. Which would never come. Meanwhile, Ian Selwyn, gallant soldier, awarded the Military Cross, posted on special assignment in Central Asia, would be blown to pieces by an IED, and brought home to a hero's funeral. The body parts in the morgue would get a Christian burial. The media would have patriotic fodder for a few news cycles. Every cloud had a silver lining.

CHAPTER 23

"For oats, you need a ladle"

PAUL AND ALICE had left the station and were walking along a traffic-clogged street. Paul explained that the metal serpents and beasts had machines within them that enabled them to move without horses or oxen. No end of wonders, thought Alice, awestruck.

A cab soon pulled over, and Paul hustled Alice inside.

"Where to?" asked the cabbie, eyeing Alice with evident appreciation.

"West End. Just drive. I'll let you know."

Alice watched as James pulled out of his pocket a small black square and make it glow, just as she had seen the mad people do earlier. But she knew James was no Tom o' Bedlam.

Paul dialed an international number as the taxi eased away from the curb. He leaned in close to Alice's ear and whispered: "Say nothing." Alice nodded and smiled. She would do whatever James asked. He was the bravest knight on God's earth. Paul's call connected. He tapped the object three more times, then spoke: "This is 553-2HG6-Paul-439."

Buoyed by their escape, Alice was no longer unsettled by acts of sorcery. It was the way people lived in this world. She would master it too, in time. Paul spoke. "Put me through to section...Is Rick there?" Then Alice was startled. The square in his hand spoke back, though she could not understand what it said.

"Chief Almaraz is on vacation."

Rick never took a holiday. Paul's worst fears returned.

"Let me speak to Wendy."

There was a pause. "She's sick today. May I help you?"

His section had been compromised, or worse. "It's complicated. I'll text."

He hung up, knowing that they were tracking his movements through the phone. He could leave the phone hidden in the taxi, which would buy him some time to find a bolt hole. But he wanted to get a better sense of the scale of the conspiracy he was up against, and how fast its response time was. He started drafting a text. Alice leaned against him for a closer look at the mystical square.

"No quill or paper, yet you make words..."

"More sorcery," he replied as he felt her warmth press against him.

Paul realized that he was becoming comfortable with her delusion. At the core of this personality was an innocent child full of sweetness and compassion, ostensibly the polar opposite of the anger-driven Jane. Alice projected an aura unlike any girl he had ever known. Yet he sensed that the two of them were essentially alike. What had embittered Jane?

"What do you write?"

"A test." He could see the word had no meaning for her. "A trial," he added.

Alice nodded. That was something she understood. "For whom?"

"Our enemies." He completed the message and hit send. "Bring me in ASAP. Excelsior Hotel, Marlin Street. London. W.C 2."

Alice smiled. Her knight was plotting revenge.

***

As the sky lightened, Paul and Alice sat in a cafe near a window with a view of The Excelsior across the street, which Paul had designated as the pickup point. Paul's eyes constantly roamed the street. If anyone suspicious approached, the kitchen was close by for a fast escape. At the sound of footsteps his head turned quickly to see a waitress arrive with a tray. He was a little jumpy. Food would be good for them both. He had not eaten since the previous afternoon. He'd been running on adrenaline till now, but a great weariness was seeping into his bones.

The waitress put down a plate of poached eggs, bacon, sausage, tomato, baked beans, and toast in front of Alice. A clog of cholesterol, thought Paul.

"It's a feast!" Alice exclaimed.

"Well, thank you," said the waitress, placing a bowl of oatmeal and fruit in front of Paul. He was a health food fanatic even when starving. Alice ignored the cutlery, scooping a poached egg into her mouth, using toast as an all-purpose tool.

"Mmmm...Surely, our Queen don't eat this well."

The waitress gave a nervous smile and left. Paul watched Alice's ravenous consumption for a moment, then to make the girl feel more comfortable, dug into his oatmeal with his fingers, ignoring its heat. He licked them clean, and looked at Alice. "For oats, you need a ladle." She passed him a spoon.

He had almost finished his oatmeal when cars full of security personnel arrived outside the Excelsior Hotel. Men ran inside. Paul caught sight of one of their adversaries, standing talking on his mobile.

Jones was pleased to be in on the arrest. He would soon have this troublemaker in the bag and regain Nelson's confidence. He was unaware as he ran past a waste bin at the door that inside was Paul's discarded phone, luring them to his apparent location. Across the street, Paul now had visual confirmation that he was totally compromised; whoever controlled his section had relayed the phone's coordinates to his enemies in London. No help would come from Langley, only a death sentence and an unmarked grave. He got to his feet, threw some money on the table, gulped down the remaining fruit juice, then pulled a protesting Alice, her mouth full of toast, towards the kitchen exit.

146

CHAPTER 24
The Girl with Red-gold Hair

THE SQUEAKY WHEELS of a prison cart, escorted by horsemen in chainmail, approached the west gate to the Tower of London. Two semi-conscious figures, a man and a young woman, lay chained to opposite ends of the cart. The man stirred with a groan. The woman's eyes opened. They blinked, then she gasped with shock. She was no longer in the underground railway tunnels. She was in Alice's world. Whenever this happened before, what she later remembered was similar to fragments of a dream upon waking. However long and complex the dream, only bits and pieces were retained. But now she was actually there, continuously, second by second, minute by minute, in Alice's body, wearing Alice's clothes, experiencing Alice's life as it was happening. Yet she was still herself: Jane Benedict, history student at the University of London.

Jane became aware of the painful spot on the side of her head. Someone must have hit her. Omigod! No…no…this was not right…this wasn't happening. This wasn't a fleeting image from Alice's world. Now she herself was in the mainframe, in Alice's life, which did not seem to be headed in a positive direction.

"Not happening!" Jane yelled as she strained against the chains. They were real and it hurt. Then she looked at the man chained at the other end of the cart, his clothes torn and filthy like hers, his dark hair long and caked with dried blood, his face bruised, but unmistakably that of the man she had clung to between thundering trains just moments before.

"Jesus Christ!"

"Alice, don't blaspheme!" said a shocked voice. "The Lord will not aid us if you take His Name in vain." This was James De Fries, the local Robin Hood and love of Alice's life. His voice had the easy tone of the southern English countryside spiced with French accents acquired from his schooling in Paris.

Jane sobbed. "I'm not meant to be here…It's just…good dreams, bad dreams…" She shouted out, "I'M NOT MEANT TO BE HERE!" Jane recalled her wish to know the answer to the crazed conundrum of her life. This wasn't the answer she wanted.

James looked at her in horror and pity. "Oh, sweet Alice, have they stolen your wits?" Or worse, was she indeed possessed?

"It's Jane! My name is Jane!" she screamed at him, more in panic than anger.

James was at a loss for words. The cart stopped in front of the west gate. The spiked portcullis started to rise. The mechanism squealed its complaint. The prison wagon passed through and the portcullis slammed down as the vehicle stopped in the outer courtyard to the Tower. Guards dragged the woman and the man out by their chains, pitching them into the mud. Two more guards approached carrying ragged sackcloth hoods to place over the prisoner's heads. Jane resisted, screaming abuse. A guard kicked her in the stomach to quieten her.

"Alice! Be silent! Say nothing, girl!" James implored as she gasped for breath.

He prayed she had enough wits left to contain her madness, lest they kill her outright. The hood went over Jane's head. Its stench almost made her retch but the semi-darkness helped focus her thoughts on why this was happening to her. She calmed herself with the notion that she would wake up soon as she always did, remembering only fragments. Perhaps when the hood came off, she would be back in her warm, comfortable, book-strewn flat, ready for tea and toast, and many satisfying hours writing her paper. Vicious intruders would not interrupt her. They would be confined to whatever part of the multiverse they had come from. Or whatever. Everything would be back to normal.

But when the hood did come off, Jane's nightmare persisted. She found herself kneeling chained to a ring in the floor of a spacious chamber surrounded by monks and priests. Shafts of sunlight streamed in from high windows. James was nowhere to be seen. Jane looked round at the man behind her who had pulled the hood from her head, a tall man around fifty, wearing black robes and an ornate golden pectoral cross. To the assembled clergy, he was Fernando Córdoba, Dominican Inquisitor and special emissary of Prince Philip of Spain, sent to ensure England's reconciliation with the Roman Church. He bore letters of authority from Queen Mary to combat heresy in all its forms. Consequently, the English clerics treated him with deference.

Jane looked at him in astonishment. His face was that of her kidnapper, Suit. Their features were identical. It was a handsome face. Deep set and knowing eyes, a long sculpted nose that flared at the base, carved cheekbones. That slightly disdainful curve of the mouth. How could he be here? "I know you!" she exclaimed. Then it dawned on her. She must be part of some psychiatric experiment, a lab rat for some new mind-altering chemical. That was why they had abducted her. Of course! Rage exploded and she lunged at him. "Bastard!" But the chain restrained her an inch short of his elbow. Córdoba had calculated just where to stand, and remained motionless while others stepped back. This further reinforced his authority in the eyes of all. Except Jane.

"What have you given me?" she screamed. "You're testing some new drug, aren't you? You've filled me full of weird shit and now I'm hallucinating! What makes you think you can get away with kidnapping me?" Her strident tone, strange words, and pronunciation made it hard for the assembled clergy to understand her. But there was no doubting her ferocious lunacy. She added: "Fuck all you shrinks or spies or whatever you are and your fucking God complex!"

A collective shudder at the blasphemy. Everyone made the Sign of the Cross, Córdoba last, when all eyes were on him. He would turn their deference into respect and fear. He would bring this wretched English church under control. He signaled a guard unnoticed by Jane, who had now whirled round to harangue the crowd of clergy.

"You! What are you looking at? Come to see the crazy person, eh? Are you real?...Is anything here real?" Jane had much more to say, but was abruptly gagged from behind. She began to flail, rage, and sob beneath the gag. Then she noticed a young woman of about Jane's own age standing in an alcove; she was simply but elegantly dressed, a crucifix dangling from her neck. But it was her red-gold hair that made Jane really wonder whether someone had given her psychedelic drugs. Why would a genuine historical figure be part of the delusion? From her studies, Jane knew of a young woman with legendary red-gold hair who was imprisoned in the Tower of London during the reign of Queen Mary: Princess Elizabeth, daughter of Henry VIII by Anne Boleyn. What year was that? 1550-something-or-other? Elizabeth had come to the Tower not as a guest, but as a prisoner for interrogation awaiting formal charges of treason. And indeed, Jane saw, two men-at-arms stood a short distance behind this striking-looking girl.

Córdoba addressed the assembly: "Plainly this witch is possessed by the demon Superbia, that most dangerous entity from Hell, who causes women and the lower orders to question their station in life. She may infect others. What we must decide today is whether to exorcize the demon *before* the witch is burned, so that the child has a chance to repent and attain salvation."

Jane howled through her gag. Averting their eyes, the clergy began to confer amongst themselves. The other woman in the chamber looked on the unhappy madwoman with pity. Why was she chosen for this wretchedness? wondered Princess Elizabeth, putting aside for a moment her own misery and fear. She was caught in a different trap; she prayed she would not be brought as low as this poor creature. Death would be better than madness or possession. And death might indeed await her if she were not careful.

Jane saw that the girl with red-gold hair was the only person in the room who stared at her with sympathy, not disdain. Then a courtier approached from the hallway into the chamber, a nobleman, to judge by his clothing as he neared the central shafts of light emanating from the high windows. He seemed to be between forty and fifty. Jane wondered whether she could identify him. Ever the historian, she thought ruefully. Was he a known historical figure? If she could hear him speak, that might provide some clues. She stopped cursing beneath the gag. The nobleman stood beside the Princess. After a formal nod acknowledging her rank, he spoke. "As you see, madam, I promised you another lady-in-waiting."

The Princess felt a tightening in her throat. Had this evil man scoured the byways of the realm to find such a wretch with whom to torment her? A lady-in-waiting who was either demented or possessed? The Princess stared straight ahead, pretending to ignore the cruel implication, though the prospect did terrify her. Madness and possession could be contagious. Who was this Giles De Fries to threaten her? A jumped up rural poppinjay, who had sold himself to Philip of Spain. Indeed, there was a rumor that he had stolen his nephew's inheritance, and had had him condemned as an outlaw before he could appeal his case to the Queen.

The Princess glanced at the gagged and chained girl, whose rage had turned to tears. "She is unsuitable," she said flatly, as if responding to a serious offer.

Sir Giles decided to end the bear-baiting and speak plainly. "You have but to sign the documents," he demanded "and your sojourn here will end."

"I will not, Sir," Elizabeth said curtly. She turned and left the chamber. Sir Giles signaled the two men-at-arms to follow.

The hood was again placed over Jane's head. She felt more frightened and isolated than ever. Inside its gloom, Jane heard the chanting of lugubrious prayers. She calmed herself, the better to direct her analytical powers to this latest predicament. The psychotropic drug-induced hallucination theory had evaporated. The bruises and caked blood on her body were real and days old. How long had she been in this condition? Medications always gave her a detached, otherworldly quality. Whereas now, she felt drug free and clearheaded. Like others who have found themselves in dire circumstances, Jane became focused on the possible existence of a higher power, and whether that power intervened in the daily outcomes of life. Jane could use some intervention just now. So she whispered quietly in the back of her mind. "Hello…are You there? If You are, please help me. I want to go home…" There was no blinding flash, no Saul of Tarsus moment. But there was something. Like a door had opened, letting in a light breeze. She heard footsteps approach. Two men paused nearby, engaged in earnest conversation.

Then everything became clear to her.

CHAPTER 25

Within the Weightless Cocoon

PAMELA VAN DOREN reclined in her spa suite on a Singapore Airlines flight from Dulles to Heathrow, brushing aside a strand of coppery hair so that she could gaze down at the ocean. She knew that the flight path took her over the North Atlantic Garbage Vortex, as it was known, an archipelago of discarded plastic, chemical sludge and other debris trapped between the four currents of the North Atlantic Gyre. There were two similar vortices in the Pacific, imperceptible by satellite photography because most of the pollution remained just below the surface of the ocean, but extended, it was estimated, over an area twice the size of Texas. Governments lamented the damage done to marine ecology, but international waters were considered someone else's problem.

Pamela was not content to be a voice crying in the wilderness, hurling jeremiads at the world's problems. She had the wealth to be part of the solution. A year ago she had decided to fund a cleanup technique which, instead of nets, employed floating booms to divert rather than catch the debris, then used surface currents to direct it to specially designed collection platforms. Initial tests with a boom strung between two vessels a mile apart had produced impressive results, and allowed marine life to roam freely beneath the boom. The ultimate plan was to create a concave boom sixty miles across. Four such booms attacking each of the plastic vortices could eradicate the plastic swamp engulfing the Pacific within five years. Another company Pamela was funding was developing cheap biodegradable packaging to replace conventional plastics. She had signed the contracts and green lit the next stage of development just before leaving Washington.

Pamela stretched and yawned. Ah, the little victories. She had not felt so relaxed in months. The disturbing thought entered her mind that she could get used to a sybaritic lifestyle, having nothing more to worry about than what she would wear throughout each day. Even that she could leave to others to decide, if she chose. Simply enjoy her immense inheritance and leave the world to its own troubles, from which wealth would insulate her. No stress, no effort, all pleasure. Not the ever present consciousness of the world's suffering. *Weltschmerz*. The constant companion of her thoughts.

Pamela wondered why she had always identified more with people outside her class than within it. She couldn't remember an age at which she had not been concerned that each of the inhabitants of the globe should have good and plentiful food, fresh water, decent surroundings. When she was a child, her parents and their friends wrote off her altruism as juvenile naiveté, but it had stuck. It had become the driving force of her life; her existence would lack meaning without it.

Yet she was tired. Exhausted, in fact. So were her assistants, Emily and Paige. This is why she had set aside a few days for their self-indulgence. Each had a spa suite to herself and had been visited by a manicurist. Pamela wished that the flight were longer, so that they could have a little more time in which to be suspended in this weightless cocoon. After a few days' recreation in London, however, she was scheduled to address a conference in New Delhi. Her paper was written, but she could not discipline herself to work on its delivery quite yet.

There was a knock on the door of the cabin and a female flight attendant stepped into the suite to pour her coffee. As she did so, Pamela suddenly thought of a wording change to the speech and reached for her iPad, bumping the carafe the attendant was carrying. Coffee spilled onto Pamela's jacaranda blue cashmere sweater. The attendant was aghast. "My pardon, Madam. I am so sorry." Pamela could feel the woman's anxiety mount as she helped her mop up, and hastened to reassure the attendant that it wasn't her fault at all.

"Please don't be concerned. My fault. I've always been absent-minded and a little clumsy."

"I'll inform my supervisor of this accident," the woman offered.

Pamela shook her head; she didn't care that the sweater was ruined and couldn't live with herself if the woman lost her job over something so petty. And that she herself had caused. Pamela begged the woman not to mention it to anyone; she'd intended to shower and change her clothing, anyway, before arrival in London. They introduced themselves to one another and chatted until Pamela could sense that the attendant, Jazreen, felt relaxed. Before disembarking, Pamela went out of her way to commend Jazreen to the chief steward for her gracious service. An encouraging word, a helping hand—what does it cost?

CHAPTER 26

Plan B

BACK IN THE homeless encampment, Mr. Broken Teeth was cooking a sausage on a fork over an open fire, already feeling the social benefit of having frightened off those idiot coppers that had come barging in a couple of hours earlier. His status in the camp had gone way up. Footsteps were approaching. He hoped that it was that plump girl he had had sex with the other day. Of his recent conquests, she was by far the best lay. He would share the sausage with her. He laughed at his crude double entendre. Just as he looked round, a hood was thrust over his head, and he was dragged away.

Soon afterwards, Brandt slid the razor wire barrier to one side and led the handcuffed hooded man into the temporary cell of Nelson's forward HQ. He had expected more trouble with his prisoner, but the hood was an effective demoralizer. Mr. Broken Teeth was meek as a lamb when they took his fingerprints and a blood sample. Brandt removed the hood. Mr. Broken Teeth blinked, then saw the stark concrete walls and floor. The sole furniture was a cot, a table and two chairs. Whatever was on the table was covered by a white cloth. Being the man he was, Broken Teeth decided on defiance. "So…this is where you torture...well, do your worst. You won't get nuthin' out of me."

Brandt approached the table and slowly peeled back the cloth revealing plates of oysters, roast beef sandwiches, fruit, chocolates, and a six pack of Newcastle. "Are you hungry?" asked Brandt cheerfully.

Nelson entered the basement cell where their backup plan was housed. Brandt was supervising Mr. Broken Teeth as he consumed the last of the food. In fact the man did not have many teeth, Nelson observed, and was unlikely to be identifiable by dental records. By the look of the remaining teeth he may never have seen a dentist in his life. His fingerprints had not come up on any U.K. or international database. He was a non-person, as they had anticipated. Malleable clay.

Broken Teeth had cleaned every plate. Crumbs and orange peel were all that remained. He lifted a buttock and broke wind loudly. Satisfied, he looked at Nelson.

"So...what's this all about?"

Nelson smiled engagingly. "Do you want to be on television?"

Not what Broken Teeth had expected. But he knew that there had to be some reason they were buttering him up. Nelson went on to explain that he had been selected to be part of a secret new government program that would be unveiled to the public the next day. Hence the need for confidentiality. He would have to remain here in this facility until the ceremony. Creating public awareness of the issue of homelessness would be the first step in the government's program. He would be given clean clothes, job training and shared accommodation with other homeless people. A camera team would follow him twenty-four hours a day. He would be a spokesperson for the issue, and his initial media interviews had been scheduled to take place nearby sometime in the following morning. He would be paid a weekly salary of 2000 pounds for a year.

Broken Teeth gaped. Had he died and gone to Heaven?

CHAPTER 27
The Global Players Club

TWENTY MILES AWAY at Heathrow's Terminal 3, an arriving 747 slowed to a halt beside its disembarkation gantry. Outside the Customs and Immigration Hall, a man watched the ebb and flow of arriving passengers: Charles Farrell, an upper level section chief from Langley, who used the London Embassy as his coat rack whenever he was in town. It was ostensibly his liaison role with the U.S. Secret Service that had brought him to London this time. Glasses, thinning hair, he had the bland look of a bank manager, which belied his violent history as a field agent. Now he was running his own department specializing in cyber warfare.

Farrell had been recruited by a global investment group early in his CIA career and had performed well in any task they set him. They considered he had the balls for this operation. He agreed with his clients that "the incident" could not take place on American soil. It was decided that the United States' closest ally would provide a better venue. Greater plausibility, more sympathy from the public. Farrell mulled over their decision to have Pamela van Doren assassinated. Pity she was so young.

To soothe a vestigial twinge of conscience, Farrell placed Pamela van Doren within a broader context. Human affairs,

Farrell reflected, were decided by a handful of families, who controlled the tidal forces of economic power. They were above nationalistic rivalry and political ideology. Their wealth, by inheritance and acquisition, was incalculable. Capitalism, communism, socialism were labels for competing population control systems, changing like the seasons, watched over by these Olympian gods of econometrics. And there was no corner of the Earth they did not reach, influence or adjust. Because, in their view, they owned the Earth, their spherical garden estate floating in space, which they would plant, weed, and tend in their own way. And frack. And mine. And poison. Whatever. Pamela van Doren, herself from one of these families, was beginning to subvert this arrangement through radical environmental populism. Farrell's clients would compensate him well for silencing her permanently.

Farrell looked up from these reflections to see Nelson approaching through the crowd. He and Nelson had partnered in several off-the-books ventures over the past decade. The team had a track record. Pamela van Doren's trip to London had provided an opportunity that Farrell's clients had been looking for. Farrell was to supervise her elimination and steer the subsequent inquiry in the right direction. The payout for all concerned would be huge. Huge. Now his responsibilities were beginning to gnaw at Farrell's liver due to problems he was only now hearing about from the British operatives of the European Security Taskforce he was running.

Nelson reached the arrivals gate and stood beside Farrell. He had left Brandt to take care of things in London while he tried to calm the nerves of his fellow conspirator, a man who was, by personality, easily aggravated. Their conversation was somewhat like a Kabuki play, two scorpions shadowboxing behind a polite veneer.

"My people tell me your EST people have had problems," said Farrell.

" 'EST', indeed. What is, is. Nothing that can't be fixed. Your CIA Boy Scout was a complication we should have known about."

"Agreed. Something for review when the job is done."

Some element in their surveillance of the Ratcatchers had failed and the person responsible would regret his error. Severely.

"This girl, was she the best choice?"

"At short notice, yes," said Nelson with a hint of emphasis. He was not going to let that one pass. There had been far too little development time for an operation of this complexity. "Middle class university level female. History of mental disturbance, whose flawed judgment caused her to be seduced into aiding terrorism. No family. Fitted the profile."

"Do you have a backup?"

"Of course. Brandt is preparing him now."

"Him?"

"Homeless nutcase. We've done blood and fingerprints. Untraceable. We can give him a radical identity after the event. But things are coming back into line. We'll have both up and running soon, and make a choice."

"Where will the…incident take place?"

"Somewhere public. Small blast radius, minimal collateral casualties."

"But some casualties?"

"Unavoidably. There have got to be a few to make the operation seem like a terrorist attack and not a targeted assassination."

"Well, try and keep it low. We want to minimize the heat." Farrell was reassured by Nelson's impervious confidence. But Nelson had better be aware of the consequences of failure. "This is a pivotal moment, commander."

"You deliver your end, I'll deliver mine," replied Nelson smoothly. He was looking forward to his quarter of a billion dollars and penthouse in Dubai. Courtesy of the Black Vault.

"You will be well taken care of when the time comes."

Just then, doors to the customs hall slid open and a smiling Pamela van Doren emerged accompanied by her two assistants and an airline employee pushing a cart filled with elegant suitcases. Pamela had promised Emily and Paige a break from Washington as a reward for their hard work, a weekend in London visiting tourist hotspots, before participating in a conference on urban subsistence farms and indigenous seed stocks in New Delhi. Tonight, a revival of Richard III at the Old Vic. Tomorrow, a visit to the Tower of London. Sunday, the British Museum. The tour and travel arrangements had been booked in advance online; thus, surveillance of Pamela's communications by Farrell's cyber team had given her intended assassins the opening they needed. Time and place for a terrorist outrage.

Nelson and Farrell spotted their target, whose bright coppery hair made her immediately recognizable.

Game on.

CHAPTER 28

Mr. Broken Teeth

IN NELSON'S BASEMENT HQ, a man could be heard howling like a baby. Handcuffed to a post, a naked Mr. Broken Teeth was being washed down by Brandt using a garden hose attached to a spigot on the wall. Broken Teeth had been no lover of bathing even when he was sane. He hated getting wet, having spent too many freezing days and nights with little shelter becoming soaked by the rain. He wailed his complaints, as Brandt scrubbed away the detritus of years.

"Stop whining, you big girl..." growled Brandt.

An hour later, Brandt was turning Broken Teeth's shaggy mop into a stylish cut. He was now dressed in a smart suit, and stared at a hand mirror propped up on the table. He looked handsome. "Not bad..." Broken Teeth admitted. Brandt judged that Broken Teeth would not immediately seem out of place when slipped into the crowd at the critical moment. Unless he grinned.

"My Dad was a barber," said Brandt.

"Name wasn't Sweeney Todd, was it?"

Broken Teeth chuckled at his own wit. Brandt smiled in response. Good, let's keep the conversation light. "How did you know?" he asked, snipping at the sideburns.

"I've slit a few throats myself..." declared Broken Teeth with a degree of pride.

Brandt took that in. No doubt the loony was boasting. But, for sure, they would not be vaporizing a total innocent. Of course, there had always been collateral damage in these kinds of operations. It was a given. Brandt's conscience, usually impervious, had been pricked a little initially by the choice of Jane. Slender, beautiful, little more than a child. Not many years older than Brandt's own daughter. But with the potential for dynastic wealth at stake, he had put it into perspective. All the others they had ever "processed", the euphemism of their trade, had been bad guys, according to Nelson. National security said so. Or, if it was a corporate job, then those fellows had pissed off somebody important, which was tantamount to the same thing. The girl was unfortunate collateral damage, but Brandt would have few qualms about ridding the world of this fellow.

When the plan was first laid out, Brandt had asked Nelson, "You sure we're in the clear on this?" considering the extensive inquiries that always followed terrorist attacks. "Hide in plain sight," he recalled Nelson saying with steely confidence. He and Farrell outlined how the inquiry, with a supporting media campaign, would operate. Inevitably there would be interagency finger pointing. But Nelson and Brandt would be protected men, woven into the fabric of the cover story. The bomber would be identified as a mentally-disturbed British girl, or, if she did not pan out, the vagrant whose hair Brandt was neatly trimming. A body with a credible back story was key. The predetermined report of the inquiry would be a mirror reversal of the truth, in which the victim became guilty and the guilty became heroes. But it would be plausible, given the times.

ISIL had gone underground after being defeated militarily in Syria and Iraq. But bombings and shootings from terrorist groups of all kinds, sectarian and secular, throughout the globe and even in security-tight Moscow, meant that the total eradication of extremist violence was many years off. This bombing would be viewed as the latest in the never-ending succession of senseless atrocities.

The public always preferred a simple story with recognizable villains. And heroes too, like Nelson and Brandt. As would be depicted by a breathless media, the combined efforts of the British division of EST and the CIA had almost prevented the terrible event. Without their efforts, it might have been far worse.

"We're going to be heroes, Angus. Rich heroes. Trust me." Nelson reasoned that even if both governments knew the truth, it would be in the geopolitical interest of neither Washington nor Whitehall to question the report and open Pandora's Box. To them and to the inhabitants of Mount Olympus, it would be risky to open up matters so damaging in their implications that confidence in institutional authority of any kind would be undermined.

166

CHAPTER 29

"Much suspected..."

PRINCESS ELIZABETH HELD a diamond ring between two fingers and contemplated scratching a message to posterity into a pane of glass: "Much suspected...." Her apartment in the Bell Tower was small but well appointed. Decent food and drink were provided. She was treated with the deference due to the Queen's half-sister. She was nonetheless a prisoner under suspicion, locked in at night, escorted at all times, denied an audience with Mary. Thomas Wyatt had wrought such mischief with his ill-fated rebellion! The Queen's ministers possessed damning correspondence in which Elizabeth's name was mentioned. But she had not engaged in treasonous activity; letters she had purportedly written were forgeries. Her accusers would not present her with evidence. They questioned her repeatedly on matters about which she knew nothing. All that she did know was that her future was uncertain, that she might share the fate of her mother, Anne Boleyn. So today she was considering leaving a record incised in glass, a brief *apologia pro vita sua*. Before she could act, she heard the jangle of keys outside the door. She slipped the ring back on a finger.

The door to Princess Elizabeth's room opened and guards thrust a dirty, unkempt girl inside, the young woman possessed by the demon Superbia, whom Sir Giles had brought her to see an hour before. Elizabeth had thought his offer of a new companion another of his cruel japes, aimed to intimidate her into signing a document renouncing any future claim to the throne, in return for pardon and freedom. Elizabeth, in fact, did not want the throne, especially if claiming it meant war with Philip of Spain and the Habsburg Empire. She was tempted to live a more private life, in comfort and peace. Yet just as she had resisted passing through the Traitor's Gate, she would resist this vile suasion, although she knew that there would be a rising penalty for refusal. Elizabeth recalled with horror and fear seeing the rebels' heads on spikes. She wondered how much more she could endure. Now Sir Giles had made good his threat and had placed the female demoniac within her very chamber. The Princess commanded the guards to remove the girl. They ignored her and left.

Elizabeth turned to face the mad thing crouched on the floor. It raised its head and fixed her with an eager look. The princess shuddered with fear. Demons could leap from one captive host to another. She might become mad and be put away for the rest of her life. Perhaps that was how they connived to discredit and dispose of her. She was doomed unless God intervened. The possessed creature rose to its feet. Elizabeth shrank against a wall, holding up the pendant crucifix she wore, intoning a prayer to ward off the unclean spirit.

"I renounce you, Satan, and all your works! I adjure you, angel of iniquity, ancient serpent. Leave without any harm to body or soul..." The Archbishop of Canterbury had taught her this prayer in preparation for her confirmation. The possessed girl started to move toward her. Elizabeth's prayer faltered. "You have power to tempt, not to possess...not to possess!" The demoniac moved closer. Elizabeth thrust the crucifix out towards the thing: "Please God, come to my aid, do not permit me to become possessed!"

The demon stopped inches from the crucifix and spoke: "If I am a demon, the cross will burn me." The voice was refined, yet odd in timbre. It was known that demoniacs could speak in other dialects and tongues. Elizabeth's extended hand trembled. But she held it out resolutely.

Jane bent forward. She gently kissed the crucifix.

"See? No smoke, no fire. I'm not a demon, not even a witch. I'm just... passing through."

Elizabeth was now confused as well as frightened. The Cross did not lie. Surely not. Jane felt composed, if a little excited, quite unlike how she had felt an hour before. She had experienced an epiphany.

After the golden-haired young woman had been escorted out of the chamber, and they had hooded Jane again while the assembled clergy chanted, Jane's two principal persecutors had conversed in front of her as if she were not there. Who would listen to a madwoman's tale in any case? Jane had learned that she was to be used to frighten the Princess Elizabeth into submission. Then it had come to Jane; that perhaps she was not experiencing a drug-induced fantasy after all, rather, that she had somehow actually been transported to the era that had fascinated her since childhood and had become the obsessive focus of her studies. Somehow she really was present at a critical point in the Princess Elizabeth's detention. There was a purpose to this impossible situation. She, Jane Benedict, was there to use her historical knowledge to change things, to reverse an improper outcome. She was the tool of cosmic forces beyond understanding. Perhaps there really was a higher power. At last she had found a meaning for the pain and strangeness of her life. It was all intended to bring her to this moment. So when guards came to escort her to the Princess' quarters, Jane did not resist. The realization of her destiny now made her almost giddy with excitement.

"You're terrified. I would be too," said Jane with as much reassurance as she could muster. "I'm pretty scary on a good day. They put me here to frighten you. Heard them talking. But, don't worry, I am here to guide you."

Elizabeth lowered the crucifix. There was some sense in her ravings. Jane stepped back.

"Wow, this is fantastic. You're precisely like your portrait, but younger. You really are Good Queen Bess…or you will be."

The Princess stiffened at the familiar tone. "I am the Princess Elizabeth, daughter to the late King Henry, half-sister to the Queen," she said, a little steel hardening into her voice. "No stranger should enter my presence head unbowed."

Jane lowered her head. Slightly. "And *your* head may fall from your shoulders like your mother's did…unless you listen to me."

Images of beheading had a particular potency for Elizabeth. Early in childhood, a cruel governess had recounted the fate of her mother as a caution against disobedience. She told of how Queen Anne had requested a French swordsman to carry out her execution, due to the poor reputation for accuracy of British axe men. It was a clean death, though legend had it that when her severed head was held high the crowd saw her lips moving, begging good King Henry for pardon. Like other children of executed persons, the manner of her mother's death lurked in the back of her mind, and in her nightmares. But Elizabeth found that she was not offended by the madwoman causing her to imagine it again for the thousandth time. The madwoman's speech was strange, yet it was clearly the result of education, in a regional dialect Elizabeth had never heard before. Yet there was a sincerity to her.

"You're fairly frightened now, right?" Jane continued, a grin all over her face, her epiphany making her a little manic, "I started to wig out myself, then I had a flash. Blinding flash. Everything made sense."

None of this made sense to Elizabeth, but she no longer felt threatened by the girl.

"I'm here for a reason…I'm here to help you survive, so that you can do all the great things you are destined to accomplish. You must continue to defend yourself. 'Much suspected by me, nothing proved can be. Quoth Elizabeth Prisoner.' " Jane had read an account of Elizabeth's inscribed message just the previous week.

Elizabeth gasped. How could this mad girl quote what she herself had only thought about writing? Only God could know what she had not yet written.

Elizabeth sank to her knees and crossed herself. "Have you been sent to me by God?" she asked.

"As strange as it may sound...I think I may have been, yes," replied Jane.

Elizabeth started whispering a prayer in Latin.

"I'm suddenly...happy," Jane felt obliged to tell her. "I know, I'm sounding crazy. I mean, I know I *am* crazy, but in a good way. You see...there may be a God...and She loves me after all!"

Jane giggled at her own blasphemy. But the Princess did not hear. She was lost in prayer, thanking God for sending her a guide.

CHAPTER 30

Crossing the Line

"I'M ON THE track of a terrorist plot. I don't know what the situation is, I just know that something is going down."

Paul was talking on the bedside phone in a large hotel in Mayfair, not far from the U.S. Embassy in Grosvenor Square. It was early afternoon. He was not ready to go to the embassy and demand a hearing till he made contact with someone he could trust. Right now he was being blocked by a low-ranking official. By the man's tone, Paul could tell that he was being dismissed as a crank.

Alice, dressed in new pajamas and a hotel robe, had just enjoyed a delightful hot bath and was now gleefully examining shopping bags of clothes that her James had bought for each of them, spreading them over the twin beds. Among other things, he had chosen a grand gown for her. It was finer than any fabric she had ever touched and shot through with glorious color. She glanced at him with love as he spoke, then listened more closely. Alice had accepted that in this kingdom of sorcerers people were able to talk to each other from afar, but the concern in his voice worried her.

To distract Alice and forestall conversation while he considered his next move, Paul switched the TV from the Internet back to normal programming. He had explained television to Alice as a magical window on other people's lives. Earlier he had flipped channels through a range of programming, offering quick explanations of each. Talk shows were council meetings where people discussed the needs of their townships. Alice soon caught on. Wildlife documentaries showed where game could be hunted. Cartoons were paintings come to life. What a world, she wondered. Was this magic eye showing her to others just as she watched them? She touched the screen and jumped then giggled as static electricity crackled.

"...look I am not a crank," Paul insisted, not that Alice understood. "Crank" to her was a word for epilepsy, so what he was saying made little sense to her.

"I am CIA undercover...my name isn't going to mean anything to you, with all due respect!" Paul realized he was letting his frustration show. "Look, I'm sorry...I need to talk to the Embassy's senior secret service...hello...Hello! Jesus!"

"James!" said Alice, crossing herself, "Blasphemy is a mortal sin."

Paul sighed and was silent for a moment. He lacked the inclination to play along. "Look. I need some sleep. You do too. Whichever bed you want, I'll have the other. I'm taking a shower. Don't leave this room."

Alice stared at him blankly. Paul turned wearily to the bathroom and shut the door. A few moments later Alice heard the sound of water running. How did they draw water to their chambers so high above the ground, creating pools and waterfalls? she wondered. And how did they provide water that is instantly hot? Alice moved to the bathroom door. She had worked out how to turn the handles that gave entry to doorways. Paul hadn't locked it. He wanted the fastest access to the room if he heard sounds of trouble. She opened the door an inch and peeked in. Silhouetted through the frosted glass of the shower, she saw water cascading over James' black hair, his lean muscular body. Alice blushed and smiled and closed the door.

A few minutes later, Paul, wearing his robe, quietly slipped out of the bathroom. He saw Alice, eyes closed, curled up on the farther bed. He put his head at the foot of the nearer bed so that he would sleep with a clear view of the door.

But Alice was not asleep, as he realized when she lay down beside him and hugged his back.

"Alice...what are you doing?"

"I want to lie with you." She slipped her hand inside his robe and caressed his chest. Paul placed his hand over hers and moved it away.

"That would be wrong."

Alice hugged him tighter. Her James was so noble. " 'cos priests say so, while they sin themselves?"

Alice's proposal was an unexpected development for Paul. In the field, a dispassionate, goal-oriented attitude to relationships was required. Somehow this disturbed girl had penetrated his defenses; against all his training, he wanted to nurture her; yet he was meant to be ready to cut her loose to whatever fate circumstances dictated if her continued presence endangered the mission. On the other hand, it now seemed that she *was* the mission. And he did care about her. It didn't help that she was acting out her delusion in a new and provocative way.

"Because it would complicate things," he sighed.

Alice looked away. There was silence for a moment. Finally: "It is time, James. There may not be another."

He realized that he was tempted. It was possible, even probable, that he would be dead tomorrow. And the girl, too. Certainly, enough people were determined to bring that about. This could be his last chance for intimacy with someone who loved him. And she was exceptionally desirable. But he blanked that thought out. He knew that he had to close this discussion without confrontation. He couched the truth in oblique terms.

"It's not that..." he started, about to admit that he was attracted to her. Then changed tack: "You don't know me. You think you do, but one day you'll see things differently. Sleep now."

Alice put it down to his exhaustion. "You're too tired to think clear. You'll know your mind better when sleep is done." She lightly kissed his bruised neck. "My poor love."

Paul was glad that it was settled. For now.

"Sure. Now go back to bed."

"This is where I wish to couch."

She clung to him tightly. Paul was too tired to argue further. "Be my guest." They both fell deeply asleep within seconds.

A few hours later, Alice moaned in her sleep. Paul was instantly alert.

"Alice, what is it?" But she did not wake. Her body twitched, then he realized that one of her legs was hooked around his thigh and pressed against him. The moan became little gasps. Paul knew that he ought to disentangle himself, resume propriety, put distance back into the relationship, but somehow he could not. If he woke her, then the issue would come to the fore again. Perhaps she would soon sink back into deeper unconsciousness, then he could move to the other bed. At least that was how he rationalized his decision to let her go on rubbing against him, gently, rhythmically, while he watched little sparks of pleasure flicker across her face. He felt involuntary arousal, and struggled to remain motionless.

He knew that he had crossed the line.

CHAPTER 31

" 'I am but mad north-north-west.' "

JANE AND ELIZABETH sat together, talking earnestly like any two girls of the same age, divisions of rank dissolved by the apparent supernatural occurrence. Jane had asked her about her relationship with her half-sister Queen Mary, fifteen years her senior.

"When I was a girl she taught me cards and riding, how to play the lute. She was a kind sister. It galls me to the quick that she believes me a traitor, yet they will not let me see her till I confess to what I have not done, and sign away my birthright."

"You will see her," insisted Jane. "Demand it over and over. When you do, my advice is this: Keep any dissenting beliefs secret in your heart until the time is right. Be the grateful child she remembers. Survive to be Queen."

Elizabeth's eyes lowered. "I do not wish to be Queen."

Jane knew that the person to whom she was speaking had a backbone of titanium. But at this point the Princess Elizabeth was frightened. And so young. She needed to be persuaded to embrace her destiny. "Mary is ailing," said Jane. "She will not bear a living child. You will be Queen in a matter of years. You will reign for over four decades. You will be one of the greatest monarchs England will ever have known."

Elizabeth looked at her astonished. "How can you know these things?"

Suddenly Jane shivered, then gasped.

"What troubles you?" asked Elizabeth.

"I don't..." Jane's breathing quickened.

"Are you ill?" asked Elizabeth.

"I…haven't been feeling myself lately…" An ironic laugh was all she could summon before sinking to her knees.

"Guards!" Elizabeth cried out.

Outside the door, Córdoba and Sir Giles had been waiting, disturbed that the Princess' initial protests had given way to quiet conversation that neither could hear. Now she was demanding that they give medicine to this sick girl. It would seem that the Princess was in no way cowed by her encounter with the demoniac. Quite to the contrary. The guards looked to Sir Giles for orders. Exasperated, he waved them in.

Jane recognized that she was experiencing the unmistakable sensations of arousal. Although technically a virgin, Jane was no stranger to self-pleasure. It enabled her to maintain her independence. How could anyone know the ways of her own body better than she? Relationships led to pain. She did not need anyone for sex. She had told that to the shrinks. But they scoured her sexuality repeatedly, probably more out of prurient interest than for therapy.

Sex had been the last thing on Jane's mind while she was instructing the Princess Elizabeth on her future role as Queen. Jane had been exuberant, convinced that she had discovered her own destiny through securing that of Elizabeth. Then suddenly the air was being sucked out of her lungs, and her brain was folding in on itself. All signs indicated that she was about to lose consciousness and depart through the portal. But the familiar pain of transition had turned into inexplicable waves of erotic pleasure. As the guards dragged her out, and her mind spun like a giddy carousel, she heard herself gabbling unintelligibly. Jane could read six languages and it was none of those.

The guards became frightened. Once out of the Princess' cell, they dropped the witch to the flagstones and stepped back.

Córdoba stared at the writhing, moaning girl with contempt and no small degree of apprehension. The course of madness could not easily be predicted. They had made a mistake. One best reduced to ashes.

Then Elizabeth stepped out from the doorway. "Take her to a physician, that she may be healed," she said in a surprisingly strong voice. She locked eyes with Sir Giles and gave him a look of mortal enmity. "And from you, sir, I again request… nay, I demand an audience with my sister the Queen that I may address the charges against me. I demand it without delay. Arrange it, Sirrah." Without waiting for a response she turned and went back into her quarters.

"Lock the door!" snapped Sir Giles at the dumbstruck guards.

Córdoba saw that Sir Giles' plan had failed. The Princess would stand firm. He was losing faith in this strutting English knight and his boastful promises. His use of the witch was an extravagant idea, and those rarely work. He should never have consented to it. Córdoba stepped forward and looked down at the wench, who was now caressing her nether regions. As an Inquisitor, he had much experience with the disgusting practices of the possessed. He knelt down to observe more closely.

"Is it plague, sire?" one of the frightened guards asked.

"Not plague...possession and madness," pronounced Córdoba.

Jane giggled. " 'I am but mad north-north-west: When the wind is southerly I know a hawk from a handsaw,' " she quoted. "Whoa! Shakespeare hasn't even been born yet..." She squealed with laughter, then another wave of pleasure swept over her.

Jane looked up at Córdoba but saw only Suit, her captor. Arrogant bastard! I'll bring you down a peg or two. She seized the Inquisitor's ankle. Before he could ward her off, she had grabbed his clothing and started pulling herself up his body. As he staggered back, she locked her legs around his thigh. "Oh! Oo! I'll hump your leg like a dog!"

Sir Giles could not help being amused at his Spanish confederate's discomfiture. "It seems the little bawd has taken a fancy to you."

Córdoba had never in his life permitted a woman to touch him in this manner. Rage at his defilement welled. He punched the side of her head with all his might and she fell senseless to the ground.

CHAPTER 32

A Small Island of Trust

SUDDENLY PAUL FELT Alice convulse and jerk upright, wide awake. After a moment's disorientation, the girl became aware that she was lying on top of Paul. Her expression changed to shock. Paul realized that she was Jane again.

"Oh, my God!" she whispered, then rolled off the bed onto the floor. She sprang up, angry, confused, backing towards the bathroom. "How could you do that to me?"

"Do what?"

"You were raping me."

"You've got it all wrong," said Paul, getting up on the other side of the bed, his arousal evident.

"Then what's that?"

Paul did not want to go there. He struggled to be reasonable. "Jane, you are still wearing pajamas, I did not touch you." That produced a mocking double take from Jane but he continued. "It wasn't you. It was Alice. You became Alice again, and she needed to be close to me."

"So Alice made you do it."

"You could say that. I probably should have moved away. But I was afraid to disturb her. Alice is so vulnerable."

"Fuck Alice!" yelled Jane as she ran into the bathroom and locked the door.

Oh, shit, thought Paul, crossing to the bathroom door. He pressed his ear closer and heard a sniff from inside. Improbably, Jane was weeping.

"Look. I'm sorry, Jane, I'm sorry. You were a virgin yesterday, you're still a virgin today. It was a misunderstanding. That's all."

In truth, whatever contact they might have had was at the moment unimportant to Jane. There were larger issues. Normally she remembered fragments of her visits to Alice. This time nothing. Not a single image. Which frightened her. Why had the pattern changed? And it was now after dark. How long had she been gone?

"Where are we?"

"Hotel in the West End. We lost them in the underground. I'll take you to the U.S. Embassy first thing in the morning. We'll tell them everything we know. You'll be protected. You'll be safe."

"Safe?" she asked, with a derisive snigger.

"Yes, absolutely."

There was another silence. She blew her nose. Then he heard her voice again, fighting back a sob.

"Do you know what it's like to be me?"

Paul said nothing. She needed to talk. He needed to learn. A stream of angst poured out of her. "You know, to be smart, really smart. But without warning you're wrenched out of your life, then bingo! You're back. You just remember a few tiny pieces…and everyone's staring at you like you're the village idiot. Or a liar. Then you try and explain…'Oh, sorry, I just had a past life experience. Or something. I'm fine now, really…' and they say 'Of course, dear,' while looking at whoever brought you, as if to say—how could you bring this thing into my house? But then you say—no really, I'm fine, and you try to explain the multiverse to them and their eyes glaze and they can't get away quickly enough, so they don't catch what you've got."

So that's how she rationalizes Alice, thought Paul.

"And you can see that scarcely-veiled distaste in their faces... You have a mental defect. Your brain, your core, your very soul is poorly manufactured. You are defective and will one day be a burden..." The sob finally broke through.

Paul waited for her to cry it out. She needed the release. The tears died away. "I don't look at you as a burden, Jane," he offered.

"How do you look at me then?"

"Like you're Alice's twin sister, and I'm going to try to protect you like I'm trying to protect her."

"You could be James' identical twin, you know."

"Yeah, so I've been told."

There was another silence. "I don't know what's real anymore," Jane stated, calmer now. "Are we all just figments of our own imaginations? Unravel that paradox. Am I real? Are you?"

That was too big a question for Paul at this particular moment. Despite a few hours' sleep, he was still bone weary. He sighed. "We're real, and the people who want to kill us are very real," Paul answered. "Powerful people. We're in a world of shit right now, Jane. So if I'm to stop them, I need my forty winks. You can stay there if you like, I'll leave a pillow and some blankets at the door, or you can come out and take the other bed. Your choice."

"Whatever..." was the reply. He heard the shower start. Good, it will help her sleep. Paul lay back, putting a pillow under his head. He was asleep immediately, only to jolt half-awake as the bathroom door opened. Jane, in her robe, walked past him to the other bed.

"Fed up with being a virgin anyway," she said. She curled up facing him, a sad wry smile on her face. They stared at each other for a moment from their separate beds.

"Jane, I'd be grateful if you refrained from removing any of my body parts while I'm sleeping."

She liked his sense of humor. Humor could be such a peephole into the soul. In fact, now she liked everything about him.

Especially those eyes. "Very well. I declare you a scissor-free zone."

Paul laughed spontaneously. She had wit, goofy though it was. And wit was endearing. His laughter released a laugh from her. They looked at each other in silence for a moment. Paul felt that they had achieved some common ground at last, a small island of trust. "Goodnight," he said and rolled away to face the door. If he could maintain her in this mood, when she told her story at the U.S. Embassy in the morning, she might be believed. Within minutes, they were both sound asleep.

CHAPTER 33
Quite Contrary

GUARDS DUMPED ALICE on the floor of James' cell like a sack of grain. The impact stirred her from unconsciousness. James could see that she bore the marks of beating. He lunged forward, but his ankle was chained to the wall. He fell short of Alice, just inches from his hand. Then he decided to wait till the guards were gone before trying to rouse her, in case she was still possessed.

"Alice?" asked James tentatively after the door clanged shut. He prayed it was Alice, not the snarling loon of the morning.

She groaned, then the pain of her abuse melted at the sight of him. "My love." James was relieved that the demon had left her. "Where are we?" she asked.

"The Tower…I have demanded Queen's audience, by right of birth. We shall be summoned on the morrow."

James advised Alice to say nothing unless addressed by the Queen. His stepfather had served the Tudors well over years. Now at last he would receive the justice that he deserved.

They slept denied the comfort of an embrace. In the morning, a ewer and basin were brought to them so that they could to bathe their hands and faces. Then Alice and James, their hands chained, were led to a large hall full of courtiers and men-at-arms. At the end of the hall was a raised dais supporting a richly-carved throne. A small and slight woman, looking older than her thirty-eight years, with wan solemn features and piercing blue eyes, sat stiffly upon it, regally dressed but unattractive: Queen Mary, daughter of Henry VIII by his first wife, Catherine of Aragon.

Alice heard a bailiff intone "Bring forth the prisoner!" James was led forward, while Alice remained. Three guards stood beside her, halberds a thrust away if she were to give trouble. They intended to take no chances with the possessed. Alice watched as James arrived at the foot of the dais and bowed low to the Queen.

"Last I saw you, James De Fries, you were but eight years old," Queen Mary remarked in a voice unexpectedly deep and gruff. "A wide-eyed boy on his first visit to court, clinging to his mother's hand."

"I am flattered that you remember, Your Majesty," replied James summoning as much humility as he could muster as a bulwark against the Queen's reputed short temper.

"I was fond of your mother, God rest her soul, so it pains me to see you here, accused of treason and the consort of a proven witch."

"She is no witch, Majesty. I am no traitor." James chose his words carefully. "I rose against corruption, not the Crown."

"Your uncle claims otherwise." Her tone had soured.

"He claims my lands as well, bequeathed to me alone by my stepfather."

"You should have settled with him, divided the estate. He has much influence at court."

"None has such influence as you, Majesty." James meant to acknowledge her omnipotence, yet the Queen read it as flattery, which she always enjoyed but by which she was never swayed.

"True. A fine silver tongue in that handsome head," she said tartly.

"You have no more loyal servant than I…" said James then wondered if this were a misstep. Had he invited a test?

"So say all around me," the Queen replied.

Yes, flatterers all, thought James, pigs jostling for position at the trough of plenty. How he despised them, yet now he had sounded the same.

Queen Mary addressed the bailiff: "The girl." The bailiff signaled the guards to lead Alice forward. This was not what James wanted to happen.

"We will make a test of your loyalty," pronounced the Queen. "Witch or not, this village girl, child of a common headsman, is unworthy of a man of noble birth." James' heart sank, but he knew he dare not show it.

Alice arrived, buoyed by the summons. James' suit must have found the Queen's favor. She dropped to her knees in obeisance. Queen Mary noted her beauty, but not with approval. James saw in the Queen's face envy tinged with bitterness. The trap was closing around them.

"Give her up, and I will look favorably upon your case," said the Queen with a light smile. Though pain knotted her stomach at the thought, Alice would accept the sacrifice, if it restored her James to his rightful station. She prayed he would not contest the Queen's wishes.

James understood that if the only way he could save Alice's life was by sacrificing their life together, he would do it. "Your Majesty, your will is my command."

Queen Mary continued: "Give her up to face the penalty prescribed by law, and I will dismiss all charges against you and restore your lands."

James could forswear the woman he adored in order to save her. This was different. A chill pervaded his being. Consign an innocent who loved him to a terrible fate, then be rewarded with all that he had been fighting for. Such calculated cruelty. To make him complicit in her death...

In fact, cruelty was not the Queen's purpose that day, though it was often required of a ruler. Cruel though it might seem, witches had to suffer a foretaste of eternal hellfire in public so as to warn and to save the people, lest their baser instincts drive them away from God. The duty of the Monarch was to protect Holy Mother Church and the sanctity of Her teachings. The decisions of royalty reflected God's purpose and were not to be questioned, whatever their consequence. In childhood, Mary had memorized the New Testament. The Bible was explicit on this point. Romans 13, verses 1 and 2: *Non est enim potestas nisi a Deo quae autem sunt a Deo ordinatae sunt itaque qui resisit potestati Dei ordinationi resistit.* "For there is no power save from God; those powers that exist are ordained by God; and so, whosoever rebels against power rebels against the mandate of God." Such was the authority of Kings. And Queens.

Yet her own right to rule was being questioned. When her late father King Henry, having succumbed to lust, had broken with Rome, he had compromised the divine mandate that maintained the power of the dynasty. He had broken faith with God. Although she had loved him, Mary was certain that his foul-smelling ulcerous death was a foretaste of the sulfurs of Hell. Misfortune and rebellion had followed his demise. The souls of her subjects were in peril. God would continue to punish England if she were to fail to return the English Church securely to Rome. Heaven wept over its heresy; crops rotted in the fields, causing famine and unrest.

So the Queen had many other pressing issues to manage today, and competing factions at Court through which to manage them. She needed the cooperation of the Inquisitor Córdoba. That was essential. The girl must die. Córdoba had made that clear. She needed Sir Giles De Fries to continue ruthlessly to stamp out rebellion in the southern counties, and attempt to discover whether her half-sister Elizabeth had been involved in Wyatt's conspiracy. The continued loyalty of Córdoba and De Fries was paramount, of greater import than the life of a peasant girl and the alleged theft of inheritance, of which crime Sir Giles was no doubt guilty. The blood feud within the De Fries clan must end. She had told Sir Giles in a private audience that after the girl was burned, she would rescind her promise to restore James' lands, and would instead replace them with lands of greater value in the North, near the Scottish border. Thus the two men would be kept apart while familial wounds healed. Besides, she needed strong commanders to keep the Scots at bay. She looked at young impetuous James De Fries. He would soon forget the girl. There were peasant trollops aplenty, where he was going, if that was his taste. And given his reputation, he would establish firm bonds with the local population, and do all in his power to protect them. Which would serve her purpose against the borderers.

James sank to his knees beside Alice. He would beg if he must. "She has done no wrong, Majesty."

"She is a peasant...guilty of witchcraft," the Queen explained, as if speaking to a child. "Do this as a token of your loyalty to me."

Alice addressed the Queen uninvited. "I am no witch but I accept my fate."

"I do not," James said hastily, hoping to nullify her offer. "Our fates are bound together."

The Queen was shocked, not by the peasant girl's lapse of decorum. She had expected a wailing plea for her life. Or more mad ravings, the like of which had been described to her. The mad were sometimes entertaining to watch, like cats with bells tied to their tails. So she did not expect this self-sacrifice, spoken with quiet, almost serene, resignation. This was not how Satan's vessels comported themselves. There was more to this than met the eye. But larger issues vital to the Crown were at stake. Witch or no, the girl must burn.

Alice heard James and was distraught. "No need for us both to die." Alice loved James for his nobility of spirit. Yet she wished he would shed it now. "Do as her Majesty asks..."

James was gripped by a quiet anger. "It is a vile bargain. I will not."

The Queen did not appreciate his scorn: "So much for loyalty to the Crown."

Alice dissolved into silent tears. As the headsman's daughter, she had seen the apparatus of power at work. For the poor folk dragged under its grinding stone, there was no mercy. She knew that she was doomed. Must James be as well?

James had hoped that an honest examination of his suit would be sufficient to exonerate him. As for Alice, she was no witch. Mayhap a trifle touched from the beating she had received. But she was her true self now. James knew that he had one remaining option. "Majesty," he announced so the whole court would hear, "I demand the right to trial by combat against my accuser."

The Queen stared at him. This a development she had neither expected nor desired. Yet she could not deny James' customary right before the court. The outcome was no longer predictable. That occurred to Alice, too. Perhaps they were not doomed after all. The Queen bowed to the inevitable.

"And trial by combat you shall have." She turned to the bailiff. "Summon Sir Giles De Fries."

CHAPTER 34

Sword and Buckler

THE DOORS OPENED and Sir Giles De Fries, who had been waiting in an adjacent chamber, appeared. He bowed low to the Queen then strode across the flagstones to arrive at a respectful distance to her left. He bowed again. The Queen nodded. Then Sir Giles turned to give James and Alice an elaborate mocking bow.

"Greetings, nephew. And outlaw. And plaything of the Devil's whore. Your new titles become you. I accept your challenge. My choice of weapons will be sword and buckler."

James was surprised by his uncle's enthusiasm for a death match against a man his junior by a score of years. His thoughts turned to the moral dilemma he would face in their conflict. While his uncle had no compunction about killing him, could he kill his stepfather's brother? James had wished for revenge many times. Now the moment had come. He had appetite for victory more than murder. As guards removed his chains, James resolved to leave his uncle wounded, not dead. He glanced at Alice, as they led her from the center of the room. This was the girl for whom he would die, if it were God's will. But his cause was just. And God favored the just.

Sir Giles turned to the Queen. "Your Majesty, may I present Cedric of Winchester, my champion." A muscular giant of a man stepped out of the crowd and bowed to the Queen. Sir Giles had anticipated his nephew's predilection for heroics. There was no way young James would accept the Queen's proposal. So Sir Giles had borrowed one of Córdoba's personal guard, a champion swordsman in England and Spain.

The Queen noted Sir Giles' foresight. Alice saw that James would be fighting one of the men who had tried to violate her. But she wanted no revenge that risked James' life. James himself was outraged.

"Champion?" James shouted for the whole court to hear. "God's Blood, fight me yourself, coward!" The supercilious grin on his uncle's face infuriated him more. Now he really did want to kill the spineless cur. There were many in the hall who privately agreed with James, but they raised not a murmur. Sir Giles did indeed have much influence at court. The courtiers understood that they would be witnesses to the judicial murder of an innocent man. But to survive in politics, honor must sometimes be bent.

"It is my right to appoint a champion," snapped Sir Giles, "It is yours also. Summon your champion."

"I fight my own battles," James replied with contempt. He turned to the Queen. "Majesty, I declare Alice Craddock of Farnham to be my betrothed. If...when I prevail, and receive the pardon the law dictates, that pardon shall extend to all members of my family."

The court was hushed. Alice looked at James. She had never loved him more. Queen Mary's jaw tightened. She looked across the hall at Alice, her face sorrowful, but glowing with pride. There was a purity about the girl, a commodity so rare that young James was prepared to die for it. The Queen sighed. In a court packed with dissemblers and wastrels, it was a shame to lose a capable young man. He deserved hope at least, in his final moments. She would give him that much.

"If God decides that your cause is just and gives you the victory, then pardon is hers also." However, she saw little contest between this young nobleman and Cedric, battle-hardened mercenary for the Hapsburgs and champion for hire, so her ruling was immaterial.

The Queen arose, and turned to a senior advisor, the Duke of Norfolk, who was hoping that this task would not be assigned to him. "Norfolk, see that the contest is fairly conducted, and advise me of the outcome."

"As you command, Majesty," Norfolk responded.

The assemblage bowed as the Queen left the hall, followed by her ladies-in-waiting. She was not pleased by these developments. But it was a busy day. There were other matters to address.

Norfolk ordered the two combatants to prepare. An oval was cleared in the center of the hall. Alice, her hands still manacled in front of her, quickly stepped forward, and before her guards caught up, reached edge of the circle of spectators close to the Duke. Alice would rather witness than listen, whatever the outcome. Norfolk saw the defiant pride in her face. He saw no trace of the raving spitfire about whom he had been told. Unfortunate child. He nodded his assent. Two guards flanked her while another stood behind.

Stewards brought forward two dueling swords, their blades three feet in length, with quillions at the hilt curving back towards the pommel to protect the fingers. James had trained with a similar weapon at school in Paris, and had fought friendly bouts for wager. But he had never used a weapon in earnest until confronted by the assassins his uncle sent, who drew daggers against him on three sides. He had proved to be more accomplished with the dagger than they. Accompanying each sword was the buckler, a round shield, steel-rimmed and studded, a mere twelve inches in diameter. Held by a leather strap, it was used to both to ward off blows and to deliver them at close range. James and Cedric took their weapons, and were allowed time at separate ends of the hall to stretch their limbs in swings and lunges. After a brief interlude, Norfolk ordered them forward to the center of the wide ring of spectators.

"Are the combatants ready?" asked Norfolk.

"Aye," both men replied. The hall fell silent.

"To first blood?" asked Norfolk, trying to steer the combat against a mortal outcome.

"To the death," said Cedric immediately. Cold. Expressionless.

"To the death," echoed James, unsurprised.

"To the death, then," said Norfolk, with discernible regret.

Each raised his sword in salute to Norfolk, then to his opponent. James made the Sign of the Cross, then kissed the base of the blade at the hilt, before sweeping the weapon in a low arc across the floor. I raise my blade to God to give me victory, said James to himself, and I point to the ground where I will put you. But James knew that he had a serious task ahead of him. Cedric of Winchester was a professional, powerfully built and a half-foot taller than he.

"*En garde*," the Duke of Norfolk announced. Each assumed the position. "*Allez.*"

The swordsmen started warily circling each other, watched by all, but by none more intently than Alice. A steward brought Sir Giles his requested goblet of wine. He hated to admit to himself that his nerves needed steadying. The combat was a foregone conclusion. Or was it? In the past few weeks fate had reversed a number of his assumptions. He had underestimated the inner strength of the Princess Elizabeth. His manipulations had secured for him her undying hostility, rather than the renunciation of any claim to the throne. His failure legally to eliminate the Princess from succession as promised would anger Phillip of Spain, who had already paid him a substantial advance in gold coin. There was a limit to how long he could prevent the audience with the Queen that Elizabeth had now demanded. That issue would come to a point soon. There would be fancy footwork ahead.

Footwork indeed underpinned a swordsman's victory. Agility of the feet was more important than strength of arm. Balance and maintaining correct distance were key. As James and Cedric circled, each gauged the other's stability and reach. Cedric made a sudden step forward to assess the reflexes of his opponent, who jumped back, lurching slightly before straightening into guard position again. Typical, thought, Cedric. These young nobles who fancy themselves with the sword do not take the time to develop the automatic stability that was a standard discipline of his own generation. They were seduced by the new gadfly style of fighting made popular by Portuguese fencing masters. This would be short work.

Alice's heart raced as Cedric launched a series of feint attacks, before thrusting high to James' shoulder. But James did not hop back as expected. His feet remained locked firmly in place. He parried the blade, stepped forward, and thrust to the belly. Only Cedric's speedy counter parry prevented a serious wound. As it was, the tip of James' blade, parried downwards, nicked Cedric's thigh. Cedric sprang back. A flea bite, but an indication that his opponent was a better swordsman than he had at first pretended to be.

A running battle then ranged back and forth across the oval. Alice had seen her brothers compete in the quarterstaff championships each year at harvest time, but she had never seen a duel with swords before. Thrust, parry, riposte, disengage, circlage, coupe…James and Cedric unleashed every maneuver and deception, causing gashes, blows from shield and elbow, building to a furious interchange of clashing Toledo steel. Both men paused, breathing hard, bleeding from superficial wounds. Alice was breathless too. She hated to see the tiny trickles of blood that streaked James' arms and torso. Cedric and James stared at each other. Men of the sword have respect for one another's art regardless of allegiance.

"We are well matched," said James.

Cedric nodded. "Aye, 'tis a shame I must take your life."

Cedric attacked once more. He would wear his opponent down with brute strength while keeping a careful distance from the blade that had scratched him more times than expected. He would beat that blade hard, followed by a series of multiple disengages, so that his opponent could not be certain from which side of the line his next lunge would spring. In this way, he began driving James close to where Sir Giles was standing. Sir Giles would know what to do next. As the spectators backed away from the swinging weapons, Sir Giles moved with them, deliberately spilling his wine on the floor as he backed away. Cedric then adjusted the angle of attack so that James' withdrawal would take him across the puddle. This caught the eye of Norfolk across the oval. Alice saw Sir Giles tip his goblet too, but his purpose did not become apparent till a few moments later when James' fighting retreat reached the wet flagstones. The result was as intended. His back foot, the anchor to his posture and his guard, suddenly slid. James fell to one knee. Cedric immediately slashed his exposed shield arm, cutting tendons, rendering it useless. The buckler fell to the floor. Relief and spleen boiled within Sir Giles. Finish him now. Finish the whelp.

Alice screamed at the wound. That revitalized James. He parried the next thrust, sprang up and went back on the attack, trying to disregard the pain radiating from the arm now hanging by his side. He feinted low, drawing Cedric's blade down, then cut high, landing a sweeping gash across Cedric's forehead. The big man recoiled. Blood ran into his eyes. He could not see. He slashed at empty space as James sidestepped. He was at James' mercy, no longer able to judge distance. But James could not kill a helpless man. He dropped the tip of his blade onto Cedric's heart, and held it there for all to see. Cedric parried wildly, but James evaded and placed it there again. The crowd of courtiers were in suspense, waiting for the fatal thrust. This was not the expected outcome.

"Strike or forfeit!" commanded the Duke of Norfolk. The Queen would blame him if there was not a clean finish to the affair.

Instead, James turned to Sir Giles. "Fight me! Coward! Fight me!" He would not kill his uncle, merely humiliate him, force him to plead for mercy. James strode towards his uncle, extending his weapon.

Sir Giles backed away. As the tip of James' sword homed in, Sir Giles grabbed the ten-year-old page boy standing beside him. The boy hitherto had been enthralled by the combat. Suddenly he found himself lifted up and proffered as a shield. The child screamed. James hesitated. Cedric had now wiped the blood from his eyes and was closing on James from behind.

Alice saw the danger. Her manacles did not prevent her from snatching a dagger from the scabbard of the distracted man guarding her. She lunged forward to help James, who continued to yell his challenge. The page boy squirmed in Sir Giles' grasp and begged for release. The shameful character of Giles De Fries had now been exposed to the entire court. They would reconsider their support of such a man. Then Cedric arrived behind James, thrusting his blade into his back. Alice slammed the dagger into Cedric's kidneys an instant too late. As blood filled James' lung, his last image was of Alice calling his name, her face suffused with horror and grief.

198

CHAPTER 35

It Was the American

"JAMES!" ALICE WOKE with a start, gasping for breath. Alone in bed. She scanned the room for him. Then the bathroom door opened. Paul appeared, a towel round his waist.

"God be praised!" exclaimed Alice, running to hug him. "I have seen something terrible. There is treachery ahead. Trust no one, James. I beg you." Paul found his arms instinctively folding around her. But inwardly he was dismayed. Alice would make his task all the harder. He needed Jane. Where had she gone?

***

In the Tower, guards flung the witch onto fetid straw lining the cell. As they chained her to the wall, she whispered as if to some unseen presence. "I'm not meant to be back...it was just a one-time thing, right? I did what I was meant to do...why am I back?"

The guards left hastily. As they slammed the door bolts home, Jane tried to make sense of what had happened. She had awoken on the floor of a large hall, onto which it appeared she had just been thrown. Scattered groups of people were clamoring at one another. Foul smelling men unlocked the manacles on her wrists, twisted her arms behind her back and clamped them on again. There was blood on her hands. Literally and figuratively. Jane understood from verbal abuse, accompanied by cuffs to the back of the head, that she had stabbed the greatest swordsman in England. And there he was lying a few feet away in a pool of blood with a dagger protruding from his back. Face gashed. Eyes wide open looking right at her with a fixed accusing stare. How the fuck did I do that!!! Then she recognized him as The Giant who had helped kidnap her from her flat, and had tried again at a townhouse and then on a train on the Piccadilly Line. What! Jane's brain went into temporary meltdown.

She had seen a man standing nearby, dressed in elegant doublet and hose. The same nobleman she had seen standing by the Princess Elizabeth. He walked up to a group of courtiers, but they turned away from him. Then Jane recognized her kidnapper, Suit, dressed in priestly robes, explaining to a distinguished elderly man that the witch was already condemned to death, and that the demon inside was too dangerous to be allowed to remain in this world any longer. The witch must be burned as soon as a bonfire could be made ready. Guards had jerked Jane to her feet.

It was then that she had seen the other dead body lying on the flagstones. It was the American. No! Alice's James.

CHAPTER 36

Locked Out

EARLY THE NEXT morning, Paul was weighing whether or not to take Alice with him to the U.S. Embassy. Although Alice looked perfectly presentable—more than presentable—in the new dress, Paul needed her as Jane. He pulled out bottled orange juice, cheese and crackers from the minibar, and handed them to her. She must be hungry. Perhaps she would forget her self-imposed role for a moment.

"Cheese."

"Oh cheese!" said Alice, her eyes lighting up. She snatched the package and bit through the wrapping, trying to chew it along with the cheese. "Wait" he said, grabbing a piece of the plastic sticking out of her mouth, and slowly extracting it, leaving the cheese which she continued to chew with little grunts of enjoyment. No, he decided. Safer to go it alone.

"Alice, there's something I have to do. I will be away a couple of hours. You must stay here."

"Let me come with you."

"There is too much danger. You will be safe here."

"James, don't leave me… I pray you."

"I must...it is my duty."

A knight must do his duty, she knew that. She nodded sadly.

"I will return soon. Then the danger will be gone," he reassured.

She remained disconsolate. Then he had an idea. He took the Gideon Bible out of the bedside drawer and handed it to her.

"Here...you can read, can't you?" Alice gave him a look, pretending offense, but was glad of The Good Book.

"I learned my letters, silly. You know that. I will pray for you, pray for us both."

"You do that. Now, very important. Stay in this room. Do not go outside for any reason. For *any* reason. Understood? I will be back. I promise."

Alice stood up, flung her arms around his neck and kissed his cheek. She was afraid to let him go, given what she could remember of the dreadful vision she had seen. Her eyes became misty as she looked into his. She was begging him to kiss her. So he did. It was meant to be a kiss of reassurance. But as their lips parted and their tongues melded, Paul felt an inexplicable glow. It was not the glow of rising lust, rather an intense fondness that lifted his spirits. It meant a great deal to Alice that this James had at last kissed her as a lover should. She broke from the kiss, took a deep breath and said, "Go now."

It was crazy that he was feeling like this. He had lost all perspective. He was still in control but she had somehow bewitched him. It didn't make sense, thought Paul, as he gave her one last look from the door, but he had to keep moving forward.

The elevator he took stopped at every floor. It was a large hotel favored by package tours. A lot of people were checking out. Paul turned from the elevator into a lobby full of arriving tourists. A large group from a Japanese girls' school was being checked in. Paul paused to scan the crowd. Lots of happy exuberant girls talking and texting amid harassed older chaperones. Then Paul froze. Ahead of him at the concierge desk was the leader of the thugs at the townhouse.

Paul had expected that they would be scanning every hotel in London. He hadn't expected them to track him down so quickly. He had checked in as Gerhart Wolfram, using a virgin Swiss passport and credit card known only to him. He had smuggled Alice in, and had not ventured outside his room till now. How long would it take for hotel staff to put a room number to the face on the photos Nelson was showing? He had to get back to Alice. Behind him, he saw the elevator doors closing on a full load. The other elevator was ten floors up. Paul drifted unobserved to a house phone behind a pillar and dialed his room. Of course, if she picks up the phone, she's a fake, he realized. It was not rational, he admitted, but he did not want her to be a fake. Yet now her survival might depend upon it.

Alice sat on the bed reading the Bible, starting with the book of Genesis. The world seemed to have changed greatly in the few days since she last attended Mass. God's children had all become sorcerers, vying in feats of magic as well as feats of arms. So she thought she ought to read the Word of God again from the beginning. The lettering on the page was hard to recognize but her memory of the Bible helped her decipher the text. She had just reached the Garden of Eden, when the object beside her buzzed loudly. She leaped away, startled. The high-pitched noise kept repeating itself.

Paul scanned the lobby. Nelson's back was still turned. Pick up, Alice, Jane, whoever, pick up.

The object kept buzzing, abrasively to Alice's ear, as she considered what to do. She had seen James speaking to this object, but it had never made this hostile noise before. Then it stopped. Alice gingerly approached for a closer look. The object buzzed again. Alice jumped back. Slowly she backed towards the door. The object kept buzzing. Instinct told Alice that the shrill noise meant that something was wrong. She needed to warn James. He could not be far away. Perhaps he was outside.

Alice opened the door as a tall slender woman in traditional Nigerian attire passed by. "What a beautiful garment," thought Alice. She had heard of Africans but had never before seen one. Impelled by curiosity, she stepped away from the door. She wanted to meet this woman and ask her about her faraway land. The door closed noiselessly behind her.

Paul listened to the continuous ring tone. So she didn't know how or did not want to answer the phone? He put the handset down and moved towards a returning elevator. Halfway there, he saw Brandt and Dr. Picton enter the lobby. The doctor's presence meant they needed Alice alive for a while longer, which heartened Paul a little. He had to get upstairs.

Nelson and Brandt had emailed Paul's photo, supplied by Farrell, to every hotel in London. They had already gone through a dozen false hits. Then a clerk from this hotel contacted them, positive he had registered the man in the photograph sometime the day before, but with the high volume of guests couldn't connect the man to the room number. Brandt exchanged an exasperated glance with Nelson, who was waiting none too patiently for the clerk's memory to kick in.

Brandt's eyes cruised the bustling lobby. A movement through the crowd caught his eye. He could not be sure if the dark-haired man in the windbreaker was their target, but he was taking no chances. "Wait here," he growled at Picton, then headed off.

No pretense any longer of anything other than We Own You, Dr. Picton thought wretchedly. Just when he had escaped the violence of the other night by the skin of his teeth and was done with this miserable business once and for all, Nelson had summoned him to this hotel, making it quite clear that to refuse would be a fatal mistake. How long was this going to go on? Regardless of what they had paid him in the past, he had rendered his services; he was not on open call.

Brandt saw the man he was following disappear through a Staff Only door. He did not look like an employee. Brandt quickened his pace.

On the sixth floor, Alice walked down the corridor and caught up with the woman who had attracted her curiosity, Ms. Nkruma, CFO of a growing IT company.

"Are you an Ethiope?" Alice asked.

"What?" The woman stopped dead in her tracks.

"Are you an Ethiope?"

White people, she thought. "Oh, no," Ms. Nkruma said, taken aback. "I'm from Nigeria."

"Do you miss your village? I know I miss mine." Alice smiled nervously "May we talk? I have a fine chamber."

Ms. Nkruma gave Alice a long, quizzical look, then strode away, muttering pejoratives in her native Hausa about the crazy British.

Alice, saddened by the rejection, walked back to the door of her room. But there was no handle on the outer side, as there had been on the inside. Alice pushed to no avail. She was locked out.

206

CHAPTER 37

A Village Gull

BRANDT PEERED ROUND the corner into the hotel laundry. Thick bundles of washing were piled everywhere. Three laundry staff were busy loading and unloading noisy washers and dryers that lined the walls at the far end of the room. Brandt entered, flashing his security services ID. He strode past an L-shaped stack of laundry baskets, overflowing with towels. Paul had wedged himself behind them, his hiding place not meriting more than a glance by Brandt.

At the same time, Alice was wandering the maze of corridors, quite lost. All the doors looked the same. She now understood why James had told her not to leave the room, and was upset with herself for disobeying him. Yet she must find James, because something was wrong.

Paul, peering through layers of towels, saw laundry staff shaking their heads in answer to Brandt's questions. Paul looked around. A possible avenue of escape was in the small adjacent alcove where the laundry chute disgorged sacks of washing from the upper floors. Paul lay flat, then slithered back along the wall and into the alcove. He raised the hatch, climbed into the chute and let the hatch swing shut again. Then a bag of laundry from above landed on his hunched shoulders.

Alice wandered worried. She had not meant to leave the chamber; it had shut her out. She had so much to learn. James was nowhere to be found. Rounding a corner, she saw a group of young girls laughing and joking. Their language was foreign, almost musical, as though they were singing to each other. They had pale skin, hair as black as James', and dark eyes of unusual shape. Alice stared at them amazed. They were the most beautiful girls Alice had ever seen. She joined them unnoticed. When the door in the wall opened suddenly, the girls passed through into the small room beyond it, and Alice impulsively followed. She remembered now: this was the magic chamber that she and James had entered which could move all over the castle. It would help her find James.

The Japanese girls pressed the button for the lobby. Like the rest of their party, students from a strict private school in Osaka, they were traveling in school uniform. Because of the quality of their clothing, Alice saw their social status as higher than hers, and automatically bowed her head to them. The teenagers were amused and returned the bow, giggling. Not what Alice expected, so she bowed deeper this time. The girls giggled again and bowed once more.

"We visit London first time. Is this you first time?" asked one of the girls. Alice found her voice pleasing, even if the pronunciation of words was strange. They must be from across the sea. Perhaps they had seen her James. She would confide in them.

Brandt had searched everywhere except the laundry chute alcove, which he entered gun drawn. As he did so there was a low noise, like a thump. He looked at the chute. Big enough for a man to hide in. His finger closed round the trigger. He reached slowly forward, placed his hand on the handle, and quickly opened the hatch. Just two bags of laundry, the top one perhaps the source of the noise he heard. As he was about to look up, a bag of bedding dropped to the bottom of the chute. Satisfied, Brandt shut the hatch and moved away to search elsewhere.

It was Paul who had dropped the bag. He had kept it with him for that purpose. He had wedged himself horizontally between the walls of the chute above the hatch, and was working his way up. Another four feet and he would reach the hatch to the next floor.

Nelson had finally made progress. It was against hotel policy to divulge guest's information without a warrant, but the repeated use of the words "national security" proved effective. The concierge gave him the room number assigned to the man in the photograph, just as Jones and two other security agents arrived. Nelson dispatched them upstairs immediately. Then he dialed Brandt for an update. No sign yet.

Nelson turned to a sullen Dr. Picton. "Go to the far end of the lobby. Check out the function rooms. Call me if you see either of them. I will check the coffee shop and return."

"I am not one of your staff. I am here for medical matters only," said Picton stiffly.

"You are here for whatever I say," was the curt response.

"You've no right to blame me for this."

"Just do what I tell you immediately I tell you to do it, and everything will be fine." Nelson gave Picton a hard look then strode away to check out the coffee shop.

Jones and the two accompanying security agents hurried into a half-full elevator and hit the button for the sixth floor. The doors closed and they ascended just as the adjacent elevator arrived, from which the Japanese teenagers emerged, followed by Alice. The girls skipped off towards the exit, giggling and waving goodbye to her. Although they knew something was lost in translation, the English girl's story sounded so romantic to the Osaka teens. They were big fans of Most Extreme Elimination Challenge back home. Maybe her boyfriend would win the British version of the show.

Alice looked across the vast greeting hall of the palace, hoping to catch sight of Paul. She stiffened. The man with the face of Sir Giles De Fries, whom people here called Dr. Picton, stood there. He was clothed in grey cloth, expensively woven.

Alice snorted her disgust. Her persecutor was walking with his back to her toward some rooms with double doors. It did not take Alice long to decide to settle the score once and for all. She followed him at a discreet distance. Now she knew for sure that James was in danger. Perhaps she could help. She would ambush one of their enemies and strike him down.

Dr. Picton passed a kitchen staffer, wheeling a cart full of cutlery for the daily roast towards another function room. Then the staffer got a call. The man stopped, the customized ring tone indicating that it was his girlfriend rather than his wife. He turned away from approaching hotel guests to take the call. Alice saw the opportunity, reached over and acquired a long serrated carving knife.

Picton stood in the doorway of a large darkened banquet room. The door had been left ajar. Perhaps she was in here. He flicked the light switches. Only the globes at the far end of the room went on, casting some light on a couple of dozen tables. She could be under any one of those tablecloths if she's in here at all, he thought, and he certainly didn't intend to check them one by one. Instead he called out: "Alice! This is Doctor Picton," trying for honey, while achieving peevishness. "We only wish to help you, Alice! Come out." His words obscured the sound of Alice's shoes on the carpeting as she slipped into the room behind him, knife at the ready.

"If you're there, come out," Picton continued, his eyes sweeping the shadowy tables ahead. "It is for your own good. Trust me, I know what is best for you. We will take care of you."

Alice was now close enough to ram the knife into him. But she found herself hesitating. Somehow she could not stab even a man she hated in the back. At the critical point, the rage that had driven her was checked by conscience. Yet she was the daughter of a headsman, the very instrument of community vengeance. What was the matter with her? Perhaps an instant later she would have taken her chances on the Day of Judgement, and thrust the blade into his black liver. So consumed was she by indecision that she did not hear Brandt run in behind her.

Picton reacted to the sound. He whirled round to see Brandt grabbing Alice, clamping his hand around her wrist, forcing her to drop the knife. Alice realized that God had intervened to save her from mortal sin, and was grateful, even though she had been recaptured by these hateful men.

Picton was furious. She was going to kill him! How dare she! "You mad little cunt!" He balled his fist. He wanted to punch her in the face, but a forbidding look from Brandt restrained him.

" 'Vengeance is mine, saith the Lord. I will repay,' " Alice quoted contritely, ignoring the pejorative.

"Quite right, Alice," said Nelson approaching.

Alice reacted to the sound of the Inquisitor's voice with resignation. The end was at hand. Nelson continued to speak to Alice, while putting on a surgical glove.

"But as you know, the Lord works in mysterious ways, His wonders to perform."

Nelson bent down to pick up the fallen knife.

Picton thought: Oh My God! Surely he is not going to kill her in broad daylight, in a West End hotel right here in front of me? These people are out of control. He was about to protest when Nelson grasped the knife and in one fluid motion rammed it into Picton's solar plexus. The doctor bent double, sucking in air with an agonized wheeze. Amid the pain of his dying moments, he heard a voice of belated self-reproach. He was already a prosperous doctor before he had succumbed to Nelson's blandishments. His life, so full of achievement, with greater wealth and honor ahead, was now to be cut short and end in ignominy through his own folly. Nelson twisted the blade, thrusting it upwards, puncturing the aorta, then pulled the knife out. Blood streaked the gleaming chrome and dripped from the tip. Picton pitched over dead. Alice squirmed in Brandt's grip, expecting the next thrust. But Nelson laid the carving knife on the carpet, careful not to smear the girl's fingerprints on the hilt.

"You can let her go now, Angus." Brandt released Alice.

She saw no point in trying to run. She had just seen the Inquisitor Córdoba murder his ally, Sir Giles De Fries. "You... are a man of God," she stammered, " 'Thou shalt not kill.' "

Previously, Dr. Picton had filled Nelson in on Alice's delusions. For Nelson, another piece of the puzzle fell into place. *Oh; so she thinks I'm a priest. Perfect. I can use that.* "Justice, Alice. I am empowered to kill evil men, just as your father was." Nelson locked eyes with her. The girl was apparently tormented by confusion. *Excellent.* He was pleased that she was in her Alice persona; it would make it easier to get her out of the hotel under his control, if he managed it skillfully. He would offer her what her heart most desired: reunion with her lover. Then he would require a series of simple tasks from her that she believed would achieve this goal. "I am the righter of wrongs," said Nelson.

Alice now understood that the only way that she might save James would be to give herself up to their enemies who had hounded them from one world to another. She took a deep breath and straightened her posture: "You condemned me as a witch; why should I trust you?"

"I am a different man now, a better man."

Brandt's thoughts were elsewhere, as they generally were when he was dealing with the dead. He hid the body from view with a tablecloth draped to floor level. He fantasized momentarily about the body being discovered later that day in the middle of a wedding banquet, and mass panic breaking out. The bride screaming, waiters dropping trays of dishes, everyone dashing for the doors. Some taking their wedding gifts back. He chuckled ruefully. *You think of the craziest things in this job.*

Nelson gestured the way out. "My Lady...?" Alice nodded her compliance.

Brandt watched, in awe of Nelson. *He could sure pull the chestnuts out of the fire.*

Alice knew that she was caught in a trap. But she seen many a river eel lie quiet then slip from the net as the catch was hauled aboard. The James of old was dead. Nothing could change that.

She would face whatever came to save the James of this world, even if it meant sacrificing her own. She would play the village gull he took her for. She would bide her time.

24

CHAPTER 38

Revolving Doors

IN THE MEZZANINE laundry room, Paul struggled to make his way, inch by inch, up the chute to the next hatch. He was almost there. The hatch opened. Three laundry sacks, one large, two small, were pushed out onto the floor. His hand grabbed the rim. Then Paul hauled himself out, panting from his exertions. He looked around cautiously and moved off into the mezzanine.

Paul concealed himself beside a pillar and looked out over the railing. To his shock and dismay he saw Alice crossing the lobby escorted by two of their pursuers. Alice was walking between them, keeping up with their brisk pace. She showed no signs of being under duress. What had happened? Had they somehow turned her? Was it Alice or Jane? He raced to the stairs.

Nelson and Brandt were heading through the crowd to the entrance. There was still time to connect the package with the target as per the original plan, but they needed to launch soon. Jones was waiting near the lobby doors. He and Nelson exchanged a look. Jones nodded. He was to continue watching the hotel for a while in case the American was still hiding there. Jones hoped that he would be the one to trigger the capture, redeeming himself in Nelson's eyes for letting the American outmaneuver him. Jones remained scanning the lobby as Nelson guided Alice into the revolving doors to the street.

In spite of herself, Alice reacted to the doors with glee. She turned to face the glass door that had bumped her from behind. It's like skipping around the Maypole, she thought. She did not step out when the doors opened to the street. Nelson reached for her too late to stop her continuing for another whirl around. A giggle of childlike joy broke through her anxiety.

Nelson and Brandt extracted Alice from the revolving door, and ushered her into a waiting Lexus. Was she Jane now? Paul asked himself. Not likely, judging by her second circuit around the revolving door. He had slipped out of the hotel's side exit and was watching discreetly from the corner. Or could she be a new personality he hadn't encountered yet? Paul watched the car drive off. He'd lost her. Paul refused to believe that Alice would betray him. But Jane? He could not be certain. Maybe they had persuaded her that he was rogue and not they. It was possible. But if he was to save her, he could not think about that now. He had to figure out a way to penetrate the conspiracy and strike at its core. Why this girl? How were they planning to use her? Something deadly was going down, and soon.

***

Minutes later, a taxi pulled up outside the U.S. Embassy in Grosvenor Square. Paul got out and paid the driver. While the gate guards processed a prior arrival, he waited in line, using the instant calm breath method to fight back the tension he felt showing in his face. He needed to appear composed and rational if his improbable tale was to be believed. When summoned, Paul walked forward, gave his name, and announced that he was carrying a weapon in a back clip. Within seconds two sub-machine guns and a pistol were pointed at his head.

Paul was led to the CIA interrogation room deep under the embassy, off limits to staff. He sat alone at a table. Agents took his gun and phone, locked him in. A camera was built into the table to record interrogations, but nobody had come to commence the process. Perhaps the notion he could just walk into the embassy and summon the cavalry had been naive. Paul spoke right into the lens.

"Hey! Anybody out there? Terrorist alert! Something is going down. Something bad, if you don't act quick! Jesus, guys! This is important."

Silence.

An interval passed. Then a slightly aggrieved voice came from the speaker beside the video camera in the interrogation room: "Why are you here?"

Paul was at last getting a hearing. He quickly debriefed.

Then the voice interrupted: "Our files show no record of authorization for you or any other agent to engage in a covert operation in England, which I would remind you is one of our staunchest allies."

"That's nonsense," replied Paul, "Call Rick Almaraz' office right now. The number in case you don't..."

The voice cut him off before he could continue. "Section Chief Almaraz died in a car accident yesterday. Who else can corroborate your story?"

Paul had feared that his mentor was dead but confirmation hit him like a hammer. Grief momentarily overwhelmed him. Paul struggled to regain composure. His worst fears were realized.

Two men in the next room watched Paul on a video feed. Paul was being covertly subjected to voice stress and micro-expression analysis. The interrogator was Josh Levinson, a former agent turned independent security contractor, carrying out work the Agency wished done at arm's length. Farrell had been his handler for three years and Levinson had always delivered. So when he found out there was a Ratcatcher meddling with their plans, Farrell brought in the toughest men he knew to plug the leak.

Levinson put his finger onto the screen highlighting an involuntary twitch in Paul's cheek. Stress. Farrell nodded.

So this was the man who had caused so much trouble. Smart enough to run rings round some top British operatives, but dumb enough to walk into the lion's den and offer up his head. Well, that would take about five minutes to arrange. He wouldn't wait. He would clean up this loose end himself. Farrell switched off the microphone, and turned to Levinson.

"Go quiet for a couple of minutes. Is your team ready?"

Levinson nodded.

"Then come into the room," Farrell continued, "offer sincere apologies, say you've had a call from Langley, they have confirmed his story, the rogue agents involved have been intercepted, you have a car waiting to take him to where they are being held for identification. He'll ask you about the girl. Keep saying you have no information. Make sure he's never found. Same as the others. Are your guys up for that?"

Levinson nodded again. "An extra 50K each, sure." That was only reasonable for the third termination, dismemberment and incineration he had organized for Farrell this week.

"25," said Farrell firmly, "Don't be greedy." The sudden steely undertone made Levinson reflect a moment. He always tried to negotiate the best deals he could for his team, but Farrell was a good customer, he wasn't going to jeopardize the relationship.

"25 it is."

Farrell didn't care about the money. His financiers had trillions at their disposal. It was the principle of the thing. The costs of privatized covert ops had been skyrocketing in recent years. People always had their hand out, asking for more, when really they should count themselves lucky to be working.

CHAPTER 39

At the Dorchester

IN HER SUITE at the Dorchester Hotel, Pamela van Doren stood in front of a mirror, holding a handwritten list of bullet points, rehearsing answers for the Q&A that would follow her talk at the conference in New Delhi. Spontaneity takes practice. She would be announcing the opening of a seed bank that she had funded for propagating and distributing indigenous, non-GMO seed stocks at radically subsidized prices to urban farmers on the Indian subcontinent, a program set later to be expanded to included subsistence farms and, ultimately, large commercial operations.

Pamela always wanted to hear the weight of her words as they sounded out loud, rather than inside her head. She tried changes of phrasing and cadence. More gravitas here. A lighter touch there. Her summation had to be fluid and well-reasoned, constructed through a series of interlocking sound bites. Every answer had to be quotable, yet fireproofed against media distortions.

Pamela put the finishing touches to her makeup, arranged her distinctive red-gold hair in a casual up do, grabbed her hat, jacket and shoulder bag and stepped out of her suite to join Emily and Paige for a champagne brunch. Then off to the Tower. What fun!

CHAPTER 40

The Millstone of Justice

NELSON DROVE, ALICE beside him, Brandt in the back. Alice's stomach was in knots. Wicked knots. Brandt sensed her unease. "Dinna fret yourself, lass," he said, using his soft Scottish brogue. "You'll join him soon enough." He caught Nelson's sardonic smile in the rearview mirror. Gallows humor helped him deal with the "processing" aspect of their work, which was troubling Brandt more than usual this time.

Alice nodded. She was trying to puzzle out what was happening, and how she should act. Now that she was becoming accustomed to the miracles of this world, her mind was freed to think more deeply about her situation. What most perplexed her was that although people from her old life had reappeared here, they seemed to be unaware of it. The Inquisitor Córdoba called himself Nelson; his henchman Cedric, Angus. And the rest. She was not convinced that Nelson remembered his other life at all; he was merely trying to dupe her. Even her James insisted that he was a man named Paul. Why could she alone see who these people truly were?

It became hard to think. The noise from outside their carriage became oppressive, unlike anything she had ever heard. She heard the sound of a dozen grinding mills, punctuated by a sharp high-pitched unearthly keening. Giant moving iron trees were lifting loads to the top of a castle that people were building in a street full of castles. Alice felt assaulted by unnatural sounds, sights and smells.

Nelson's car pulled up outside the abandoned building next to a large construction site in the London Docklands, Nelson's secret HQ. He turned to look back at Brandt, who nodded.

"Won't be long," Brandt said as he got out of the car.

Nelson remained with Alice. He watched Brandt unlock the padlocked gate and disappear into the building. At the same time he checked Pamela van Doren's Twitter feed on his tablet. Her assistant Emily had tweeted "Champagne brunch at the Dorchester, then off on our way to 12 acres of History!" with various hashtags and a Smiley Face emoticon.

Alice watched as swirling images and text changed at the flick of Nelson's finger. Her attitude to sorcery was beginning to change. She was no longer afraid of these objects with strange powers. Perhaps they were akin to the Talisman of legend. She wanted one for herself.

Brandt had gone inside to put the final touches to the terrorist's lair to be discovered during the forthcoming investigation. Wearing gloves, he scattered radical literature among the laptops. Evidence of terrorist barbarism would be found on their hard drives. It amused him to place some hummus and falafel in the mini fridge. Stereotypes work. Then Brandt moved to the next room to prepare Mr. Broken Teeth for his part.

Brandt opened the padlock and slid back the razor wire fence that secured Broken Teeth's makeshift cell. Over his arm, he carried an overcoat, a smart gabardine. Broken Teeth lay on a cot, reading a girlie magazine, a mug of tea and a half-eaten hamburger on the floor beside him. Brandt placed the gabardine carefully on a table.

"What d'you want?" growled Broken Teeth without looking up.

"Got to see if this fits."

"Why?"

"For your TV appearance."

"When's that? 'cos I'm fed up with being cooped up in this shithole. I mean, are you buggers for real?"

"Just a few more hours and you will be on your way. So let's put the coat on, see that it fits."

Broken Teeth looked up and peered at the elegantly stitched gabardine. "I'm not wearing that poncey thing..." growled Broken Teeth, testing what power he might have in this new relationship.

"Would you like to smoke some hashish?" asked Brandt, as if he were offering tea and biscuits. He pulled a neatly-rolled joint from his breast pocket, and placed it on the table.

"Now you're talking." said Broken Teeth. He dropped the magazine and stood up. Brandt picked up the gabardine and carefully helped slide the man's arms through the sleeves. It was a good fit if it remained unbuttoned. Broken Teeth did not care. His eyes remained fixed on the joint. Hash was a rare commodity in the homeless squats that he inhabited.

Satisfied, Brandt handed him the joint, pulled out a cigarette lighter, and lit it for him, before stepping to one side away from the smoke. Broken Teeth sucked in a deep lungful, holding it in for as long as possible. As he exhaled, the room seemed to swim from side to side in front of him.

"This is some good shit," he said, starting to cough.

Yes, it was good shit, but in addition to hashish it contained a chemical compound that would render the smoker unconscious in a matter of seconds. As Broken Teeth began to stagger, Brandt deftly caught him and laid him back down on the cot. Out like a light. He checked his breathing, then made sure he lay stretched out comfortably, a pillow under his head. He covered him with a blanket, and tucked it round his chin, covering up the gabardine completely, then left the cell, padlocking it behind him.

Nelson chose his time alone with the girl to play his next card. He had predicted Alice's fascination with his tablet, and he placed it on her lap. Then he tentatively took her finger and guided it scrolling through a blizzard of images. Alice resented his uninvited touch but said nothing. What great skill these portrait painters possess, Alice mused, portraits that look so true to life you could imagine them talking. Then one did. Nelson had steered Alice's finger to a slideshow of photographs from the Pamela van Doren website. He touched an icon, a frame unfroze and Pamela van Doren began to speak. It was a recording of her addressing a rally in Peru on water rights. Nelson muted the sound.

Alice gasped at the sight of the strikingly beautiful woman with red-gold hair. Could it perchance be she?

"Do you see this young woman? Pamela van Doren. She has the power to help you. You will meet her within the hour."

"Meet her?" Alice stammered. What did this evil man intend by granting her an audience with the Princess Elizabeth? He gave her another name. Did he not understand who she truly was? Alice decided to keep these thoughts to herself. She would continue to dissemble. "How can I thank you, sir?" Alice asked meekly.

"You can thank me by giving me your trust. To join her, we must enter the White Tower by a secret passage."

The White Tower. To which she and James had been taken and where they were condemned. Where James had been killed. Where she had murdered. It frightened Alice to contemplate going back there. Yet she sensed that the millstone of justice was turning. To save her James this time, she would let it crush her.

CHAPTER 41

Tempus fugit

JANE PACED ABOUT her small cell, as far as her chains would permit. She gazed at the narrow barred window above her, which cast a blur of dawn light on the opposite wall. "God… Are you there?" Jane whispered to herself, in her small cell, gazing at a narrow barred window above her. "I'm going to be burnt to a crisp in a little while. Something I could live without. So if you are up there, well… *Tempus fugit*, you know… It's time for me to go back… Really is..." Jane stifled a sob. "Paul, where are you? I need you, Paul…"

These were her thoughts, as she contemplated the hour ahead with that special acuity of the unjustly condemned. Death Row, the final frontier. Jane tasted all the rage and helplessness of the soon to be terminated. Why? Why me? The hopes, the dreams not realized. A sense of futility, punctuated by leaps of false hope, and prayers for a miracle. Would there be a miracle in her case?

Jane shuddered, anticipating the flames. Then she forced herself to calm down and reflect on her life while she still had one. Hadn't she been wasting it so far? What did her life matter, if she spent it alone? Sure, she loved her studies, found meaning in activism, had more than she needed. Well and good.

But what had she gained from her fiercely-guarded independence? Figuratively, she'd been living in a cell, like this one. Self-condemned to isolation. A life sentence. Jane made a pact with the God in Whom she scarcely believed: If I live, she vowed, I'll find people who'll accept me. Accept them. Make it up with my aunt and uncle. Find a best friend. Experience romance. Maybe true love? Help people, individual people, not just humanity. As things stood, who would know or much care when she failed to show up in her own world?

Jane wondered why she had collided with the paranormal. It had turned all her notions upside down. She had entered another dimension of existence. It fired her imagination. She couldn't think of a better job for an historian than being Jane Fixit Ph.D., zapping from era to era, tightening a nut here, loosening a bolt there, keeping the machine on track. She knew she was being fanciful, but it was part of a new zest for life she felt. She wanted to go on living more at this moment than ever before. Why would the Supreme Webmaster open this portal, show her what was possible, only to reduce her to ashes within the hour?

For some unfathomable reason, it seemed, she was required to share Alice's fate. From her research, Jane knew that those condemned to burning were sometimes euthanized before the flames reached them. By garrote, a bag of gunpowder hung around the neck, and other means. None pleasant. Jane contemplated the intense pain that she knew was ahead for her. She hoped she could bear it with dignity. Then she heard the distant clink of chainmail in the corridor. They were coming.

CHAPTER 42

Riding in a Car with Boys

THE U.S. EMBASSY had given Paul back his phone but not his weapon, citing strict British gun laws. Paul was in an elevator being escorted to the basement parking lot by a man who had introduced himself as Special Agent Josh Levinson. He had entered the interrogation room to apologize for the misunderstanding, and had delivered the good news that the plot had been foiled. Paul had gone along with the apology and the explanation he'd been fed, but didn't buy any of it. It was too pat, the agent often broke eye contact, and he seemed anxious to get Paul transported to the site of the alleged arrest. Paul played along, while considering his next move.

The elevator doors to Parking Level 3 opened. At the curb ahead Paul saw an SUV with three men in suits standing beside it. They were between thirty and forty-five, and each one was built like a linebacker, like Levinson himself, who led Paul toward the group.

"This is Special Agent Paul Montgomery," Levinson called out, then turned back to Paul. "Meet my team. Paul, here's Dennis Adamo and J.R. Simmonds, and that's Tommy Sigura." Pleased to meet you was exchanged all round. Levinson gestured Paul to the back passenger door. Adamo got in before Paul.

"I had to give up my weapon, so I'd appreciate a loaner, if anyone has a spare," said Paul as he settled into his seat. Sigura sat to his right, leaving Paul wedged between two hefty men.

"Gotta get you a permit first," replied Levinson, getting behind the wheel.

"You know how funny they are about that sort of thing over here," muttered Agent Sigura.

"Won't need one today," continued Agent Levinson. "Bad guys are in the bag now, thanks to you."

"Yeah, congrats, man. Awesome work," chimed in Agent Adamo, echoed immediately by the other agents.

"Thanks. Where are they being held?" asked Paul, as he secured his seat belt, wishing he had not entered the vehicle.

"Not far. Be there in about ten minutes." Levinson hoped that was vague enough. They just needed to get him to a spot they had used before, a lane between two buildings where there were no CCTV cameras. There was a body bag ready in the trunk where the subject could be stored prior to disposal. It shouldn't take long.

"How about those Clippers? Been watching? You a Clippers fan?"

"Man, they are so strong this season," replied Paul without missing a beat. Why weren't they pumping him for information about this bizarre plot he had uncovered, Paul wondered with mounting disquiet. Sports conversation continued as the van drove off. Agent Simmonds pulled out his phone and texted something. Paul shifted suddenly in his seat to check the reaction. Agent Adamo beside him reflexively slipped his hand inside his jacket towards his shoulder holster. Paul pretended not to notice. But it confirmed that he was on his way to execution.

CHAPTER 43

"Thanks, Winnie!"

AS NELSON'S CAR approached Tower Hill, the massive stonework of the Tower complex came into view. Alice flinched in her seat. It chilled her to see harsh noon light on its stark unforgettable central edifice, the White Tower. The car turned a corner and the castle disappeared from view. Nelson pulled into the underground car park of an office building. Alice saw the Inquisitor who called himself Nelson point another Talisman and the gate barring entry opened by itself. This world of marvels, Alice wondered, was it of God or the Devil?

Few people were working that Saturday afternoon, so the lowest level of the car park was empty. Nelson parked beside the door to a storage room. Brandt pulled a duffel bag out of the trunk. Once again, Alice saw the door open at Nelson's gesture. Both Nelson and Brandt produced flashlights, illuminating stacks of boxes. Dust. Cobwebs. Abandoned. Dimly visible, there was a hole in the far wall big enough to slip through. Alice seemed to take some convincing to step inside this dark place with them, but Nelson's powers of persuasion prevailed. Or so he thought.

Only a handful of people knew of the existence of the chamber they subsequently entered. Even fewer knew how to access it. Located under the north corner of the White Tower, it was Winston Churchill's secret war room, long closed, still classified.

The official War Cabinet rooms had been constructed under the Treasury Building in Whitehall before the outbreak of World War II. When Churchill became Prime Minister in 1940, he commissioned a second secret emergency cabinet command center, for use should an invading force reach London. Churchill's sense of the dramatic drew him to the White Tower, a symbol of British power for nearly a millennium. Churchill knew of subterranean chambers thirty feet below that had been constructed during the reign of Charles I. This was the bolt hole he wanted. He ordered the chambers expanded and strengthened. A narrow spiral staircase was installed, along with an oak door that opened to the ground floor. A sliding steel door was installed behind it, sealing off access from above. Here in this historic venue he would direct the defense of London and fight to the end if need be. Churchill and his military leaders could enter through a secret tunnel constructed from Tower Hill Tube Station, half a mile away.

As it happened, Churchill only visited the chamber twice as the threat of invasion receded. Early in the Cold War it had been briefly considered as a government command center in the event of a nuclear exchange but was ruled too small and shallow and was abandoned. Under Prime Minister Thatcher, all Churchill wartime memorabilia was relocated to a special section of the Imperial War Museum for public display, and the tunnel to the forgotten bunker was bricked up. The plans to Churchill's private lair were in the classified section of MI5's data bank. Nelson had discovered that the original tunnel passed right beside what was now a corner storeroom located at the basement level of an underground car park not far from the Tower. There were barely three feet of earth and construction rubble between the wall of the storeroom and the wall of the tunnel. It had been an easy matter for Nelson and Brandt to breach both walls, create access to the tunnel and set up the abandoned war room as the forward staging area his plan required. They passed through the tunnel into the chamber.

Having quickly set up the staging area, Nelson watched security camera coverage of the Tower ticket office on a widescreen laptop. At precisely 1:00 p.m., a limousine pulled up outside it. Pamela van Doren and her assistants Emily and Paige stepped out. One of them paid the driver, while the other texted their assigned personal tour guide. A well-dressed young man exited the ticket office to greet them. After shaking hands, he showed them the day's itinerary on a tablet. Nelson noted that Ms. van Doren was wearing a chartreuse bomber jacket and a stylish cap, covering her signature mop of fiery hair.

Nelson had hacked into the Tower mainframe and had key surveillance cameras inside and out available on his screen. He clicked on another icon and the guide's itinerary came up. First destination: Tower Grounds with the Ravenmaster. Second: Jewel Room. Third: Hall of Kings. Nelson watched as the tour guide led the party towards the main gate. He estimated that it would take just under an hour for them to progress to where he wanted them.

The text from Simmonds came in. Nelson was much relieved as he deleted it from his phone. The last serious loose end—the American—would be disposed of like the others. Nelson scrolled through security cameras on his laptop. Everything was tight. Time to take a quick break. He stepped out of the curtained alcove where he had been working into the large stone chamber of the War Room, where arched pillars supported a low ceiling. It was lit by battery powered lanterns they had placed at each corner.

"They have him," Nelson whispered to Brandt.

"Glad to hear it." Brandt's police work had taught him that the people who get caught are people who leave witnesses.

"Call Jones. Tell him he can stop looking. He's to go back to base and text me from there."

Brandt put his Bluetooth back in his ear. Nelson turned his attention to Alice, who was crouched over a tattered map of

1940 Europe that lay in a corner. Through the dust she made out the word London. Was this what England looked like from the heavens? It was so small, and the island beside it so big it could not be contained within the parchment.

"She OK?"

"Like a kid with a new toy."

Brandt had given Alice a pocket flashlight as a distraction and she had been exploring her new environment with awe. It was a jumble of furniture deemed too awkward to move when the bunker was abandoned. She stood up and played the torch beam across the wall. To have a shaft of light at your fingertips was better than holding a torch of rushes that oft sent a spark into your face. It illuminated an affectionate cartoon of Winston Churchill, drawn in boot polish by one of the workmen before they sealed off the access tunnel in 1985. "Thanks, Winnie!" was inscribed below in surprisingly neat copperplate. Britain's wartime leader was depicted with a cigar in one hand and a scotch in the other. Alice had never seen a cartoon. As a country girl her access to visual depictions of people was liturgical. Saints in stained glass. Revered. Serene. Yet these lines on the wall so captured the spirit of a man full of pride and determination. The tunnel had frightened her at first but Brandt had tried to buoy her confidence by telling her stories of the legendary English hero who had built this secret passage and had won a great war. She looked at Brandt across the room. The big man had just placed a blue and silver jewel the size of a peach stone in one of his ears, then walked away talking to himself. Such odd customs.

CHAPTER 44

Time for a Different Sort of Life

NELSON STUDIED ALICE, looking for signs she might revert to the girl he had kidnapped. None so far, but it hardly mattered now. He had her in his grasp at target point. He could make it work, even if she did change back into Jane. He had a cover story ready that would persuade Jane to ascend the staircase from the chamber, and enter the Hall of Kings in the Tower. Or he'd just break her neck. Whatever. He would detonate by cellphone when the security cameras showed the target was within the blast radius. His phone pinged. A text from his junior agent. He walked away.

Jones was parked across the street from their temporary base, the soon-to-be-demolished derelict building adjacent to a large construction site. Jones clicked off his call from Nelson. "Yes!" he exulted. Nelson had given him a critical task to carry out, namely kill the vagrant they had taken as plan B, then call the disposal subcontractor. A text followed with a direct link to the number to call. When Nelson had recruited Jones, he had pointed out that a time would come when he would be required to go, as he put it, "hardcore". Carrying out this order would earn Jones a substantial rise in pay grade. Not a problem, Jones had responded instinctively. Now the acid test had come.

Like other would-be murderers, Jones rationalized the crime as the only moral lapse of biblical proportions he would ever have to commit to secure his future. After this, he would content himself with a life of minor moral elasticity. In fact, he would have the money to do good. To compensate for his sin, he would fund charities. He would become a philanthropist with lots of girlfriends. The reverie of his future was interrupted by a passing forklift.

Once inside the building, Jones descended to the basement and found the cell with the razor wire gate, dimly lit by a fluorescent tube in the far corner. Jones peered inside. The unconscious man was lying on a cot, as Nelson had said. Jones unlocked the razor wire gate, slid it closed behind him, and pulled out his Glock. He was not taking any chances. Putting his cellphone down on the table, he approached the figure on the cot. Jones tentatively lifted the blanket. Mr. Broken Teeth looked like a city businessman in a smart suit and an elegant if slightly flamboyant gabardine overcoat. He was quite unrecognizable as the man they had acquired the day before. Jones prodded him in the leg. No reaction. All set then.

They say the first one's the hardest, Jones reflected, yet at this point, it didn't feel hard at all. The real question was whether to shoot him in the head or the heart. Better the heart, less mess for the cleanup crew. Suddenly Broken Teeth bolted upright and grabbed Jones' gun hand, twisting it violently. Before Jones knew it, the weapon was pulled from his grasp and pointed straight at him. Whatever the drug was that they had given him, it was no match for a constitution forged in the worst meth pits and crack squats in town, Broken Teeth would later boast. Not that anyone ever believed his tall tale.

"Are you here to kill me?" Broken Teeth hissed.

"No, no. I was just checking on you…" stammered Jones, backing away.

"Liar," said Broken Teeth, shooting him in the stomach.

The bullet severed nerves at the base of Jones' spine, and he fell to the ground paralyzed from the waist. Broken Teeth could not wait to shed the gabardine. "Why'd you people want me to wear this pouffy thing? Stupid." He tossed the coat onto Jones. "Here, you have it, I'll keep this," he said slipping the Glock into his jacket pocket. "And this," he added, grabbing Jones' cellphone. "Thanks, it's been a blast." He strode out of the room without looking back.

Jones struggled not to hyperventilate. There was no sensation in his legs. The pain in his stomach was bearable if he did not move. He pushed the gabardine off his face, and as he did he became conscious of square objects sewn into the lining. He reached for a zippered pocket and frantically worked it open.

Broken Teeth paused at the exit to the building. He reconsidered keeping the Glock. Maybe it was time for a different sort of life. He took it out and tossed it aside.

Jones gaped at what he had pulled out of the coat pocket, a cellphone taped to a detonator. A lightning bolt of realization shot through him. Shit, oh shit! He was never going to be rich. He'd never have all those girlfriends. He was expendable. With his peculiar sense of cruelty, Nelson had ordered Jones personally to make the suicidal call that would trigger the detonator, thinking that he was calling the cleanup crew.

Walking away from the building, Broken Teeth examined the sleek high end phone he had taken from the table. He saw a text alert on the screen. It read "Call 07700900999." Why not, he thought, hitting the call icon.

The second ring triggered the explosives. Jones was blasted back through the razor wire gate like brie though a cheese grater. The sound of the explosion and the dust and smoke that issued from the basement vents went unnoticed in the smoke and noise of the adjacent construction site. The remnants of Jones' body would be discovered in the terrorist cell's HQ. The plan was that it would be revealed to investigators that Nelson's unit had been on their trail, closing in, but arriving just minutes too late to prevent the bombing of a famous British monument, despite the heroic death of a junior agent who had discovered the terrorists' lair and taken them on singlehandedly. Sacrificing

Jones would ensure that Nelson's unit received a pass at the enquiry.

Oblivious to the explosion, Broken Teeth dropped the phone in a gutter. Useless piece of crap. Don't need that, either. He walked away a free man, feeling more alive than he had in years. The phone rang a few moments later.

Nelson and Brandt listened as the phone went to voice mail. Brandt was somber faced. He had considered Jones a weaselly little shit, but his death was nonetheless regrettable.

"Had to be done," said Nelson. Brandt, nodding, remained silent.

CHAPTER 45

Descant of Agony

THE SUV SPED through the West End streets, heading east. Paul was telling baseball jokes, causing his fellow travelers some amusement. He had successfully assessed their cultural interests. Adamo and Sigura, both New Yorkers, exchanged a wry look. They couldn't figure why the kid had to die. He was funny. But they had a job to do. Best not to think about these things. Not if you wanted to move up the food chain. Paul continued to play the role of the agent who believed his mission was over and would be mentioned in dispatches for his part in its success. But when Levinson turned the vehicle off the main road down a side street between two office buildings, Paul realized that this was the moment. The agents would have expected a sudden move earlier, in the middle of traffic, and believed their charade was working. Paul understood that plausibility and timing were vital. His survival was predicated on commitment, unhesitating follow through and surprise.

In a lightning maneuver, Paul released his seat belt, dove forward, while twisting to face upwards not down. He had gauged the position of the handbrake and the distance between the two front seats. With one hand he grabbed the wheel of the SUV, swinging the vehicle across the lane toward a parked delivery van. With the other hand, he plucked the Sig Sauer P226 from the belt of Agent Simmonds in the front passenger seat. He had noted when he got into the SUV where each man carried his weapon; back clip, shoulder or belt. He had also noted that the driver, Levinson, had an ankle holster in addition to his back clip. He would have to watch for that.

Paul's ability to multitask had impressed his superiors during his CITP training. While he was playing the sucker, he had mapped the interior of the vehicle, calculating the spatial relationships between occupants, and potential trajectory of bullets. He scanned the instrument panel. Front and rear airbags were operational. They would be the equalizer he needed. Almost as soon as Paul got Simmonds' weapon clear of the holster, his thumb flicked the safety catch, and his finger found the trigger. He put a bullet into the man's inner thigh as he pulled the gun away. Simmonds gave a deep guttural gasp and fainted. Despite Levinson's struggle to dislodge his grip, Paul had his hand clamped on the wheel, immovable. The SUV slammed into the back of the parked delivery van, as Paul intended. The agents in the back seat had tried to grab Paul and pull him back, instead of immediately drawing weapons. Then the impact of the collision triggered the airbags, knocking the gun out of Adamo's hand and preventing Sigura from aiming. Paul had braced himself for impact, so lost no time. In quick succession he placed the muzzle of the Sig Sauer against Sigura's kneecap and fired. Paul could see Levinson beside him reaching down for his ankle holster, trying to push the airbag aside. Paul swung the gun onto Levinson's extended elbow and fired, shattering the humerus at the joint, then swiftly swung it back to put a bullet into Adamo's nearest knee, then another into Sigura's foot. Paul's next bullet deflated the driver's airbag, allowing him to smash Levinson in the face with his gun, stunning him. Paul then pulled himself up, reaching over the back seat airbags to club both flailing men in the head with his pistol butt till he could grab their weapons. The vehicle reverberated with shrieks of pain and vows of vengeance, in a weirdly musical descant of agony and rage.

"Where's it fucking happening?" Paul screamed at Levinson, when he had collected weapons and phones from each groaning man into a gym bag he took from the trunk. They were all still alive, though the one he had shot in the thigh might bleed out if help did not come soon. Paul saw many faces at office windows looking down on the lane. Police would not be far away.

"Tell me where," ordered Paul, "and I will speak for you at trial." Levinson remained silent. "It's over. You've lost. Help yourselves by helping me. Where is she?"

"Tower of London!" shouted Adamo from the back seat.

"Shut up!" yelled Levinson.

Adamo ignored him. "The White Tower. Better hurry. Show's on."

Paul shouted: "What show?"

Adamo said, "The girl's wired..." His words spluttered. Sigura had cut his throat.

Paul heard the sound of approaching sirens. He quickly locked the gym bag full of evidence in the trunk and pocketed the car keys. He knew he couldn't take a gun where he needed to go. Paul sprinted back up the lane to the street.

CHAPTER 46

A Conspiracy of Ravens

PAMELA VAN DOREN, Paige and Emily had lucked out. The weather for their day at the Tower was cool yet sunny. It was great to let go of the stress and just be tourists. The first item of the girls' itinerary was to meet with the Yeoman Warder Ravenmaster of the Tower, a sympathetic and humorous man whose relationship with the renowned birds was uncanny. The girls strolled with him through the greensward. The Ravenmaster repeated the legend that there had to be a conspiracy of ravens, a flock of at least six birds, in residence on the grounds or both the Tower and the British monarchy would fall. The girls had the rare privilege of feeding and stroking one of the tamer ravens. Glossy blue-black feathers, piercing gaze. Such intelligent creatures! They thanked the Ravenmaster, and their tour guide led them toward the Jewel House.

There, the strains of Handel's Coronation Anthems set a regal tone for viewing the Crown Jewels. Hearing that all day must drive the attendants insane, Pamela thought. She gazed at the opulent display before her. Of all the treasures in the Jewel House, the Cullinan Diamonds particularly fascinated her. Cullinan I, the Great Star of Africa atop the Sovereign's Sceptre, and Cullinan II set in the Imperial State Crown. It wasn't the brilliance of the jewels that most impressed Pamela, but their history. The original Cullinan Diamond, before it was cut into nine large pieces, was easily twice the size of any previous diamond at the time of its discovery just after turn of the twentieth century. The miner who dug it out, Thomas Evan Powell, handed it over to his boss, Frederick Wells. Wells received £3,500 for it; as far as Pamela could work out, Powell got zip. Its current value was estimated at 400 million dollars.

"Inflation," Pamela observed wryly to herself.

She thought about miners in Africa dying before their time earning pennies for perilous work so that the elites of the world could indulge their appetite for conspicuous consumption in the unending competition for status. Pamela was well aware of the ironies of her position; self-consciously, she fingered the large white solitaire scintillating on her own right ear. Of course she would modify how she expressed that publicly, or she would be tagged a Marxist, and her ideas would be buried under a ton of media snark. Pamela wasn't a Marxist. She was all in favor of capitalism. It just needed to be practiced with a moral compass, capitalism with a conscience.

CHAPTER 47

The Plum-Colored Coat

BRANDT HANDED ALICE a mug of strong milky tea which he had poured from a thermos. It was the only sustenance they had available. All trace of their presence here would go back into the duffel bag they brought with them to be removed when the job was done.

"Thank you, sir," said Alice with a quick bob of her head. She sipped at the unfamiliar warm liquid. Tea. It tasted robust and sweet. Only the rich could afford such a drink.

"Glad you like it," said Brandt with a smile, adding "my Lady." In her old life, Alice would have regarded that as mockery, but the big man seemed sincere.

Nelson was in the curtained alcove connecting a slender cell phone to a detonating device with wires extending from the lining of an elegant plum-colored velvet ladies' coat. The explosives were now armed. He carefully replaced the completed device into a pocket in the lining, zipped it up, then rendered the zipper inoperable with a penknife. Just in case she got curious.

Alice shivered and rubbed her arms. She was wearing only the gown of fine material in which she had left the hotel. So she was pleased when the Inquisitor, the man called Nelson, walked over carrying a coat made from rich fabric.

"You're cold, Alice. Put this on." Nelson gently took one of her hands, slipped it into a sleeve. "For this important occasion, we have made a special coat for you." He placed it over her shoulders. She was glad of its warmth.

"It is lovely, but weighty," said Alice.

"It's a handsome garment. You want to look well when you meet the Lady, don't you?"

Nelson guided Alice to the railing at the foot of the narrow staircase that led up to the steel door at the top. He felt like an executioner escorting the condemned onto the scaffold. What manner of men were official executioners, Nelson wondered, like the headsman the deluded girl claimed her father to be? Did they enjoy what they did? Nelson himself no longer received visceral pleasure from the act of killing as much as he did intellectual satisfaction, combined with the adrenaline rush that came from a vigorous game of racket ball.

Alice believed, as she followed this man, that she was a lamb led to slaughter. But facing the unknown beyond that door might be her only chance to save James. Nelson set about opening the heavy steel door resting on runners set in a groove. It had not been opened in decades, prior to his test run a week ago, when he and Brandt spent several hours oiling its moving parts so that it would operate smoothly and quietly when the wheel mounted on the door was rotated. After an initial strain requiring the better part of his strength, the wheel turned and the steel door slid aside. Then he slowly turned the ring mounted on the oak door. They had done similar work to oil away any creaking. The door gave way silently.

Alice felt a gust of warm air waft over her face. She heard the sounds of distant voices in the hall beyond, but all she could see ahead was a high wall made of parchment stretched across a metal frame and mounted on wheels with pictures and writing inscribed on its other side. Nelson led her out to stop behind this twenty-foot long mobile exhibit, a guide to the Hall of Kings, presented to visitors as a giant parchment. In a recent remodeling, two double-buttressed pillars were installed, to increase support for the floor above. In a gesture to authenticity, they had been assembled from rings of the same Kentish rag-stone from which the White Tower had been built nearly one thousand years before. The displays of life-sized wooden horses, figures of kings, and suit upon suit of royal armor had been reorganized into four aisles, spanning the chamber. This wall, facing the aisles, had suffered some discoloration due to water damage and so became a good position for this exhibit.

For Nelson's purposes, the exhibit concealed his access point, enabling him to bypass the explosive-detecting sensors that screened visitors at the entrance, and made the ideal forward vantage point for the final stage of the plan. Nelson would walk her to the corner from which there was a good view of the central aisle down which all visitors passed. There he would wait till Pamela van Doren and her entourage entered the aisle. Then he would send Alice out to meet her. Brandt was downstairs at the laptop watching the progress of the van Doren party on the security camera output.

"Moments away," texted Brandt.

As Nelson waited, he felt an inner glow soothe the tension that always accompanied the mission critical stage of an assignment. He was minutes away from earning a quarter of a billion dollars. When and only when news media listed Pamela van Doren among the dead would an escrow account in the Cayman Islands, programmed via a special algorithm, automatically wire the money to accounts Nelson had set up in Moscow, Shanghai, Dubai and Berne. He would tough out the enquiry as a hero of the war on terror, retire a year later, and live like a king.

"Soon," he said, smiling at Alice.

CHAPTER 48

In the Hall of Kings

JANE VOMITED ON the ground as she was dragged on a sledge towards Tower Hill past a jeering mob. When they had taken her from the cell, a guard, who alone among her escort had looked on her with pity, had placed a copper jug to her lips. She had taken some deep gulps of sweet wine mixed with brackish water. As they neared the hill, the sight of the stake at which she would be burned had unnerved her.

Was this always to have been the place of Alice's destiny? A small patch of ground where her life would be extinguished? The trunk of a freshly cut pine tree had been embedded in the ground. Logs and bundles of sticks were piled high at its base. A heap of fresh green straw was nearby. Sometimes executioners would put green straw on the bonfire so that the condemned would pass away from smoke asphyxiation before the flames reached them. If she had to die, Jane wanted to do it with dignity, but she feared that courage would fail her in such a barbarous death. There was a strange buzzing in her ears, an otherworldliness separate from the terror she was feeling.

***

Alice leaned against a wall of the Hall of Kings in the White Tower. A little lightheadedness had come upon her, and she heard a humming sound. Don't go wobbly on me now, thought Nelson standing at her side. Nelson had a plan for the eventuality of Alice losing her nerve. If necessary, he would snap her neck, place the body behind the center of the exhibit, and detonate when the van Doren party stopped in front of it.

"Target," read a text from Brandt. Nelson put his eye to a tiny peephole he had cut into the faux parchment.

And there she was, at the far end of the hall, Pamela van Doren, global environmental activist, flanked by her assistants and the Tower guide. Nelson noted she that had shed her cap and let down her conspicuous mane. A gaggle of fellow tourists had spotted her, and were following at a short but respectful distance, stopping wherever she stopped, observing her reaction to each exhibit. They would add a few more to the body count, Nelson thought, establishing the event as a terrorist attack on a symbol of imperialism rather than a targeted assassination.

"The Lady is here," Nelson said to Alice, as he steered her to the corner of the exhibit.

She peered round and was startled for an instant by the sight of a hall lined with pennants, beneath which stood knights in full armor, some on horseback. She heard no clanking of cuirass, or whinny of horses. Then she realized that the steeds were brightly painted wooden effigies, the helmets and breastplates empty of their knights.

"Look. At the far end of the hall. Pamela van Doren. Do you see her?"

Alice's heart leapt at the sight of the Princess' red-golden hair. "Yes, may I go to her now?"

Perfect, thought Nelson. "Approach respectfully and make yourself known to her." He gestured Alice to go.

Alice stepped forward to an uncertain future without a backward glance.

Nelson stepped through the oak door at the top of the staircase to join Brandt in the War Room, but found him rushing up the stairs. "The American's alive! Here."

"What? Fucking idiots! How could they…?" No time for that. Professionalism kicked in. He turned back to peer through his peephole. Alice was progressing down the aisle as intended. "We can still fix this, Angus," Nelson said confidently. "He can wait. Just head him off. Keep 'em apart. I won't blow till you're safe. It's a big ask Angus, I know. Trust me."

Brandt trusted Nelson as he always had. No time for debate. The plan teetered at mission critical. He could save the day. Brandt nodded then stepped through the door without a word. He checked his weapon, transferred the Bluetooth to his other ear, filtered into the crowd.

Nelson ran down the stairs to reach his laptop, quickly scanning all cameras covering the White Tower, inside and out. No sign. He dialed Brandt. "He's not at the south end. Try sweeping north." Brandt knew to avoid the central aisle where the plan would climax at any moment. After detonation he would lawfully detain this interfering dickhead and shoot him dead.

Nelson enlarged the camera angle that covered Alice's progress towards the target. "Nearly there, twenty seconds tops." At that time their paths would converge and put Pamela van Doren within the blast radius. It was not a big bomb. The planners surmised that modest loss of innocent life would be mourned and fade from public memory but the destruction of a beloved monument would not. They wanted the scars to be minimal. Hence the bomb sewn into Alice's fashion label coat delivered a guaranteed kill zone of only twenty feet. Nelson wanted them closer than that. He moved a cellphone on the table nearer the laptop. A number was displayed on the screen. All he had to do was hit send, and that was seconds away. Then he saw Alice sink to her knees forty feet shy of the target. "Not yet!" he heard himself shout at the screen. "Jesus Christ!"

The target was standing in front of the statue of Charles I. Pamela was discussing with their guide the only English king to be beheaded by order of Parliament, when her assistant Paige nudged her arm, directing her attention to a girl kneeling in the hallway facing them with her head bowed and her hands clasped in supplication. Was she a stalker? Her assistants were concerned. There had been a few back in the States, where Pamela was always accompanied by low key security. They hadn't thought they would need it for a private weekend in London. *A taste of things to come, I guess,* thought Pamela.

Alice had knelt when she did because her mother taught her so. *Approach ye fine folk,* her mother had said, *not as nigh as a four-horse wagon unless bidden.* So Alice waited on her knees in silent prayer. *A troubled girl,* thought Pamela. *She looks harmless enough.* She talked down her assistants' concerns and moved towards Alice to assist her. Alice looked up. The Princess Elizabeth beckoned with a welcoming smile on her face. Alice arose and made a courtesy.

"That's more like it," Nelson said to the screen. He had moved into a new mental zone. Every second expanded. He clicked onto Brandt's Bluetooth. "Angus, get behind a pillar. Face west." "Copy that," replied Brandt. Then something caught his eye.

Nelson stared at the security camera output. Pamela van Doren was now just within the blast zone. Nelson placed his finger a millimeter above "Send" and told Brandt: "Detonation in five…f-" The word froze on his tongue.

The security camera showed a figure dash into the central aisle, grab Alice around the waist, and carry her off at the run and away from the target. A second later another figure, Brandt, charging through in pursuit. Nelson stayed his finger just in time. While there was a chance that Brandt could herd them back toward the target, he would not detonate. At the same time, panic had broken out in the hall. Paul had screamed "Bomb! Everybody run!" at the top of his lungs. Nelson saw Pamela and her assistants scurrying in the direction of the exit with other panicked tourists. "Talk to me, Angus! Are they close? Back away!" But Brandt's Bluetooth had been swept from his ear by a hanging pennant. Chaos cluttered the security screens.

"Angus! Gotta blow! Find cover!" No response. He dared wait no longer. Instinct took over. He pressed "Send" harder than was needed. An instant later he saw a blinding flash behind the southwest pillar. Screams pierced the smoke and dust.

CHAPTER 49
A Drilled Tooth

JANE FELT HER arms being wrenched back to be chained behind the stake. She watched soldiers pour oil from buckets on the surrounding circle of bundled sticks and logs. Oil slopped on the ground all around her. "God help me...please," she begged. The crowd parted and Inquisitor Córdoba appeared. He stepped onto the firewood stacked to make steps up to the stake.

"God will come to your aid," said Córdoba "if you confess before the people. Confess that you and the Princess Elizabeth have together engaged in the foul practices of witchcraft. Repent of your sins and beg God's forgiveness through me."

"If I do this...you will save me?" Jane whispered through her tears. She realized that she had been set the same moral challenge she had faced earlier. And had faced successfully. Nothing had prevented Elizabeth's reign. It was an historical fact. Unless Jane now changed the outcome.

"You will be saved from the pain of hellfire today and forever," said the Inquisitor. "You will be set free to give evidence at her trial. You will be given property and a stipend. I give you my word as a man of God."

A hideous death, or wealth and property. A simple choice. Not to mention the tempting opportunity to remain a 21st century mind in a 16th century environment. To unravel then re-weave like Penelope the threads of history by the simple utterance of a few words. And who better qualified than she? Power. The most seductive temptation of all. The power to play God.

***

Alice was shocked when her James suddenly appeared yelling her name, lifting her as if she were thistledown. Surely the Princess would be offended by such behavior. But when she saw the desperation in his face she knew they were in mortal danger. He shouted other words, beyond her understanding, as people all around began to scream and run away from them.

When Paul had reached the Hall of Kings, he had cruised the closest aisle of exhibits looking everywhere for a sight of Alice. He had ignored a slight figure in a purplish coat moving up the center aisle. Then he caught the proud line of her chin, the bright flowing hair. It was Alice, and he grasped what the coat was for. His gut clenched. He leapt forward, ducking under an armored horseman to reach the center aisle and intercept her.

"The coat is poisoned. Get it off!" Paul screamed, peeling it off her, and dragging her round a thick double buttressed pillar away from the crowd, and out of view of Nelson's laptop. From the corner of his eye, Paul had seen Brandt in pursuit, closing in fast.

Brandt hoped that Nelson could still see him, now they had lost communication. He paused at the pillar to peer round, weapon pointed, then stepped forward. At the same time, Paul had ripped the coat off Alice, and he swung it back round the pillar, falling at Brandt's feet. Brandt recoiled instinctively, but knew Nelson would wait till he got clear. Then he heard the ring tone. Paul pushed Alice further round the pillar, hoping that it would deflect the blast, which came a second later with a deafening crack.

Nelson scanned the security cameras. Exhibits had been blown over. Smoke and dust obscured the body count, but they would help cover his next move. He turned his attention to the terrified crowd now jamming the exits. He spotted Pamela van Doren at the fringe of the crowd around the North East door. She was hugging her two assistants, comforting them. Nelson's mind raced, ego overriding reason; though, in truth, reason had left him a long time before. He hoped that Brandt was unscathed, but could not think about that now. He could still fix this. It would make for a tougher inquiry, but he could ride it through. He would find a concealed vantage point, shoot the target dead, then wound a few others, casualties apparently caught in the crossfire of a gun battle with surviving terrorists. The confirmed death of Pamela van Doren from whatever cause would trigger the gush of money into his accounts. Desperation and greed rationalized risk.

Paul lifted his head from the flagstones, as dust and plaster rained down from the painted ceiling. The blast had fractured the mighty pillar behind them, blown chunks of masonry from the corner, but the structure held. Paul had taken Alice to the floor, each instinctively trying to shield the other, as the explosion split the air.

It was louder than any blast Alice had heard at the contest of cannonry on Farnham Common. She wondered if more shot and shell would be flying overhead. She had given up trying to unravel the mystery of this world. She was on a bolting horse, plunging through a nightmare. She just had to hang on. Her James would know what to do. For a brief moment she had no desire to get up, comfortable on the flagstones, pressed against her beloved, now returned to her by God's Grace. She gazed into his green eyes, their faces inches apart. Surely God would not take him from her again.

Nelson stepped out through the oak door into the chamber. In addition to his pistol he had brought with him an Agram

2002, a Croatian submachine gun with a 22 round clip, favored by terrorists, ideal to be the culprit weapon if required. He peered through the peephole, trying to get a fix on his target.

Paul pulled Alice to her feet, dragging her back to the fractured pillar. He did not know how many adversaries he faced. The epicenter of the explosion was the safest place to seek cover. The only casualty Paul could see was Brandt, who had fled as far as he could from the fallen coat before the blast blew off his left leg at the knee.

Brandt lay on his side, looking back at the bleeding stump, as he crawled towards his fallen gun. He had trusted his partner, and had trusted wrong. But he knew that his real mistake had occurred years before when he had succumbed to Nelson's invitation to join him in entrepreneurial security. Now he had ruined his life and his family. He could not live with that. Brandt's fingers reached for his gun, and he placed its muzzle under his chin. As he fumbled for the best angle, Paul reached in and snatched it from his grasp. Brandt looked up. The American who had outwitted them crouched down to examine his leg.

"We need you alive." Beside the American stood the girl who moments before had been totally under their control.

"Why should he live?" she gasped.

" He's our witness. Trust me on this, Alice," said Paul. Trust, she would forever.

Paul continued. "Help us and I will speak for you." It took no persuasion. Brandt's loyalty to Nelson now lay with his missing leg.

"I need your belt," said Paul, reaching down to Brandt's buckle and unhooking it. The steady trickle of blood from the stump became a squirt as Paul heaved the belt loose. Brandt, a proud man, suppressed a howl of pain.

"Let me do it," insisted Alice. Paul looked at her in surprise. "My Da taught me." Her father, because of his trade, which oft called him to lop the hand off a thief, was considered an expert on ruined bodies. When the blacksmith's son fell under the wheel of the ale wagon she had watched him tie a leather thong above the stump of the severed foot and clean the wound. The boy lived to resume his trade. Such acts had earned the Craddock family a measure of goodwill in the village. Alice took the belt and fashioned a tourniquet round the leg as confidently as a surgeon might. But Paul was no longer surprised by anything Alice did.

"How many?" said Paul checking the clip in Brandt's gun.

"Just Nelson," said Brandt, suppressing a groan as Alice knotted the belt tight.

"Nelson?"

"My boss." Paul turned to Alice. "Stay here."

He turned back to Brandt. "Don't mess with her, trust me on this." Then Paul ran back to the fractured pillar.

Brandt's stump had stopped bleeding but a new pain afflicted him, his deadened conscience regaining sensation like the nerve of a drilled tooth.

"Will you ever forgive me, lass?" asked Brandt.

"I will," said Alice. "But God may not," she added after a moment's thought.

CHAPTER 50

Vengeance Is Mine

"WILL YOU CONFESS?" shouted the Inquisitor Córdoba once more. The crowd that had amassed around the pyre on Tower Hill was hushed, awaiting her answer. Many who had attended earlier burnings hoped that the witch would remain defiant, some in sympathy with her, some because it would make for a better spectacle. Jane was silent for a moment. The weight of her decision bowed her head. She whispered. "Hear my confession…"

Murmurs of disappointment ran through the crowd. Córdoba bent closer to her. "Speak loudly. The rabble must hear you."

"I confess…" Jane started, then she yelled "I confess that I want you to go straight to Hell!" She swung her foot and kicked him in the groin. She would not betray the Princess Elizabeth. She would not betray Alice. She had a responsibility to see things through as they were meant to be. Jane had found her reason for being.

Córdoba lurched, missed his footing and tumbled backwards to the base of the bonfire. This provoked a huge laugh from the people, who rarely saw but always relished the embarrassment of authority figures, particularly clerics. When the

Inquisitor got to his feet, he saw that oil had smeared his fine robes. He glared at the witch with loathing.

"Die screaming, then!" He never had any intention of honoring a promise to a vessel of Satan. If she had made a good confession, he would have shortened her demise with the green straw. But not now. No. She would taste the searing pain of eternal damnation in this world before she entered the next. He gave the signal. Two men came forward with burning torches. Jane knew that her agony was at hand.

***

Paul scanned the fallen debris of the Line of Kings. There was an armored horseman left standing, and using it for cover was the rogue agent who had ordered Paul's hanging.

Nelson had found his firing position, and was scanning through the chaos for the target. Paul saw the man level a submachine gun, as if taking care with his aim. Paul pointed and shot instinctively. The bullet struck the breastplate of the knight. Nelson ducked and pivoted round the backside of the horse. But the shot had had the effect Paul wanted. It spooked the crowd. Every person in the hall, including Pamela van Doren and her companions, hit the ground.

Nelson cursed and directed his attention to this new threat. He blazed away at the pillar, the source of the shot. To his surprise, and to Paul's, the impact of the bullets delivered the coup de grace to the splintered pillar. The central column split diagonally and pitched to the ground with a deafening crash and a cloud of dust. Paul dived for cover as Nelson fired another salvo. Paul knew that he had to draw fire away from Alice, and ironically, from the other man who had been trying to kill him for two days. Close by he saw steps leading down to a darkened adjacent chamber. A sign saying *The Fate of Traitors to the Crown—Opening Soon'* barred the entrance. Paul ran toward it and dived head first down the steps as a burst of gunfire chewed up the flagstones at his heels.

"Nobody leave the building!" yelled Nelson, unseen by the crowd. The crowd pressed together, cowering near the exit. He fired another shot at the wall above the doorway for emphasis. "Terrorists are hiding among you. Stay where you are! Don't move! Help is coming!" They'll keep. He reloaded and headed in pursuit of Paul, laying down short bursts of suppressive fire into the darkened room as he approached.

Paul knew that he was outgunned. He ran through the hall to the far end looking for a hiding place from which he could take his best shot when his pursuer was silhouetted at the entrance. The first exhibit was a low platform on which stood the wax figure of a hooded executioner, with a traditional headsman's block at his feet, on which he rested the tool of his trade, an antique long handled axe with a single-edged iron blade. Beyond that was a simple gallows still under construction. It would give him cover and a clear sightline. He took up a position in the shadows beneath it.

A burst of gunfire from the corner of the entrance splintered a wooden beam above him. Paul rolled away. When he looked up, he knew that he had missed his chance. His assailant was inside, somewhere in the shadows. He decided to crawl to an exhibit against the back wall where he could not be outflanked. It was a recreation of punishment for the crime of heresy, burning at the stake. The wax figure of a young woman was chained to a post on top of a pile of logs and kindling. A sign beside it read: "Anne Askew, aged 26, executed July 16, 1546."

As Paul edged forward, his foot caught a can of nails beside the unfinished gallows, pitching them onto the stone floor. Their tinkling sound betrayed his position. Another burst of gunfire sprayed the wall just above him. Paul instantly took aim at the muzzle flash, and squeezed the trigger. Nothing. The extractor on the right side of the slide had been damaged when the explosion had thrown Brandt to the ground. The casing of the shot Paul had fired at Nelson remained jammed inside. As he frantically tried to pull the slide and eject the cartridge, a silhouette loomed over him. He pointed the pistol at it, bluffing.

"Drop your weapon!" Paul barked with as much confidence as he could summon. Again he squeezed the trigger. Nothing.

Nelson leveled the Agram at Paul's head: "This won't look good on your record."

Then Nelson sensed a presence behind him. He swung his weapon round. It was smashed from his hand by the blade of an axe, which sheared away three of his fingers. Alice stood before him with the face of an avenging Fury. She had tested the headman's blade with her thumb when she picked it up. It wasn't nearly as sharp as her Da's, who prided himself on his ability to take off a head with a single stroke. Some headsmen needed three or more swipes. But Alice did not care. She would smite him as many times as it took to send this evil caitiff to Hell. Nelson stumbled back with a howl as the pain kicked in. Alice lunged and swung the axe in a mighty down stroke, bisecting Nelson's right shoulder down to the lung. He fell back against the pile of logs, his mouth filling with blood. This was not the death Nelson had always imagined for himself. Alice stepped to one side and swung the axe laterally, taking Nelson's head off at the Adams apple. It fell to rest between his legs. Paul gaped at her, splashed with Nelson's blood. He struggled to process the sudden turn of events.

Alice nodded to herself. Her Da would be proud of her handiwork. Then her shoulders arched, and her body shivered.

"Alice…?" croaked Paul, wondering whether he might be next. Then he saw that her gaze fixed on the wax effigy chained to the stake above her. She dropped the axe.

***

The circle of fire round the stake was closing in on Jane. She moaned as heat began licking at the calves of her legs. Inquisitor Córdoba stepped forward to catch her eye. Yes, he wanted to teach the witch that since she had defied him she would die in torment.

Bundles of burning sticks hissed and crackled. A spark flew out. It landed on the Inquisitor's oil-smeared robe. It immediately caught alight. Córdoba beat at it with his sleeve, which also ignited. He stepped back into a pool of oil, slipped and fell to the ground. The puddle beneath him lit up. Flames shot up his leg, finding his silk undershirt, a secret luxury he allowed himself. Within seconds, Córdoba was ablaze. The crowd backed away. The witch could kill even from the stake, it seemed.

But Córdoba did not die, not immediately. It would be seven more days of agony and delirium before Spain's principal agent at the English court would breathe his last. The conspiracy to eliminate the Princess Elizabeth from succession would die as well. Later, as Queen Mary succumbed to fatal illness, Sir Giles De Fries would flee to Spain. But newly-crowned Queen Elizabeth's reach was long. The ungallant knight would die after drinking Gascony sherry laced with arsenic.

Soldiers ran forward and beat out the flames on Córdoba's robes. Jane heard the Inquisitor shrieking in the agony he had promised would be hers, yet she felt no pleasure at the sound, or the sight of him writhing. The feeling of otherworldliness had come over her again. She looked round at the fire behind her. The flames were licking her bound hands, yet she felt no pain. Not even heat. In fact, she felt its reverse. Cold. Intense cold. Perhaps this was the programming of the mind/body complex when undergoing a dreadful death, Jane speculated, a merciful delusion blocking out pain. She felt a force coursing through her. Then her vision blurred and pixilated. She heard men shouting commands at her. Telling her not to move or she would be shot. Then everything went dark. Yet again.

***

Armed police had burst into the White Tower. Pamela van Doren, naturally calm in a crisis, though this one had stretched her nerves to the limit, directed them to where the last gunshots had been heard, then resumed tending to the wounded.

The police descended the stairs and switched on the lights illuminating the chamber that now contained real horrors as well as simulated ones. Paul was holding Alice close, with his other arm raised in surrender.

"Don't shoot! I'm CIA Special Agent Montgomery. Get an ambulance!"

Probably a bit late for the fellow without his head, thought the leading police officer as he approached, submachine gun leveled. But Paul was looking at Alice's hands, which were gripping his arm tightly. They were no longer pale. They were bright red, and large blisters were forming on them.

Alice suddenly stiffened. She uttered one word, "James!" Then she fainted dead away.

CHAPTER 51
Alice and Jane

A TAXI PULLED up outside Hammersmith Hospital in South London. Paul got out, wearing a smart suit he had just bought himself from Oliver Spencer, and carrying a bunch of pink and cream roses. Due to a delayed shock reaction, the girl had been unconscious for almost a week. Doctors had been worried that she might be sinking into a coma, but Paul had been told that this morning she had awoken, weak, but apparently coherent. Her first questions had been about him.

Paul walked through a bustling hospital corridor till he reached a security door, guarded by a uniformed policeman. He showed his ID and was admitted. A nurse placed his flowers in a vase. One Mr. Hannay, a senior official at the Home Secretary's Office to whom Paul had previously outlined the little that he knew of the conspiracy, was there to greet him.

"How's she doing?" Paul asked.

"Sleeping a lot. The blisters are healing surprisingly well. Burn specialist says there should be little to no scarring."

"Good."

"Your meeting with the Prime Minister today has been brought forward to 4:30. A car will be sent for you." The invitation had been a reassuring sign that Paul would not be swept up in the brutal housecleaning currently taking place on the other side of the Pond.

"I'll just see how she is, and then we'll talk."

Paul picked up the vase of flowers, and headed down the hallway. He entered her room quietly. The girl lay asleep, her bandaged hands across her lap. Paul looked at sunlight playing on the spill of fine fair hair across her forehead. He placed his vase of flowers by the window, where the light would bring out their color. He leaned over and kissed her on the forehead.

"Alice..." he whispered in her ear. He saw a faint smile crease her lips. Paul sat down at the end of the bed. A few seconds went by, then she sat bolt upright with a gasp. She looked at Paul.

"Oh!...it's you!" There he was. Hair dark as jet and those emerald eyes.

It was Jane who had awoken.

"How are you feeling?" he asked, much as a doctor would.

"Fine, I think...I just sleep and sleep..."

"That's what you need."

She looked at his pebble grain shoes, his neatly pleated slacks, and cashmere jacket. "Nice duds. Going to meet the Queen?"

Paul smiled. "The Prime Minister."

"Oh..." Jane looked toward the window, noticing the flowers. "I was interrogated this morning. Apparently, my fingerprints are all over an axe at the Tower of London. When are they going to charge me?"

"With what?" he asked.

"Oh...Unpaid parking fines, being a suicide bomber, that sort of thing," she answered lightly, though in truth she was terrified that she'd be facing consequences for something she'd known nothing about.

"They're not," Paul said flatly. "No charges. At all. You're a hero. That's already been decided. You'll have to give evidence at a secret hearing. Tell whatever you can recall. Just a formality."

"So, I'll be free…?" Jane was stunned. "What about… that Lizzie Borden moment I heard about this morning?"

"That's our little secret. Ours and the CIA's. We're good at forgetting things."

"Human rights, national sovereignty, stuff like that," Jane said with a wry smile.

Paul thought for a moment, seeking common ground. "It's a complicated world, Jane. Sometimes we make things better, sometimes we make them worse. This time we made them better." It was the best he could summon. There was silence as they looked at each other for a moment.

"Well, thanks for saving my life."

"Thanks for saving mine," he said with equal gratitude.

Another silence. His feelings for this girl had not diminished in the intervening week, during which he had studied all available information on Jane Benedict, gifted undergraduate at the University of London. Alice was the one who had initially captured his heart. Yet he sensed that in some way Alice was still present in the wan but smiling girl leaning on her elbow beside him. It was hard to define quite how, but Jane seemed to Paul to be complete now. Paul was drawn to Jane as he had been drawn to Alice, even though he had to admit that he could scarcely claim to know either one of them. There were many things that he wanted to say to Jane, but this was not the time.

"I'm going to let you rest. Just wanted to be sure you were OK." He got up and moved toward the doorway.

"Paul. Will I see you again?"

He was hoping she would ask. "If you'd like that. Tomorrow, then?" He grinned, and gently shut the door.

Paul walked down the hospital corridor reflecting on the week's events. He scanned his tablet for the latest media coverage. There was gratitude that casualties at the Tower were limited to one death and eleven injured, two seriously, one of whom was Brandt, whom media hailed as the Wounded Hero of the Tower.

After consultations between Downing Street and The White House, it had been decided that the truth was too monstrous be made public, as Nelson had predicted. Exposing the bombing as a false flag operation could undermine confidence in institutions of authority. While intelligence agencies in both countries introduced new safeguards and oversight procedures to identify rogue behavior, the decision was made, albeit with some distaste, to run with the story of the daring EST/CIA operation that had prevented a terrorist attack from being much worse, one in which senior and junior EST operatives gave their lives. Thus Nelson died as he had always imagined he would—*universally admired*—fueling the media's need for human stories, in the lack of details of the bomber's plot, which were designated classified due to ongoing anti-terrorist operations.

The absence of the bomber's fragmented corpse was remedied by changing the labeling on the body bag containing Selwyn's mangled remains, previously identified as "John Smith Killed by Train." Rather than receiving a hero's funeral, his relics were cremated as those of a perpetrator of atrocity, identity unknown. The reputation of Ian Selwyn, however, would be enshrined in memory as that of a hero of the War on Terrorism. EST Junior agent, Willem Jones, would be accorded similar treatment.

Angus Brandt had confessed everything he knew about this and other unauthorized operations he'd carried out under Nelson during lengthy interrogations. Publicly, he was billed as the hero who confronted the bomber, losing a leg in the process. To the few who knew the truth, he was scum. In return for his cooperation and silence, Brandt received the best medical care, was given early retirement, and put on a generous pension. He would live each instant as an imposter. Every time someone stopped him to thank him for his service, when his kids looked at him with pride, his wife with gratitude, he would be tormented. The conscience which Alice had revived in him like the nerve of a diseased tooth would flare into agony. People would be mystified, months later, when he put the muzzle of a

Glock into his mouth and fired. The inquest would attribute his suicide to PTSD. His grieving widow and children would be left, as Brandt had always planned, well-to-do and respected.

Wounded CIA private contractors Levinson and his surviving crew were shipped to Ramstein Air Force Base in Germany for urgent medical attention. They would never be seen again.

Senior CIA analyst Charles Farrell was arrested for arranging the murder of Section Chief Rick Almaraz, allegedly to avoid prosecution for unspecified corruption. National security would require the case to be heard in camera to protect classified material. Farrell would spend twenty-three hours a day in an isolation cell and the remaining hour slumped in a small exercise yard, endlessly reliving the chain of disasters that had brought him to this place. Who let him down, why didn't they..? If only... if only..., till it drove him insane. Charles Farrell would wait nine years for a botched execution by lethal injection.

Pamela van Doren became the media's darling. Fellow tourists trapped in the smoky Hall Of Kings had taken pictures and video of Pamela and her assistants Paige and Emily, as they tore strips from their own clothing to bind wounds and comforted traumatized survivors till paramedics arrived, in the process creating viral video history. The issues she championed would become debate fodder on every TV screen in the world, the very outcome the conspiracy had been designed to prevent. Local politicians everywhere would see advantage in joining her demand that access to pure water and safe food was a basic human right.

The Olympian Gods would never be charged with anything, but they knew that their power had been curbed. For the present.

Paul looked up from his tablet. He saw the irony of the cover story. But his thoughts returned to the mystery of Alice and Jane.

Jane settled back on her pillow, enjoying the fragrance of the Peace roses that Paul had brought her. Nice touch. There was a perkiness bubbling within her, a sense of joy at little things that she had not felt for longer than she could remember.

As a child, Jane had imagined many colorful ways her life might turn out. None came close to her current situation. Apparently, she was an ax-murdering potential suicide bomber, pardoned without arrest or trial for actions she had undoubtedly carried out, yet of which she had no recollection. And all before the age of twenty. Not bad. What's next? If her visions of a past life were caused by mental illness, recent events indicated that the real world was even crazier than she. This gave Jane some comfort, a renewed confidence. Perhaps Alice had left some trace of herself? But what was beginning to nip at her sense of wellbeing was the dreadful fate of Alice and James, which she had shared firsthand until the last moment. Alice Craddock's reward for a short life of kindness, courage and humility was to be burned alive by evil men. The agonizing injustice of it rankled. Injustice still reigns. Jane's mood was turning dark again. A nurse came in to check her vitals and administer medication. Her consciousness succumbed to the drugs.

CHAPTER 52

The WTF Moment

JANE WAS JOLTED from sleep feeling that she had fallen heavily out of bed. Yet the floor was not linoleum, but cold uneven stone. She opened her eyes to an uncertain scene. As the blur cleared, there was James De Fries lying prone on the floor, his arm outstretched towards her, concern turning to guarded joy at her awakening. Shock stunned her like a cattle prod. WTF! She was back! Subject to forces beyond her understanding—again….Was it a time loop? Some diabolical Groundhog Day? Then it came to her with a rush. The unjust fate of Alice and James had been on her mind before she was drugged to sleep. She had wished she could have fixed it. Now she was back at the last hour in which she could fix it. Was this her purpose? Her destiny? A surge of adrenalin gave her an involuntary shiver.

"Alice, be not afraid, lass. 'Tis I. Did they harm you?" asked James, noting the mark of a recent blow. He prayed she was not the snarling loon of the morning.

"James…" Alice murmured, after a moment's silence. Jane realized that she had just made Alice say his name, as though her mind were lodged within Alice's, a curious melding that Jane had not previously experienced. She could feel Alice's thoughts and steer them into speech, yet she sensed that Alice remained unaware of the intrusion. Jane's thoughts whirred as she processed her new predicament, recalling all that had happened and would still happen unless she could prevent it. It was as if within a nanosecond she had received and absorbed a file containing Alice's life from its beginning. How much or how little should she say to James? If her approach failed, she might just be burnt to a crisp with Alice.

"My love..." she whispered, needing him to accept her as the Alice he adored, if she were to change his fate and thereby hers. As she uttered the words, she felt a warmth spreading through her, the wellspring of love Alice gave to this man. Even bruised, disheveled and dirty he was a strikingly handsome man with green eyes that seemed to bore right into her. Just like Paul. But she could not speak to him as she might to Paul. How could she predict his reaction? He might think her mad, or worse, the witch she was accused of being. This might cause events to fork in a different direction. Jane was concerned about triggering the phenomenon known in chaos theory as the Butterfly Effect. What if it was more than a theory? If she prevented pre-ordained deaths, how changed would her world be when she woke up? If she woke up…Well, she had no choice. She had to do something or die.

She reached to touch his hand, but their feet were chained to separate pillars. Their outstretched fingers remained inches apart. James gave her a rueful smile. "I have been granted Queen's audience, by right of birth." He went on to explain that his late stepfather had served the Tudors well over the years. "The Queen knows the estates are mine. I will prove the accusations against me are lies, created by my uncle to steal my inheritance."

"The Queen will deny you…"

"How know you this?" asked James taken aback.

"I heard the men talking. Your uncle and the priest. They paid me no mind," Jane said, dissembling as Alice as best she could.

"Then I will demand trial by combat and challenge my accuser."

"He will appoint a champion. Cedric of Winchester."

James, again taken aback, heard a new inflection she put on some of her words. Was she still a little touched?

Jane noted his reaction. She had spoken as Jane not Alice, an error she quickly corrected.

"How know you this?" James asked once more.

Again she lied. "They spoke of it,"

Before he could question her further, she asked: "Do you love me? "

"I do, with all my heart."

"Do you trust me?"

"Aye, you are pure and good."

"Do you believe that God may give a special gift even to the humblest?"

James could not grasp the import of her questions.

"I have God's gift of second sight. "

While Jane was not yet ready to accept fully that mankind was ruled by a benevolent deity (though the concept was growing on her) she understood the persuasive power of the word "God" to a man in whose culture atheism was unthinkable. God was her best hope to make him to do what she needed him to do.

James was shocked. "Has God given you a vision?"

"You are fighting… Winning… Sir Giles spills wine behind you and makes you slip… I saw you die."

A chill ran through him. Alice's mood was strange. Had she become bewitched? Nay, she's just a little touched from the beating she took. Or had she indeed been vouchsafed a true vision? The moment between them was broken by the clanking of keys opening the door to their cell.

"Trust me," urged Alice.

"Say nothing, Alice," said a worried James. "I pray you. Nothing."

Three guards stepped in, one carrying a basin and a ewer of water. He placed the basin between them and filled it.

"Clean yourselves," barked the guard at the door.

Jane looked at her reflection in the rippling water. This was the first time she could see the face of Alice Craddock, whose adventures she had experienced through Alice's eyes, but those eyes had never alighted on a mirror. Jane studied her features. Despite Alice's long flaxen locks and Jane's neatly cropped hair, they resembled one another uncannily. What was the connection between them? Jane felt her resolve strengthening.

CHAPTER 53
At Sword Point

THE GUARDS LED them down a long corridor lit by torches mounted on the wall. Jane turned to James and whispered quickly: "When I call your name, step to the side, left or right. Do not step back..." James stared at her. Before she could say more, a guard poked her roughly with his club.

"Silence, witch!"

A door opened to a sumptuous hall decorated with tapestries celebrating the reign of the late King Henry. Men-at-arms stood by the doorway and at the corners. Courtiers, nobles, knights, and servants were milling about conducting the court's business. A waft of body odor spiked with perfume, but rank nonetheless, emanated from the hall. Jane's nostrils twitched. Others were oblivious. At the far end of the hall was a dais where the Queen sat on her throne attended by ladies-in-waiting. A clerk took a parchment from her that she had just signed.

The hall gradually fell silent as the two prisoners were led in. Courtiers stared at them while pretending not to. They halted some distance from the throne. Jane discreetly studied the small sad Queen. Poor Bloody Mary. She burned 300 Protestants, while her father executed 57,000. History could be so unfair.

A booming voice intoned: "Bring forth James De Fries!"

The lovers exchanged glances. Perhaps their last.

"Beware Sir Giles behind you," Jane whispered as James was hustled forward, leaving her guarded by three men with halberds an easy thrust away. Jane hoped that she had instilled just enough detail into her warnings. But not too much. She had to be delicate, to minimize her interference with the flow of today's event, up until that crucial moment.

Jane watched from afar as James arrived at the foot of the dais and bowed low to the Queen. A conversation she could not hear unfolded. After a while she saw the Queen's expression change. An official called for guards to bring Alice Craddock forward. This was where it could go badly wrong, Jane knew, if she did not play her part well.

Once in the royal presence she dropped to her knees in obeisance just as Alice had. Jane ceded control of Alice's body and persona back to their owner and let events play out. As before, Alice offered herself as a sacrifice, then watched James refuse to give her up. He named her his betrothed and demanded the pardon ordained by God should he prevail in trial by combat. Again Jane felt Alice's deep love surging within her. Must be a pretty amazing man, this James De Fries.

The trial by combat was announced. The Queen left the dais, followed by her ladies-in-waiting.

"When I shout, step aside," Jane cautioned. She saw uncertainty in James' eyes. A guard pulled him away.

***

"Greetings, nephew. And outlaw. And plaything of the Devil's whore. Your new titles become you. I accept your challenge. My choice of weapons will be sword and buckler," said Sir Giles, confronting James in braggadocio tones.

From James' perspective, his uncle's subsequent announcement of Cedric of Winchester as his champion supported Alice's apparent foreknowledge, be it demonically or divinely inspired.

James' derisive reply accusing his uncle of cowardice before the entire court further sharpened Sir Giles' thirst for revenge.

"This whelp will die and the witch will burn," he growled to Cordoba as they walked away.

A long oval was cleared in the center of the hall and roped off. As James prepared for combat, stretching his sinews, hefting the rapier in each of the guard positions, getting a sense of its weight, he studied the room, the faces of the courtiers, and particularly the movements of his enemy. He observed Sir Giles conferring with his champion. A giant of a man, thought James, the biggest opponent he had ever faced. Worse, he was a left hander. James would have to profile his stance more, and strategize accordingly.

Then he saw his uncle signal for a servant bearing a tray of wine goblets to approach. Sir Giles took one, but did not drink from it. The weight of Alice's words increased.

Sir Giles carried his goblet of wine past the Duke of Norfolk, with barely a nod of deference to the most senior of the Queen's advisors.

Impudent Winchester goose, thought Norfolk, who personally had no stomach for refreshment when shortly one of two men, possibly both, would die in his presence. Norfolk did not care for Sir Giles, who was of the gentry, unlike Norfolk's own proud aristocratic lineage. He was unimpressed by Sir Giles' ambition, irritated by his overweening sense of entitlement, and disturbed by his reputation for cruelty, the latest example of which had just come to Norfolk's ears. Sir Giles had ordered that the accused witch be placed under guard at the front row of the spectators, to distract her beloved and force her to watch him die. Sir Giles lacked honour. Why the Queen showed him such favour, Norfolk could not understand. But it was prudent to hold his tongue.

Jane had been about to break away from her guards to get closer to the oval, as Alice had done, when the guards took hold of her under each arm and led her forward to the very place she would have chosen, midway along the oval, with a view of the duel in profile. She had arrived in the same place as before, but by different means. Jane realized that her intrusion into Alice and James' lives had already caused subtle changes to the details of the original event. Little ripples were spreading and each ripple might trigger another ripple, and so on. She willed it all to play out as before, until the wine was spilled. Sir Giles took his position nearby. Knowing that James and Alice were watching, he mockingly raised his goblet to them both. But he did not drink.

"En garde," the Duke of Norfolk announced. James and Cedric assumed the position in sixte.

"Allez."

***

Queen Mary had been waiting in an antechamber close by. She listened to the clash of steel and occasional gasps from the crowd. Skilled combatants were evidently in play. The poor naive boy would die with honour and respect, but she had no wish to watch. Then she heard a quickening in the exchange of blades—thrust, parry, circlage, counter parry, counter circlage and on—climaxing in a universal gasp of reaction, followed by a a hubbub of shouting.

Lord Norfolk entered, his face serious as she expected. "Majesty, in trial by combat James De Fries has prevailed."

The Queen was stunned. Her judgement had been faulty. God had given victory to the smaller, less experienced swordsman, because his claim was righteous and Sir Giles' false. False, too, Cordoba's accusation of witchcraft against the peasant girl. God would not give victory to the consort of a witch. Evidently, the Inquisitor and Sir Giles were in collusion for some reason. Probably gold. Common at court. Mary sighed. She had no time for priests who abuse their power.

The Queen got up unsteadily from her chair, wincing from a new pain in her back from yesterday's horse riding.

"Was the fight fair?"

"On that matter I wish a private word, Your Majesty."

The Duke recounted what had happened. Each combatant had inflicted superficial wounds but neither was gaining the upper hand. Then he had noticed an exchange of looks between Sir Giles and his champion. It had seemed a signal of some kind. Cedric of Winchester had begun driving young De Fries back towards Sir Giles with a furious onslaught. The Duke saw Sir Giles extend the arm that held his goblet of wine, hesitating. He was about to tip it over, when James had suddenly halted his retreat.

"When I saw Sir Giles withdraw the goblet, his intention became clear. He was waiting for the right moment to wet the flagstones beneath his opponent's approaching feet."

"By the Rood…" Queen Mary muttered.

Norfolk told the Queen how Cedric had redoubled his efforts and succeeded in moving James De Fries back towards his uncle. Norfolk saw Sir Giles extend his arm and brazenly spill the wine, uncaring whether he was observed.

"At that moment there was a scream from someone in the crowd. James De Fries sprang to his left in a crouch then delivered a fatal upward lunge from this unexpected position. So died Cedric of Winchester."

"I heard a great commotion," said the Queen. "In fact, I still hear much disputation."

"Yes, Majesty. Sir Giles would not accept God's verdict. He became enraged, He drew his dagger and rushed at the village girl. James De Fries barred his way, then advanced on him, at sword point. Sir Giles took fright and seized a young page, a boy barely twelve years old, to use him as a shield. A more disgraceful moment I have never witnessed at court, Your Highness."

Mary was equally appalled. Norfolk went on.

"Yet young De Fries dropped his sword, forsook revenge and turned away, admired by all. Sir Giles no longer has friends at court," Norfolk added pointedly, knowing his Queen.

The Queen brightened. "It is an unexpected outcome, in which I clearly see the hand of God."

***

A trumpet sounded.

Jane turned from aiding apothecaries dress gashes to James' arms, ribs and right thigh. Queen Mary entered the Great Hall. Everyone bowed. She approached briskly. The walk was easing the pain in her back. Ahead of her lay Cedric of Winchester face down, blood pooling, transfixed through the throat. His parry to James' upward lunge had been too little too late. It had merely lifted the tip of the incoming blade to his throat, severing an artery on the way out. Growing up as she had, the sight of blood did not disconcert Queen Mary. A few feet in front of the body she observed a crimson puddle darker than blood. Wine.

The Queen looked across to where James De Fries sat on a bench, stripped to the waist. Apothecaries were applying poultices to his wounds and sewing up the one deep gash on his thigh. Mary studied him. Lean, muscular, in the prime of manhood. She switched her gaze to Alice Craddock, the peasant girl he intended to marry, daughter of a well-regarded executioner apparently, humble yet with the glow of pride about her. The girl is comely, Mary admitted, without that tinge of jealousy she had felt at first sight. And loyal. She was ready to die for him. A little education and fine clothing, and the girl would soon pass as a gentlewoman. It may well be a good match. The Queen decided that a bold decision was necessary. It was time to curb the faction at court that had aligned with Sir Giles De Fries. She would knight young James De Fries and give him a new estate along the Scottish border. She needed a strong man like him to keep those cursed reivers in check.

"Apothecaries, give him good care," Queen Mary called out as she approached.

"Your Majesty," said Sir Giles stepping forward in her path, bowing low. The Inquisitor Córdoba hovered a step behind. They had conferred to determine the religious argument that might be used to reverse the verdict. Before either could speak, the Queen raised her hand.

"Sir Giles, you dared attempt interference with God's choice in this trial by combat. Lord Norfolk has apprized me of the enormity of your folly. But God sees all, and has revealed your deceit and cowardice for all to see."

She raised her voice for the court to hear. "By authority vested in me by God, I issue a writ of attainder for Sir Giles De Fries. You are hereby banished, and your estates forfeit to the Crown. If by week's end you are found within England's shores, your head shall be struck from your body."

Sir Giles looked around. Stern disapproving gazes everywhere. So unexpected was this massive reversal of fortune, Sir Giles found he was unable to form words properly, merely an incoherent stammer. The Inquisitor stepped forward.

"Your Majesty, the combat was tainted by witchcraft." He pointed at Alice. "By that creature, the Devil's whore."

Jane crossed herself and clasped her hands in prayer, an astute response, noted by all.

"Monsignor," said the Queen dryly, "are you suggesting that this humble girl is more powerful than God?"

"By no means, Majesty, not at all. In Scripture…"

She cut him off. Loudly.

"Be silent! I shall communicate with King Philip on this matter."

The prospect that he might lose his position at the court of Spain—or worse, given Philip's temper—chilled Córdoba to the marrow.

"You are no longer welcome at court," the Queen continued. "It is time you returned to Spain. Be gone by week's end."

The Queen flicked her fingers as if brushing away a fly. The Captain of the Guards stepped forward, and with a sweeping bow to Sir Giles that contained more than a hint of mockery, pointed to the door with his outstretched hand. Two guards with halberds approached as escort.

It was Córdoba who recovered first from the shock of dismissal. It seemed that Rome was now a safer destination than Cadiz. He had no respect for Sir Giles, whose usefulness to Spain over. But he would still need a witness whom he could control in his intended audience with the Holy Father. He was not done with this heretic nation yet.

He nudged Sir Giles forward. As they withdrew from the Queen, Cordoba took control of the devastated man.

"There is a Papal vessel at Cheapside. We will sail together to Rome on the morning tide."

Queen Mary watched them depart, amused that their path to the doorway led them past the two people they had conspired to destroy. The Inquisitor locked eyes with the witch, giving her a look of implacable hatred.

"You will die in a fire," said Jane as her persecutors passed by. It just sprang out of her. She had no idea why she said that. She felt such certainty in her words, yet how could she possibly know their fate?

As it happened, the Papal ship bearing Córdoba and Sir Giles to Rome, despite being well armed, was attacked by French privateers as the vessel entered the Bay of Biscay. The Papal insignia were not always a deterrent to pirates. It promised gold to those men with no fear of the fires of Hell. A lucky shot from the privateer ignited the powder magazine, and the ship was soon in flames. Sir Giles and the Inquisitor recalled the witch's parting words as a fireball engulfed them, and they suffered the agonizing fate they had planned for her. Horribly burned, they clung to floating wreckage till the sharks came for them.

James also heard her words as he watched his defeated enemies pass.

"Are you indeed a witch?" he whispered to Alice.

"Only to your enemies, my love," replied Jane with Alice's winsome smile.

James embraced her.

***

Alice would soon be her old self. Jane needed to allay James' fears, to smooth the path for Alice's future with James once she was gone. Assuming, of course, that she had a future. It turned out to be much greater than Jane imagined.

The Queen ordered an apartment in the Tower be made available to them during the period of preparation for the knight-hood ceremony, where James and five other newly minted knights would be dubbed by the Royal sword and progress up the social ladder. At the same time James would be instructed in the politics of the border region to help him integrate with the local clans.

Jane was feeling very tired. She knew she would sleep soon, then to wake in the twenty first century, satisfied she had righted a wrong, and never to return. But there was one part of Alice's future life she longed to experience. Lovemaking with James. And she knew Alice longed for that as well. James, being the man of principle he was, would probably wait at least until the bans were announced. But Jane sensed that little time was left to her. She considered the moral paradoxes. She would be cheating on Paul, with whom, it would seem, she was destined to hook up, even though their relationship had barely started. At the same time she would be voyeuring on Alice, by sharing her pleasure even though she and James would be ignorant of her intrusion.

So she desisted. Then, to Jane's astonishment, it was Alice who approached James and initiated an insistent embrace. Thus, Alice and Jane together gave their virginity to James De Fries. It was everything Jane had hoped for and beyond. Jane was just beginning to drift off, when she felt his hand running up Alice's thigh. James pulled her to him, and took her once more. All three climaxed together with such intensity that Jane blacked out.

CHAPTER 54

Jane through the Multiverse

WITH A JOLT Jane woke up. She was not lying in the hospital bed, but was seated and in motion—somewhere indoors. Everything was a blur at first. Then her vision cleared. She was in the window seat of a monorail carriage. And it was FAST. What seemed to be the Manhattan skyline was speeding past her window. What was she doing in New York? And the buildings were subtly different. Then she saw the Twin Towers of the World Trade Center. Still standing… Oh my God!

It all flooded into her consciousness: the life she had lived *before* she had intervened in the fates of Alice and James, and the life she had lived *because* she had intervened. She had full memories of both lives extending back to her earliest childhood. Jane almost passed out. Birthdays and homework and dinners, with and without her family, streamed through her mind in two rivers of consciousness, or dimensional tapestries of events. Had the threads of time been rewoven by the changes she had made, or had her violation of space/time caromed her onto another fold of the multiverse? And what about Alice and James and Paul—and everyone else, for that matter?

Jane thought about Paul. That was the only point of regret she could feel, that Paul didn't exist in her new stream of memory. She wanted to thank him. Hell—she wanted to fuck him. Oh, well. Other than that, she'd never trade this life for her old one.

She remembered everything about the life of that other Jane Benedict, orphaned pariah and eccentric yet gifted student of history, all the way to her kidnapping and the dramatic train of events that had followed. Her body, mind and persona were the same as in that other life, minus the trauma of loss. And she remembered everything about her amended life, in which her parents and brothers had somehow survived with her that freak car accident in the Alps. With her family intact, she had not been alienated and made to feel like a misfit. Universally beloved and approved, she had sailed from accomplishment to accomplishment. One thing remained the same; her interest in history was as keen as in her other life. Strangely, though, she had become fixated not on Alice's world, Early Modern England, but on the brief political experiment of the United States of America and the War of 1812 that had ended it. On reflection, she realized why.

The initiative and heroism of a young British captain in the battle of Queenston Heights had enabled Great Britain to win the War of 1812. His name was De Fries, Alexander Hartford De Fries. After his commanding officer Major General Brock was killed by a sniper, Captain De Fries had rallied the troops and led a charge that punched a hole in a vulnerable section of the American line. Fighting alongside De Fries were Mohawk and Delaware warriors loyal to the British, and forty freed slaves from the Canadian Company of Colored men. The ferocity of this attack enabled De Fries to flank the American forces, capturing large numbers and driving the rest from Queenston Heights in disorder.

Jane now recognized that Alexander De Fries was a descendant of Alice and James. That was why on this track of her existence she had been drawn to this conflict; for whatever reason, she and Alice and James were connected through time and space. And it was her, Jane's, intervention that had turned the conflict by saving their lives, with immense repercussions.

Captain Alexander de Fries' skilled command and personal valor had attracted unforeseen numbers of fresh recruits to swell the Canadian, British, and First Nations army. The victories at Detroit and now Queenston inspired the British coalition to go on an immediate offensive, attacking Washington and capturing President Madison, along with many members of Congress, before they could escape. Vanquished, the United States of America was formally dissolved by treaty and replaced by the vastly expanded United States of Canada, loyal to the British Crown. The Bill of Rights of the former Constitution of the United States and elements of its representative democracy were incorporated by negotiation into the charter of the newly-amalgamated nation.

Jane's mind reeled as she examined the twin tracks of her consciousness and their respective histories. Forget the Butterfly Effect—she had released the beating wings of a thousand eagles into the space/time continuum! Rather than perishing in battle, Shawnee Chief Tecumseh had survived the War of 1812, and the grateful Canadians had granted the First Nations peoples a permanent homeland centered on the Great Lakes. For its part, Great Britain had learned from bitter experience not to apply too heavy a hand on the American people, and an easy relationship between this enlarged New World colony and the Crown developed. In due course the United States of Canada, like Australia, became a sovereign state with full legislative independence within the British Commonwealth of Nations.

Due to its acquisition of a nation already vastly enlarged by the Louisiana Purchase, the United States of Canada was satisfied by its immediate North/South expansion, and did not seek to augment its boundaries any further West. The ethos of Manifest Destiny did not take root; consequently the indigenous peoples of the Great Plains and Southwest went largely undisturbed. The Oregon Territory of the Pacific Northwest coalesced into an amalgam of tribal peoples and British and Russian settlers. Mexico, after gaining independence, was not challenged in war by the United States of Canada, and dealt with its North American holdings from a relatively benign distance. In the South, slavery, already abolished by Great Britain, was phased out over a ten-year period and its agrarian economy gave way to the industrial model, helping the United States of Canada become a global economic powerhouse.

This New World example of peaceable coexistence inspired people worldwide, with the result that racist, colonialist, and nationalist ideologies relaxed their grip on people's minds and two world wars and countless smaller conflicts were averted. In the *Pax Canadiana*, the driver of technological change was not warfare but the amelioration of human conditions. In fact the United States of Canada drew inspiration from intact Amerindian cultures in their reverence for the natural world. Industrialization evolved rapidly toward elegant sustainability, and species extinctions and disastrous climate change were averted. Exploration of the solar system and beyond was rapidly advancing...Was the world amended by Alice and James' posterity? Or were there terrible consequences of which she was unaware? Her mind blown with simultaneous wonder and anxiety and relief, Jane's head was spinning.

The monorail glided imperceptibly to a halt at Grand Central. In her distraction as she emerged from the carriage, Jane lost her grip on the folder containing the notes for her latest paper. She turned backwards to see a man with black hair retrieving them.

"Oh, thanks!" she said to the top of his head, bent over her papers.

He lifted his face toward hers. She gasped.

There they were. Those green eyes.

ABOUT THE AUTHOR

If this book plays like a movie in your head, it's probably because Brian Trenchard-Smith has directed 42 films for cinema, video, and television. His cult favorites, Turkey Shoot, BMX Bandits, Dead End Drive In, The Siege of Firebase Gloria, The Man From Hong Kong have earned praise from Quentin Tarantino, and continue to be re-released on Blu Ray. He has presented over 50 cinema lectures for Trailers From Hell.com. This is his first novel. He lives in Oregon with his wife Dr. Margaret Trenchard-Smith, a Byzantine historian.